THE FORTUNES OF TEXAS

*Follows the lives and loves of a wealthy,
complex family with a rich history
and deep ties in the Lone Star State.*

Check in to the Hotel Fortune,
the Fortune brothers' latest venture
in cozy Rambling Rose, Texas. They're
scheduled to open on Valentine's Day, when
a suspicious accident damages a balcony—
and injures one of the workers!
Now the future of the hotel could be
in jeopardy. Was the crash an accident—
or is something more nefarious going on?

Laid-back "cowboy" Jay Cross has been
working at the Hotel Fortune for six months
now, and so far, no one has guessed his secret.
He's happy to be "just Jay"—especially since
Arabella Fortune likes him just the way he
is. But once the truth gets out, their simple
relationship will get *way* more complicated...

Dear Reader,

Welcome back to Rambling Rose, the town that has been turned on its ear by the Fortunes of Texas, and never more so than now, when the Hotel Fortune—after fits and starts—is finally open for business. But what kind of business is actually going on at the hotel?

For Jay Cross, who simply came back to Rambling Rose to get a break from the frenzy that his life had become, it's a place to make an honest day's pay where nobody has any expectations of him other than that he do his job. If not for the local law, who aren't happy about the supposed "gaps" in his life when they look his way after one too many mishaps at the hotel, life is nearly perfect.

For Arabella Fortune, who came back to Rambling Rose with dreams in her mind directly related to the handsome Jay, the business of the day is to finally find out what he was going to tell her the night they'd met so many months ago. The night he'd been unable to finish his sentence, *I think you should know that—* She's been dreaming about a romantic ending to that sentence for months now.

But will there be romance and love in store for them? Or has Arabella been fantasizing all of these months about a man who has more secrets than Texas has Fortunes?

Hope you'll enjoy finding out!

Allison

Cowboy in Disguise

ALLISON LEIGH

HARLEQUIN

SPECIAL
EDITION

Special thanks and acknowledgment are given
to Allison Leigh for her contribution to
The Fortunes of Texas: The Hotel Fortune miniseries.

HARLEQUIN®
SPECIAL EDITION™

Recycling programs
for this product may
not exist in your area.

ISBN-13: 978-1-335-40488-6

Cowboy in Disguise

Copyright © 2021 by Harlequin Books S.A.

This edition published by arrangement with Harlequin Books S.A.

For questions and comments about the quality of this book,
please contact us at CustomerService@Harlequin.com.

Harlequin Enterprises ULC
22 Adelaide St. West, 40th Floor
Toronto, Ontario M5H 4E3, Canada
www.Harlequin.com

Printed in U.S.A.

Though her name is frequently on bestseller lists, **Allison Leigh**'s high point as a writer is hearing from readers that they laughed, cried or lost sleep while reading her books. She credits her family with great patience for the time she's parked at her computer, and for blessing her with the kind of love she wants her readers to share with the characters living in the pages of her books. Contact her at allisonleigh.com.

Books by Allison Leigh

Harlequin Special Edition

Return to the Double C

A Weaver Christmas Gift
One Night in Weaver...
The BFF Bride
A Child Under His Tree
Yuletide Baby Bargain
Show Me a Hero
The Rancher's Christmas Promise
A Promise to Keep
Lawfully Unwed
Something About the Season

The Fortunes of Texas: All Fortune's Children

Fortune's Secret Heir

The Fortunes of Texas: The Lost Fortunes

Fortune's Texas Reunion

The Fortunes of Texas: Rambling Rose

The Texan's Baby Bombshell

Visit the Author Profile page
at Harlequin.com for more titles.

This book is dedicated to my husband, Greg.
You keep me sane.

Chapter One

January

"I thought you didn't eat bread anymore."

Arabella Fortune jumped guiltily and used the corner of her napkin to cover the roll she'd dropped in her lap, where it sat next to two others just like it. She looked from the empty bread basket to meet her brother's laughing eyes.

"More bread?"

At the question, she swiftly looked from Brady to the handsome owner of the deep voice. His name badge said Jay Cross and he'd been attending to their table throughout the birthday party for her nephew. She picked up the basket, smiling into his deep green eyes.

"Yes, please." She sounded breathless and didn't really care. "If it's not too much trouble." Jay was gorgeous. And every time their fingers brushed—when he'd given her a fresh napkin after she'd dropped hers, when he'd refilled her water glass, when she handed him the bread basket for the third time—there was an undeniable zing.

And she knew he'd felt it, too. Right from the start. The way his gaze had zipped to hers...and clung...had made her certain of it.

He had long fingers. She didn't know if they were smooth or calloused, though he had a raised scar over one knuckle, long and whitish against his tanned skin, that made her think he didn't spend all of his time on a catering crew.

His smile widened and his gaze was as warm as a caress when he took the basket from her. "No trouble at all." His fingers grazed her hand and she felt butterflies take flight inside her. That brush of his fingers *had* to be deliberate. "I'll be right back." He walked away with the basket in hand.

"Why are you staring at that wader?"

Arabella heard her brother's grunt of laughter and she pulled her attention away from Jay to focus on Tyler's four-year-old face. Since Brady had been left guardian of his best friend's twins the year before, she'd become adept at telling the two boys apart. "Was I staring?" she asked innocently.

Tyler nodded earnestly. "At his butt." His young voice was piping clear. "The wader's butt."

"It's waiter. Not wader," Brady corrected almost absently. He was busy trying to keep Toby—the more rambunctious of the two children—from unbuttoning his shirt because he was too hot. It wasn't really too warm inside the hotel restaurant where the party was being held. It was January. Back home in Buffalo, they'd be under a few feet of snow, but here in Rambling Rose, the balcony doors were thrown open and the occasional breeze that flowed in was beautifully balmy. The other two occupants of their table—her brothers Kane and Joshua—obviously felt the same. As soon as they'd finished their entrées, they'd taken refuge from Toby's and Tyler's unrelenting chatter at the bar set up near the balcony and they both had their shirtsleeves rolled up.

"Not another button," Brady warned Toby before looking back at Tyler. "And don't say butt," he directed.

"At his bottom," Tyler revised obediently. But he still had a glint in his eyes. He might be the more sensitive of the two, but like Toby, his genetic makeup seemed to be half mischief.

As the only girl among five protective older brothers, handling the four-year-old variety of male was almost a breeze. She leaned closer to Tyler. "D'you want to go outside for a few minutes?"

He nodded so hard he nearly fell out of his chair.

She looked to his twin brother, placed on her other side between her and Brady in a relatively successful attempt at helping them behave during the family event. "D'you want to go outside for a few minutes, Toby?" The restaurant, Roja, was located in the brand-new Hotel Fortune and though she hadn't had a chance to see much besides her hotel room, she was sure there would be someplace where the kids could work out their wiggles.

Toby was out of his chair before she even finished speaking, and hung on to the back of Brady's while he bounced on his bare feet.

Brady looked resigned at this latest discovery. "When did you take off your shoes and socks?"

The little boy shrugged innocently.

Arabella hid a laugh and slipped off her seat, prepared to dive under the table to retrieve the items. But she'd forgotten all about the rolls she'd snuck away in her napkin and they bounced onto the carpet like a cascade of ping-pong balls.

Brady gave her a look that, lately, had been reserved for his young charges. "Subtle, Airhead."

She crossed her eyes at him and ducked under the floor-length tablecloth, dashing the rolls out of sight along with her, and fished out Toby's shoes and socks then backed out again on hands and knees.

A pair of shining black cowboy boots met her eyes.

She looked up the long legs encased in black pants and felt her face heat at the laughter in Jay's eyes as he set the fresh bread basket on the table. "Can I help you up?" He extended his long-fingered hand down toward her.

The scarred knuckle hovered near her nose and those fluttering wings inside her took flight all over again.

She placed her palm in his.

Oh, hello. Forget *zing*. Palm-to-palm meant full-on heart palpitations.

She didn't even know how she got to her feet without catching her high heels in her maxi-length dress. Maybe she just floated upward, borne on the delight of his hand clasping hers. Regardless, she found herself standing a little closer than was probably appropriate for the moment—her nephew Larkin's first birthday party. But she just couldn't make herself put a few more inches between them.

She looked up, then up some more, until her eyes met Jay's.

She'd already noticed how green they were. But standing so closely now, she could see the circle of yellow around his pupils. The spokes of darker color that radiated out to the deep green edges of his irises.

She realized he was still holding her hand. Was, in fact, grazing his thumb ever so lightly over the back of her hand.

She also realized that both Tyler and Toby were bouncing around her, impatient for the promise of an escape from the party. And that Brady was giving Jay a narrow-eyed stare. As was Brian who'd joined their brothers Kane and Joshua at the bar. Fortunately, Adam—the eldest of her siblings—was busy with Laurel and their little boy across the room or she had no doubt his suspicious glare would be trained her way, too. Instead, he and Laurel were talking animatedly with their folks.

Catherine Fortune was smiling and nodding. Gary Fortune, however, had the same sour look on his face that he wore whenever he was faced with any of the extended members of the Fortune family. One might think discovering you had half-brothers out in the world that you'd never known about would be exciting. Not for Gary, though. Arabella knew for a fact that if not for Larkin—whose very survival had been in question not even six months earlier—her dad would sooner choke than have anything to do with "those" Fortunes.

The ones who had money.

More than they had, anyway.

The ones who had success.

Also more than Gary figured they had.

But Larkin *was* his first grandchild. And the baby was now thriving. He'd made it to his first birthday. His parents—her brother Adam and Laurel—were together. Finally. Those blessings had provided enough impetus for her dad to put aside his usual animosity, at least long enough to come to Texas for the party.

Brady nudged her from behind. "You going to let the guy get back to his job anytime this century?"

She looked into those green, green eyes again and reluctantly tugged her hand free of Jay's. "I was just going to try to find a place outside for these two to get some fresh air before the cake is served."

"I want cake," Toby and Tyler both said, nearly in unison. "Cake, cake, cake!"

"Run off some energy, you know, before we give them a sugar rush," she added above their chanting.

Jay's smile widened. "There's a perfect place downstairs. I can show you a shortcut."

Fluttering galore. "That's so sweet of you." She ignored the muffled sound of disgust that came from Brady and swept Toby up in her arms. He could put on his shoes and socks outside.

"Ten minutes," she told Brady, warning him with her glare not to embarrass her. He still rolled his eyes at her the same way he'd been doing for all of her life.

She ignored him and turned with the boys to follow Jay's extremely perfect backside out of the room.

As soon as they'd passed through the door he held open for them, he let it swing closed and the chatter and music from inside went hushed.

She felt a quick dart. "Are you sure this is okay? I didn't intend to take you away from your work." Not that she wasn't going to enjoy it while she could.

His dark brown hair was short. Thick. Light caught in the glossy strands as his head dipped slightly toward hers. "Job of the day is to take care of the Fortunes," he said conspiratorially. He really did have the sexiest deep voice. "You're a Fortune, so…" He touched her elbow lightly, directing her into a waiting elevator.

She couldn't help her shiver any more than she could help the laugh that escaped. "I'm not one of those Fortunes, though, so I'm not sure this counts."

The elevator car was narrow, long and tall and had padded walls. He punched the ground floor button. "I didn't know there were a *these* and a *those*."

Her smile widened. If he'd been waiting on the table where her parents sat, he might have thought differently.

The elevator lurched softly as it stopped and the doors opened again. Jay led them through a back corridor made even narrower by tall racks sitting on one side, then pushed through another door into the fitness center. They crossed the spacious room and stepped through another door and outside onto a grassy area.

The music and laughter from the party upstairs carried easily down to them.

Toby was squirming so much she set him down on the grass. "Put these on before you move an inch," she ordered, handing him the shoes and socks.

Tongue sticking out between his teeth, he quickly pulled on the socks. The heels weren't in the right spots, but he didn't seem bothered by it as he worked on the shoes. She knew better than to offer help. He had an independent streak a mile wide. Meanwhile, Tyler crouched down and began running a car she hadn't even known he'd had along the cobbled pavers next to them.

She looked up at Jay. "Thanks for this." She gestured at the boys. "My brother's their guardian."

He looked surprised. "Sorry, I thought they were yours."

She shook her head. "Nope. No kids. Not married." She felt her face flush.

His smile widened.

Butterfly wings fluttered inside her chest. "So, uh, how long have you worked at Hotel Fortune?"

"Almost a month now. They're good folks here. *Those* Fortunes. Hey, pard, want a little help there?" He crouched alongside Toby who was still struggling with his shoelaces.

Toby duly considered the matter, then to her amazement, he shot out his small foot.

"Always had trouble with laces, myself," Jay told the boy with a grin. "So my granny kept buying me cowboy boots. Just like these." With a wink, he wiggled the toe of his boot and Toby giggled. "My mama, though, she said I couldn't play baseball wearing boots so she taught me like this." He stretched out Toby's laces in a slightly exaggerated way. "Cross 'em over in an X," he sang softly, "pull 'em down and now what's next?"

Tyler came over to see. "Bunny ears."

"Right," Jay agreed. "Only my mama called them donkey ears. Cross 'em over in an X," he repeated, in the same deep singsong drawl, "pull 'em down and now what's next? Donkey ears—" he nodded encouragingly when both boys shouted the answer "—get all crossed up. Make 'em do a somersault. Now that's done, what else is left? Pull 'em tight and kiss an elf."

The boys wrinkled their noses and hooted. "Kiss an *elf*!" Toby stuck out his other foot and wiggled it back and forth. "Do it again!"

"All right," Jay agreed, catching the toe of Toby's shoe. "But you do the laces this time."

Unspeakably charmed, Arabella watched them as Toby grabbed his shoelaces.

Jay started singing again. "Cross 'em over in an X…" He trailed off, as the twins took over the words, easily remembering the simple, catchy tune while Toby's fingers tried to replicate the motions. Jay straightened then and his eyes seemed to linger on her face.

She raised her eyebrows at him. "Kiss an elf?"

"Mom was—is—a piano teacher." His smile was so easy. So sexy with that slash of a dimple that appeared beside his mobile lips. "She never claimed to be a lyricist."

Shoes successfully tied, Toby hopped to his feet and even though Arabella would have loved to linger a little longer with Jay, she knew she shouldn't keep him. "Thanks for showing us the shortcut down here." Already the two imps were chasing each other around the grass, burning off some of their never-ending energy.

"My pleasure." He gestured at the hotel. "Afraid you'll have to use the main elevator to get back upstairs. The door we came out doesn't open from the outside."

"What time do you get off work?" The words blurted out of her and she flushed. Not just because of the impetuous question, but because of the slow look he sent her way.

"Jay." Another one of the servers from the party stuck her head out of the door, obviously looking for him. "Need you upstairs, dude." She stood there holding the door open, pointedly waiting.

Jay offered Arabella a slightly pained shrug. "Sorry."

"No." Arabella waved her hand. "I'm sorry for keeping you." She moistened her lips. "We can, uh, we can talk later." She was practically stuttering.

She really wasn't good at this. Inside her head, she pictured herself all smooth and maybe even a little sophisticated and sexy. Reality, though, fell far short.

Fortunately—miraculously—Jay didn't seem any more bothered by her awkwardness than Toby was by his backward socks. "That sounds good," he said and she was pretty sure it wasn't her imagination that his deep voice seemed to go even deeper.

"See you later, pardners," he told the boys as he went back inside. "Make sure you run enough to make room for birthday cake."

Arabella let the boys run around a little longer than

the ten minutes she'd promised Brady. But since she could see him upstairs in the restaurant through the opened balcony doors, she figured he wasn't too anxious.

Which was fortunate because the butterflies fluttering madly inside her veins needed to burn off some energy as badly as the boys did.

Lights were coming on around the property when she herded the twins back inside through the main entrance and upstairs.

Fortunately, they were just in time to see Larkin smashing his way through his truck-shaped birthday cake, earning *oohs* from the twins who raced to the table and onto Catherine's and Gary's laps—proof that they were perfectly normal little boys despite the tragedy of their parents' deaths last year.

Arabella spotted Jay and he jerked slightly when she touched his sleeve, but his smile was warm as ever. "Hello again."

Aware of his responsibilities there, she snatched up an unused coffee cup from the abandoned guest table next to them. "Fill me up?"

One of his dark eyebrows peaked. "With coffee?"

"Are you offering anything else?"

His eyes didn't let go of hers as he tilted his coffee carafe over her cup. "That depends."

"On what?"

He shook his head slightly as if he were as bemused as she. "Arabella."

She moistened her lips. "Yes?"

"I've never met an Arabella before."

Her heart had climbed into her throat and she felt almost dizzy. "Is that a good thing?"

His dimple flirted into view. Just for a moment before disappearing again. He set the carafe aside. "I've really liked meeting you, Arabella. A lot." He took her free hand in his. His thumb stroked over her wrist. She knew he had to be able to feel the insane thrumming of her pulse. "And I get off at ten."

Choruses sang inside her head. "Okay," she managed almost soundlessly.

"But I think you should know that—"

A huge screech rent the air just then, and they both jerked. A horrible rumbling juddered up from the floor as the balcony and everything on it fell away.

In the horrified void that followed, a balloon of dust rose silently in its place.

Then a woman screamed.

Followed by another.

And suddenly people ran.

Kids cried.

Jay shoved Arabella to one side just in time to avoid a chair flying toward her and she stared numbly at the cause as Brady vaulted across the room to scoop up Toby and Tyler.

She lost sight of Jay then in the melee while Callum— one of *those* Fortunes who'd built the hotel in the first place—ushered guests off the second floor.

Arabella gasped when her dad grabbed her arm in an iron grip.

"I *knew* it was a bad idea coming here." He had her

mother's hand in his other and Catherine stumbled over a spilled tray of dishes trying to keep up with him.

"Daddy!" Arabella pulled on his hand, slowing him long enough to notice her mom. She was glad at least to see the true dismay in his face when he helped her mom to her feet. But that didn't stop him from shackling Arabella's wrist again as if she were a wayward toddler and joining the exiting guests.

Outside, the sound of sirens ought to have been reassuring—help was on its way—yet it only seemed to add to the horror.

"Was anyone hurt?"

"Where's Wiley?"

"Was it a bomb?"

"Dear God, Grace was—"

"The mayor's here. She can—"

The voices swirled and Arabella saw a mountain of rubble where only minutes earlier, Toby and Tyler had been running around the bushes below the balcony.

Nausea assaulted her and she looked away, numbly letting her father pull her and her mother even farther away from the scene. He hustled them into the car he'd rented at the airport in Houston. He was muttering to himself the whole while, but Arabella barely heard.

The evening wasn't cold, but her teeth chattered hard as she looked out the back car window as her dad drove away from the hotel. Emergency lights flashed as one vehicle after another turned into the parking lot, tires squealing. She knew her brothers were safe. They'd all been inside Roja and well away from the balcony when she'd been talking with Jay.

I think you should know that...

"Gary, surely the entire hotel isn't collapsing! Shouldn't we—"

"No," her dad said flatly, cutting off whatever her mother had been going to suggest. "We're going straight back to New York where we belong."

Jarred from her stupor, Arabella envisioned her overnight bag still sitting on the foot of her bed. Because the party was being held right there in the hotel, she'd seen no reason to take her purse to the party. "Dad, our luggage—"

"Can be sent to us. It's the least *those* Fortunes owe us."

"Maybe, but I'm still not going to be able to get on a plane without ID! And that's still in my hotel room." In his present mood, she knew he wouldn't welcome any comments from her, but if they drove all the way to Houston only to have to turn around again, he'd be even more furious.

"Don't you know better than to go anywhere without your ID?" He obviously didn't expect an answer because he was swearing under his breath as he turned around and started back to the hotel.

She hadn't *gone* anywhere until he'd dragged her out of the hotel. But she was pretty sure pointing that out wouldn't earn her any points.

"How many times have I told Adam that moving to Rambling Rose would be nothing but bad news? Kane's no better. That family just invites trouble. I told you about that wedding," he said to Catherine, repeating words that Arabella had heard again and again over the past few years. "Deranged women. Kidnapping. Car chases. Now this? Those Fortunes are cursed!"

Her mother's voice was meant to be soothing. "That was years ago. What happened at your brother's wedding in Paseo—"

"Gerald Robinson is not *my* brother," Gary snapped. "How many times have I told you that?"

Julius Fortune's copious spreading of his gene pool said otherwise. Arabella kept that thought to herself, too. She'd never met Julius, who had fathered not only one legitimate son—Gerald—but at least four illegitimate ones, including her father. Everything she knew about the wealthy philanderer who'd died before she was even born was what she'd gained via the internet and snippets of gossip from her brothers.

When they arrived back at the hotel, the number of fire engines and police cars had doubled.

"Oh, dear," Catherine fretted as they slowed for a stretcher being rolled toward the opened rear doors of an ambulance. She fumbled with her purse—*she* hadn't left hers in their room—and pulled out her cell phone. "Oh dear, oh dear, oh dear," she kept moaning under her breath as she dialed.

Arabella could see her mother's hands trembling and felt another wave of nausea. "Send text messages, Mom," she advised, knowing that her brothers were likely to respond more quickly to a text than a phone call. For there was no question that Catherine Fortune was checking on her boys.

After waiting for the stretcher to be loaded, her dad pulled as close to the hotel entrance as the congestion of vehicles allowed. The second the wheels stopped rolling, Arabella unsnapped her safety belt. "I have my room key." She pulled it from her bodice where she'd tucked it and held it up.

Her father plucked it right out of her fingertips. "Stay here," he ordered, and got out of the vehicle.

"I'm twenty-five years old," she grumbled but he'd already slammed his door shut. "I'm capable of retrieving my own damn luggage."

"Don't swear," Catherine said, holding her phone to her ear. "It's unbecoming of a young lady. Oh, *why* won't Adam answer his phone? Maybe Kane."

"I told you, Mom," Arabella said with a sigh. *"Text."*

Her mother clucked her tongue and redialed. "I don't like texting. You know that."

And her brothers didn't like getting dragged into lengthy conversations with their mother that inevitably went nowhere.

It wasn't that they didn't love her. But Arabella also knew her brothers were frustrated with the chip their father had on his shoulder against the rest of the world—and of late, *those* Fortunes—and their mother's support of her husband no matter how unreasonable his attitudes were.

Was it any wonder that Arabella had spent most of her childhood with her nose buried in the books she loved? It was so much more pleasant losing herself in the excitement of a mystery or the throes of a love story than dwell on her overprotective big brothers, her old-fashioned mother and her perennially disgruntled father.

She pushed open her car door and got out.

"Arabella, where are you going?"

"Just to see what's happening." She childishly crossed her fingers where her mother couldn't see and started weaving around cars to get closer to the side of the hotel where the action was most concentrated.

Arabella spotted Jay at once.

He stood on the far side of the debris. Yellow police tape already cordoned off the area. He was looking in her direction and she lifted her hand, hoping he would notice, but she got jostled aside by the arrival of a television crew headed by a helmet-haired woman who was clearly ready to bat her pathway clear with her big microphone.

"Focus on that pile of debris and crushed landscaping," she was ordering her cameraman. "And cut back to me in five, four, three—"

Arabella looked toward Jay again.

But he was gone.

Disappointment sagged inside her.

I think you should know that...

What had he intended to say?

...I do believe in love at first sight. With you, Arabella.

Her arm was grabbed again, this time from behind.

"I told you to stay in the car," Gary said tightly. "You want to get hurt out here?"

"The person who got hurt was on that stretcher we saw." She craned her neck, trying to find Jay again.

"Police," Gary muttered, obviously not listening. He was practically frog-marching her back to the car. "Everywhere."

"Doing their job, it looks like to me."

"Yeah and those Fortunes give them plenty to do." Her dad pushed her into the back seat and tossed her overnighter in after her. "Just watch. They'll buy their way out of this latest trouble. That's what people like them do." He slammed her door shut and got behind the wheel while Arabella was trying to untangle her high heel from where it had punctured her hem. "Who would have thought that *Arabella* would be the one to show the most common sense? She's perfectly happy in New York. Not trying to act like some hifalutin Fortune."

"Gary," her mother started again. "If you just gave them a chance, maybe—"

"I don't want to hear it, Catherine."

Neither did Arabella. She closed her eyes, envisioning Jay's brilliant green ones. Remembering the touch of his hand on hers.

I think you should know that...

Chapter Two

Five months later

"Come on, Cross. Why don't you make things easy here and just confess?"

Jay shoved his fingers through his hair and stared blearily at the cop on the other side of the hardwood table.

Supposedly, he was just there at the Rambling Rose Police Station to have a "conversation."

Except he'd been sitting in this room with the detective for two hours. And even before that, he'd been sitting in the room alone for twice that long.

"Confess what?" he asked for about the millionth time.

"What were you doing that afternoon back in January when the balcony collapsed at Hotel Fortune?"

He rubbed the pain centered between his eyebrows. "My job," he said. Again. For about the millionth time.

"Which is what?"

He dropped his hand onto the table a little harder than he probably should have. The sound of it echoed loudly in the stark room.

He stretched out his fingers, mentally counting to ten, then relaxed them again and looked at the investigator, Detective John Teas. "Whatever the GM decides I should be doing."

"GM?"

"General manager."

"That's Grace Williams."

"She's the general manager now, but she wasn't in January."

"No. She was standing on the balcony when it collapsed. And every single witness that we've interviewed about that day can't recall where you were prior to that collapse. Why is that?"

Jay sighed again. If he told the detective the whole truth and nothing but the truth, would it make things better for him?

Or worse?

"I have no idea," he replied evenly. "On that particular day in January, I was one of the servers at the birthday party being held at Roja. I spent the day running back and forth from the kitchen to the banquet room."

"Doing?"

The vision of a petite blue-eyed redhead swam easily in his head. "Delivering a lot of bread baskets," he deadpanned.

The detective didn't look amused.

Jay sighed. "I served food. Cleared away plates. Poured coffee. You know. Waited tables at a birthday party." Avoided getting caught on camera when that news crew arrived after the balcony collapse.

He pushed away the thought.

"The day before I was helping out in maintenance. The day after, I was off." As was most everyone else, which the detective knew perfectly well since Jay was pretty certain the man had already questioned everyone who worked at Hotel Fortune, from the owners on down to the lowliest of low—which included Jay Cross.

Just simple Jay Cross.

"One of your coworkers stated that you were seen outside the hotel prior to the balcony collapse."

"Yes. I'd escorted one of the guests and her nephews—" he figured the description was close enough since Brady Fortune, the boys' guardian, had been hired as the hotel concierge and gossip had it that he was in the process of adopting them "—outside so the two little boys could get some fresh air."

"It was early January."

"And the weather was beautiful," Jay returned, exasperated. He shifted on the hard chair and spread his hands, palms upward. "Come on, Detective. Do you have kids? These two boys had energy to spare and had been behaving through an entire dinner. I showed them a back way down to the first floor and outside so they could run around a little."

"Near the balcony."

"The entire back side of the hotel is near the balcony," he pointed out. "What possible reason would I have to be involved in that collapse?"

"That's the question, isn't it, Mr. Cross?" Detective Teas leaned back on two chair legs, seemingly oblivious to the danger that his generous girth presented to them. He tapped a pencil eraser against the tabletop. "You're aware of the food tampering incident during the Give Back barbecue at the hotel just last month."

If the guy expected Jay to blink, he would be disappointed. "I worked the barbecue. Like usual." Except there'd been a news crew on the premises that day, too. Not to cover a disaster—though they'd gotten that in the end—but to promote the community event. Jay had spent more time finding excuses to be out of sight in the kitchen than out in the open where the reporter and cameras were.

He hadn't thought it was all that likely he'd be recognized. Not the way he looked now. But he hadn't wanted to take any chances, either. He was already living proof that life could change on a dime. And if it could happen once, it could happen again.

"Running food back and forth from the kitchen to the buffet line," the detective said with a goading little smile. "Any period of time when you were alone?"

Detective Teas undoubtedly already knew the answer to that, too. "Yes, but not for very long."

"Do you know how many people had adverse reactions to the food?"

Jay sighed faintly. "It wasn't the food. It was the pepper powder someone—not me—sprinkled on it." He also knew that everyone had recovered. That, in fact, the one individual caught on camera having an allergic reaction to the pepper had set off more of a panic among the crowd than anything, and Nicole Fortune, who was the chef of Roja, had worked very hard to prove there'd been no mismanagement.

The damage was done, though.

Like all things caught in the media, sensationalism was more popular than truth. And this—the latest of the mishaps to hit Hotel Fortune—had everyone in town, including those who actually worked there, wondering if the new hotel could even survive.

For Jay, losing the job would be an inconvenience. Rambling Rose didn't exactly offer the plentiful job opportunities that Los Angeles did, but he'd find something. He was nothing if not adaptable.

If the people looking for him, however, found out where he was, it'd cause a lot more than mere inconvenience.

"What brought you here to Rambling Rose?"

Teas couldn't really be reading Jay's mind, but he showed an annoyingly uncanny sense of timing.

"My grandmother." Jay's words were true. They just weren't exactly *the* truth. But since that had nothing to do with this situation, Jay still intended on keeping silent on the matter.

In fact, the only time he'd come close to telling someone the truth had been in January. When he'd been staring down into the otherworldly blue eyes of Arabella Fortune. Strangely enough, he'd wanted her to know all about him. Everything.

The good. And the bad.

"Your grandmother. Speaking of." The detective's voice was like a boulder dropping in the center of the image in Jay's mind, sending it rippling away. The man made a point of looking at the yellow notepad he kept to one side of him as if he didn't want Jay seeing what had been written on it. "You're living with her. Sweet deal. Sponging off an elderly woman."

Jay snorted. "Have you lived in Rambling Rose a long time?"

The pencil eraser missed a beat. "Long enough."

"Then you've probably met her. And if you've met her, you ought to know *nobody* sponges off Louella O'Brien." Jay forced a smile. "Elderly or not, she sells her homemade jam every weekend out at Mariana's Market. Rain or shine." Much to his mother's chagrin. Sandra Cross wanted Louella to move to Houston. To give up the ranch—it hadn't been a working ranch since Jay's grandfather died twenty years ago—and move closer to her and Jay's dad. To give up her gardens and her jam business and behave the way she figured a nearly ninety-year-old woman ought to behave.

Not surprisingly, Louella was having none of it. With Jay living out at the ranch, his mother had given the subject a rest. At least with Louella. Unfortunately for him, instead of calling her mother every day to nag her about moving, Jay's mother now called *him*.

"Are you talking about Lou's Luscious Jams?" The detective looked surprised. "My wife buys it every chance she gets. She says if she doesn't get out to the flea market early enough, everything's sold out in the first hour and she ends up having to settle for some other seller out there."

"Luscious Jams are my grandmother's." In fact, he could stand some of it right now, along with his grandmother's homemade bread. He was starving. He spread his palms once again. "You said this was voluntary. I've answered all of your questions a dozen times over. So unless you're going to tell me I can't, I'll be leaving now." He put words to action and stood.

The detective didn't try to stop him, which was a relief. Jay didn't particularly relish the idea of having to call a lawyer. One, it would upset his grandmother. Two, it would necessitate being more forthcoming with the lawyer than he had been with this well-intentioned but misguided cop. And even though a lawyer would have a duty for confidentiality, these days, Jay wasn't taking any chances.

He'd closed the door on the man he'd been and he didn't want it opening up again.

Teas didn't rise, though he did let his chair go back down onto all fours. "Yeah, you can go, Mr. Cross," he said in a smooth way that had probably put the fear of God in any number of suspects. He bounced his pencil eraser a few more times. "Just don't leave town."

After a decade spent in the City of Angels, Jay had acquired his own smooth smile. "I have no intention of going anywhere." He scooped up his cowboy hat from the corner of the table and jammed it on his head. He flicked the brim, mockingly, he had to admit, and walked out of the stifling room.

The police department took up only a portion of

the building that also housed the municipal courts and the motor vehicle department. Given Rambling Rose's affordability and proximity to larger cities like Jay's hometown of Houston, Rambling Rose had become quite the boutique city since Jay had been a kid. But he could still remember visiting the building with his grandpa whenever he was staying with Louella and Herbert O'Brien because Herb's penchant for collecting parking tickets had been legend.

Jay followed the tiled corridor until he reached the public lobby that all of the departments held in common and checked his motion to pull his sunglasses out of his pocket.

He didn't wear sunglasses anymore. Ergo the cowboy hat.

At first, it had seemed like a stupid thing. More symbolic than anything.

He'd gotten rid of everything that smacked of his old life after his old life had gotten rid of him.

Girlfriend.

Manager.

Career.

His trademark shades had gone in the trash the same day he'd shaved his beard and cut his hair short.

Now, he was glad he'd changed his appearance. His return to good ol' boy Jay Cross was complete.

Nobody in Rambling Rose had a reason to connect him with his old life. And if that left him with a few missing spots in his history as far as Detective Teas was concerned, Jay wasn't going to worry about it.

He wasn't responsible for the problems that had befallen Hotel Fortune, which meant there was no way that Teas could prove otherwise. Pure and simple.

The-late afternoon sun was shafting through the glass entry doors. Another thing that hadn't changed since Jay was a kid. You'd have thought they'd have at least tinted the glass by now. But no. The sun still streamed in, turning the lobby into a sauna that no amount of air-conditioning could combat.

He tugged the brim of his cowboy hat down farther against the glare and pushed through the door, quickly sidestepping the person who was hurrying to get inside.

"Sorry," a breathless voice said from behind a tall vase of flowers. "You're the second person I've bumped into."

Jay chuckled and held the door wider. "Not surprised. Those things are taller than you." He glanced around the enormous bouquet and felt the impact straight to his solar plexus.

Her hair was mostly hidden by the ball cap she wore, but the long ponytail hanging out the back was distinctively red. And though her eyes were hidden behind a pair of reflective aviator-style sunglasses, he knew they'd be distinctively blue.

Her smile widened. "Jay!" Juggling her gigantic burden, she whipped off her sunglasses.

And sure enough, Arabella Fortune's aquamarine eyes were exactly how he remembered.

It was his own damned luck that Teas was heading directly for them.

Suddenly, he felt cornered. Hemmed in by a beautiful young woman on one side and a determined cop on the other. His frustration coalesced. "What are *you* doing here?"

Her wide smile faltered, making him feel like a total ass.

"Delivering flowers," she said, stating the obvious. "What are *you* doing here?"

Even though he'd gotten good at pretending the last decade of his life had never occurred, he ought to have been quicker with a response.

Instead, he saw Teas now just a few feet away.

He saw the POLICE sign with the big arrow right behind him.

And he could imagine the horror in Arabella's eyes when she found out he was Rambling Rose's latest "person of interest."

"Leaving," he said abruptly, and backed the rest of the way out the door.

Arabella stared after Jay. Sudden tears burned deep behind her eyes.

I think you should know that...

...I'm just not that into you.

"Can I help you?"

Swamped in disappointment, Arabella let the glass door swing closed. She blinked hard before looking up at the tall man who'd spoken. He wasn't wearing a uniform but he had a police badge clipped to his belt. "I'm sorry?"

"I recognize Petunia's Posies when I see them." The officer had a kind look in his eyes and he gestured slightly at the enormous bouquet. "Usually it's the Bellamy boy who delivers them."

If she needed proof that Rambling Rose was a small town compared to what she was used to, this was it. He probably knew Jay Cross as well. Certainly better than she did.

Or ever would.

The cop was still waiting.

"I'm filling in for Todd." She knew the kid only by name. "Temporarily. I understand he's on vacation for a few weeks."

"Oh, right." He nodded. "Big Disneyland trip. I remember now. Usually Petunia gets her dad to pinch-hit when Todd is gone."

She wasn't sure what sort of response he expected to that, so she just shrugged. "All I know is she needed someone for two weeks to fill in. I'm Arabella. New in town. And—" she glanced at the delivery slip that she still had tucked between two fingers "—looking for Mrs. Jones in Central Records."

Happy anniversary, my beloved. Arabella herself had written the customer's message on the card included with the flowers.

"Third floor. Back of the building," he said immediately. "Fastest way is the stairs. Elevator takes forever."

"Thank you, Officer—"

"Detective, actually. Detective Teas." He walked away from her in a much nicer way than Jay had.

I think you should know that...

...you should never take flirting seriously.

She huffed out a breath and headed for the wide

staircase situated in the center of the lobby. The detective hadn't exaggerated about the elevator. There was a small line of people standing outside of it waiting for the bronze arrow to move on the old-fashioned dial above the door.

She could handle two flights of stairs to the third floor a lot easier than face the fact that she'd actually moved away from New York to find out exactly how Jay Cross had intended to finish that sentence.

It had been five months since that day.

Five months of weaving romantic fantasies about the words he *hadn't* said.

She found Central Records and delivered the flowers to Mrs. Jones, who turned out to be a young woman who looked no older than Arabella. She had an enormous diamond ring on her finger and gushed over the flowers.

"How long have you been married?" Arabella was afraid her smile was wistful but the young Mrs. Jones didn't seem to notice.

"One month today!"

As Arabella went back down the stairs again, she couldn't help but wonder what sort of display the girl would be getting when she and her husband reached one year.

Arabella couldn't even get a date.

And whose fault is that? Spending the last five months daydreaming about a man you met only once?

Thank heavens Arabella was smart enough not to have shared that particular fact with anyone. Her family already accused her of always having her head in the clouds. And her girlfriends were all too busy with their own love lives—ones that were much more fruitful than Arabella's.

She'd lost count of how many bridal showers she'd been invited to lately. And being asked to be a bridesmaid for the fourth time in as many months had been just one time too many.

She'd been toying with the idea of returning to Rambling Rose almost as soon as her dad had dragged them away in January from Larkin's birthday party. But when Arabella had gotten a wedding invitation from her nemesis, Tammy Jo Pendleton, something inside her had snapped. For one thing, it was a destination wedding. In Bali.

If the invitation had been heartfelt and genuine, Arabella would've felt regretful having to decline. There was no way she could afford to travel to Bali on her administrative assistant wages, which was something that Tammy Jo knew perfectly well. But the invitation had not been genuine. Tammy Jo had sent it for one simple reason—to drive home the fact that *she* was getting married to Hamilton Dawes.

Arabella might have dated Ham once upon a time but it was Tammy Jo who'd actually landed him. And now Tammy Jo was the one having the fairy-tale wedding with the most eligible bachelor in their town.

Arabella reached her car and climbed behind the wheel. She rolled down the windows to let the heat escape. Even though it had only taken a few minutes to make her last delivery of the day, the car interior had become stifling hot. Her car was old. It wasn't equipped with air-conditioning. She probably should have sold it before she'd left New York and figured out a way to get around in Rambling Rose until she could afford to buy another vehicle. But she'd been determined to prove she wouldn't be a burden on her brothers in Texas.

Because, despite what her brothers and parents thought, just because she had a head full of dreams didn't mean she had no common sense or pride.

And just what kind of common sense did it show to fantasize about Jay Cross all these months?

She twisted the rearview mirror slightly until she saw her own reflection. "Shut up," she muttered.

For once, the mocking voice inside her head obediently went silent and she readjusted the mirror and turned the key.

The engine tried to turn over, but didn't.

The car had some power because the radio came on playing the same song that had been on the radio incessantly for months now. On the long drive from New York, every time she caught a radio signal as she drove from town to town, it had been an obvious staple.

"'Givin' it all up,'" she muttered along with the singer's deep voice before she snapped off the radio. She didn't even listen to country music but the song had still become an earworm, sticking inside her head for hours at a time. "Right now I'd like to give it all up and be back home in New York."

But saying the words was enough for her to know that wasn't strictly true. She was twenty-five years old and it was time that she began doing something with her life. Even if that meant moving to Texas like half her brothers had done.

"All right, car. Don't let me down now." Eyes closed as if that might influence the outcome, she turned the key again.

Silence reigned.

She pulled out the key with a sigh and leaned back in the seat. She tossed aside her ball cap and swiped her sleeve over her sweaty forehead.

She loathed having to call Brady. Not that her brother wouldn't help. Any one of them would. But Adam and Kane both were busy with their own lives. Which was why Arabella had first broached the subject of moving to Rambling Rose with *Brady*. He'd already gone to work for the Hotel Fortune as concierge at that point and she'd had the idea that if she helped take care of the twins for him, not only would she be helping him, but also she could get by without having to pay him rent until she got herself established. She was *pretty* sure he wouldn't have tried to charge her rent anyway, but he also would have totally lorded it over her that he was taking care of her.

Only in the time since then, Brady had fallen for the twins' nanny, Harper Radcliffe.

Which meant that now, instead of moving in with her brother and his rambunctious twins, she was imposing on the engaged couple and their rambunctious twins. They even had a dog now. All that remained was the official *I do*'s.

They never said there wasn't really room for Arabella, but that didn't mean there was.

Harper was lovely and brilliant with the boys and they adored her. Once she and Brady married, Tyler and

Toby would have a new mother to care for them. They certainly didn't need Arabella's help now.

Pity party, much?

This time Arabella didn't try to shut up the voice.

She tightened her ponytail, pulled on her ball cap again and tried the key one more time with no more success than before.

Not even the radio turned on.

Nor could she roll up the power windows.

She glanced around the interior of the car. Was there anything she was afraid of being stolen, anyway?

Plus, in a town like Rambling Rose, was there even any danger of leaving a car open like this? She *was* parked right outside the police station, after all.

She grabbed the book bag that was both a holdall and purse and even though she knew it was pointless, she pushed down the door lock after she got out of the car.

She hefted the long strap crosswise over her shoulder and looked up and down the street.

She'd been in town for only a week, but thanks to Petunia's brisk floral business, Arabella already had a good lay of the land and she set off for Provisions. Adam managed the restaurant, but he and Laurel had gone to Houston with Larkin for one of his doctor's appointments. She knew they wouldn't be back yet.

Which meant Arabella could at least satisfy the hollowness in her stomach in privacy while she dealt with her car.

I think you should know that...

...I can be a rude jerk.

She picked up her pace and was breathless when she reached the cool interior of Provisions.

There were people waiting for a table but she by-passed them for one of the few empty seats at the bar. She ordered an iced tea when the bartender came over, then pulled her cell phone out of the book bag before plopping it on the floor.

She called the flower shop first to let Petunia know that she'd finished her deliveries for the day. She did not, however, tell her boss about the dead car battery. One of the only requirements for the job was possession of an operable vehicle.

Just as Arabella finished her call, the bartender slid a tall glass in front of her. "Get you a menu?"

"That would be great, thanks." She wrapped one hand around the blessedly cold beverage and took the offered menu with the other. "Say—" she quickly read the bartender's name badge "—Evan. Any auto places in town you recommend where I can get a car battery?"

Evan reeled off three places. "But," he added as he glanced at his wristwatch, "I think they all closed at five."

Great. She smiled weakly. "Thanks."

He smiled back far more cheerfully and headed off again.

She chugged half the contents of her glass while she verified that the auto supply stores were closed. Only one was still open, but it was all the way across town. She didn't have a hope of finding a ride there in time.

She heaved out a breath.

"That sounded heartfelt."

She jerked slightly, and then looked behind her to see her cousin Ashley who, along with her sisters Megan and Nicole, had opened the restaurant the year before. Arabella flashed the screen of her phone at her, displaying her search results and made a rueful face. "Car problems."

Ashley's brows knit. "Oh, no. Anything I can do?"

Though Arabella hadn't even met Ashley and her sisters until that January, she'd gotten to know all of them better in the time since—mostly via text messages. But that didn't mean she felt comfortable taking advantage of that fact. Ashley was obviously working. "No worries. It's just the battery." She wouldn't allow herself to think otherwise. "I've got it covered."

"Well, at least order some dinner. On the house."

"You don't have—"

"Please." Ashley waved her hand. "You're family. It might as well be policy."

Arabella couldn't help but laugh. "I know from Adam that half the people who come in here are Fortunes. You'll lose far too much of your profits with a policy like that."

Ashley just grinned as she gave a sideways nod to the hostess who was trying to catch her attention. She squeezed Arabella's shoulder. "I'll check on you later."

Arabella wasn't sure if it was a promise or a warning. Either way, she didn't really see how Ashley would have the time. The restaurant was already busy and Arabella knew it would only become more so as the evening progressed. Adam had said many times how impressed he'd been by their young cousins' success not only with this restaurant but with Roja in the Hotel Fortune as well.

Unsaid, at least in Arabella's mind, was how little *she* had accomplished so far.

And she was a year *older* than the triplets were.

Evan appeared again with a pitcher. He refilled her glass. "Can I put an order in for you?"

She hadn't even glanced at the menu yet. "Hamburger and fries."

"Cheese? Bacon? Avocado?"

"Yes, yes and dear God no. Pack it to go, though, would you please?"

"You bet." He slid the menu away from her and headed away again. While she waited for the food, she sent her daily reassurance to her mom—which necessitated several follow-up texts that yes, she was taking her daily vitamins, yes, she was getting enough sleep despite what Brady must have said, and no, just because she was delivering flowers these days didn't mean she'd stopped looking for a "proper" job.

Proper in her mother's vernacular meant nine-to-five with insurance benefits and a retirement plan.

By the time Catherine Fortune's questions were finally spent, Arabella had received her order of food. She gave Evan enough cash for his tip before she left.

The sun was no longer blazing, but it was still a long way from setting. On the way back to her car, she passed a bus stop and sat on the pretty wooden bench in the shade where she ate her fries and hamburger, and dialed Brady's number—twice.

She hung up both times before it could ring, though,

and finally tossed her phone inside her book bag. Calling any one of her brothers would be her last resort.

According to the bus schedule posted on a sign next to the bench, the next bus wasn't due for another hour. She could eat at her leisure, enjoy the shady spot and pretend that she hadn't foolishly given it all up in New York.

The hamburger was enormous.

She still managed to polish it off. Then she slowly dredged french fry after french fry through her mustard and contemplated whether she could stand the humiliation of returning to Buffalo so soon after coming to Rambling Rose.

On the plus side, her dad would get over his apoplectic anger that she'd defected to the "other side," which was how he viewed the rest of the Fortunes of the world.

"Need a lift?"

She looked beyond her mustard and fries to the street.

A bus hadn't stopped in front of her bench, but a dusty blue pickup truck had.

The french fry stuck in her throat as she looked through the opened window to see Jay Cross sitting behind the steering wheel.

She coughed slightly and sucked iced tea through her straw, forcing the fry down. "Not from you," she croaked.

His lips compressed and she thought he'd drive off.

But instead, he leaned over and pushed open the passenger-side door a few inches.

It was embarrassing the way her heart skittered around so easily.

She stiffened her spine and said nothing. Just raised her eyebrow. She'd perfected the motion when she'd been a teenager—a baby sister's defense against so many protective older brothers—though she figured the effort right now was pretty well lost under the brim of her baseball cap.

"Come on, Arabella." Jay pushed the door open a little wider. Wide enough now that she could see the way his shoulder stretched the fabric of his gray T-shirt. Not so stretched out that it was in danger of splitting, but definitely stretched enough to be…interesting. "At least let me apologize."

"For what?" She was rather pleased with the bored tone.

"For not saying…more…earlier at the, uh…" He looked pained. "You know. At the municipal building."

She gathered up the long strap of her book bag and tossed the rest of her french fries in the cement trash bin next to the bench before she stood.

Maybe it was childish, but she enjoyed the look of relief on his handsome face when she smiled.

Enjoyed even more the glimpse of his frustration when she turned aside and walked away.

Chapter Three

Jay swore as Arabella marched off along the sidewalk. The tail of her red ponytail bounced against her spine and a giant olive-green bag banged against her jean-clad hip with every step she took.

She looked a lot different than she had all those months ago at Hotel Fortune. But whether she was in a clinging green halter dress or jeans and T-shirt, there was still no mistaking her beauty.

He nearly strangled himself with his safety belt when he reached over to pull the passenger door closed again. He was able to troll along behind her only because there were no other vehicles parked alongside the curb, and he saw the way she angled half a look over her shoulder at him before her ponytail bounced with even more pronounced vigor.

He followed alongside her that way for two blocks before she about-faced and propped her fists on her narrow hips, giving him a glare.

He had the random thought that having her glare at him with those incredible eyes for the rest of his life would be better than having a dozen others looking at him with adoration.

Then he thought that there was probably a song in there somewhere.

He shook off both thoughts and rolled to a stop at the curb.

"I don't know why you're bothering to follow me," she said testily.

"Because I want to—" What? Apologize? Explain? "You surprised me," he said and cringed at his own lameness.

Her eyebrows disappeared from view beneath the ball cap. It was blue. Not quite as blue as her eyes. And it didn't sport the name of a sports team. Instead, it just sported an emblem of an open book.

"I didn't expect to see you," he tried again. "There."

"Where?" She lifted her arms at her sides. "In Rambling Rose?"

When the universe tosses you a nugget, you run with it. At least that's what his manager claimed.

Former manager. If Michael Devane hadn't already cut him loose, Jay would have done it himself.

"Right," he said to Arabella. "In Rambling Rose. I know I came off—"

"—rude?"

"Yeah." He cleared his throat. "I'm sorry. I never

intended to be rude. I just—" Couldn't explain. He switched course. "Are you visiting?"

She shrugged noncommittally and folded her arms across her chest. Obviously not going to make things easy for him. But then again, she hadn't started walking away from him again, either.

"I hope your visit is longer this time," he said honestly.

She looked away, presenting him with her very lovely profile. Her lips twisted slightly, revealing a dimple that he knew was glorious when it accompanied an actual smile.

"And less upsetting than last time," he added.

That earned him such a fast look that her ponytail flew forward over her shoulder. "Upsetting?"

"After the balcony collapsed." Even as he mentioned it, he wondered what sort of masochistic streak he'd developed. He didn't want to talk about the balcony collapse. Especially after his encounter with Detective Teas. "You disappeared so quickly afterward."

Her shoulders looked a little less stiff and she mumbled something.

He leaned across the cab of his truck again toward the opened window. "Sorry?"

She released her arm-clench and took a step toward the curb. Probably an unintentional one, because as soon as she seemed to realize it, she went stiff and still all over again. "I said," she uttered louder, more clearly, "my father was anxious to get home."

He was pretty certain that had *not* been what she'd muttered, but he wasn't going to call her on it. "Once things calmed down, I discovered y'all had left the hotel." He didn't add that he'd also heard through the hotel grapevine that their luggage had been shipped back to them. As if they hadn't been able to leave Rambling Rose fast enough.

Not that he believed *anyone* had been responsible for the balcony accident, but if Teas felt the need to be suspicious of someone, why couldn't he be suspicious of someone making such a quick getaway like that? The entire team working the front desk had talked for a week about how obnoxious Arabella's father had been.

She took another half step. "You checked?"

"Of course."

Her eyes narrowed as she looked at him. Then her head shook slightly and the tail of her ponytail drifted off her shoulder again. "Why?"

"Because I really liked meeting you. Now can I at least take you wherever you were waiting for the bus to take you?"

She moistened her lips. "I wasn't actually waiting for the bus. I was—" She broke off, taking another step nearer. So near that she could close the fingers of one hand over the truck door. "I was deciding whether or not I wanted to stay in town. For a while."

"I hope you do."

"Why?"

"I told you. I really liked meeting you."

She angled her head slightly. "But…?"

"But…" He mimicked the way she drew out the word questioningly. "What?"

She pressed her lips together. They looked soft and pink and perfectly, entirely natural.

Entirely enticing.

As if coming to a sudden decision, she pulled open the door and worked the strap of her bag free. She dumped it with a thud on the floor and climbed up into the passenger seat. "You can drop me off at my car. It's still at the police station. Or as you call it—" her dimple appeared, again in an unsmiling sort of way "—the *municipal* building."

Whatever it was called, Jay wanted to go back there about as much as he wanted a hole drilled in his head.

But since that wasn't something he wanted to admit, he waited for a passing car and then pulled out onto the street.

He glanced at her. "It's a long drive here from New York if you're not planning to hang around awhile."

He received the side-eye on that one. "Or maybe I just don't like flying," she countered.

"Do you?"

Her lashes swept down as she fastened her seat belt. "I haven't done all that much of it, if I'm being honest."

"I like flying."

"Suppose *you* have done a lot of it."

He tightened his grip on the steering wheel and shot her a quick look. "Why's that?"

She shrugged, seeming oblivious to his sudden suspicion. "Everyone's done more flying than me."

The tension leaked out of his shoulders. "Well, I have done enough flying to get my license."

She looked at him with even more surprise than he felt making the admission. "You're a pilot?"

"I have my private."

"Which means what? You fly private jets?"

He laughed. "No. It means I can fly a single engine in clear conditions. I don't have an instrument rating." He'd intended to get it but life and circumstances had gotten in the way.

"You're talking the tiny little planes, then?" She shuddered. "They look terrifying."

"They're exhilarating," he corrected.

"I'll have to take your word for it," she said dryly, then pointed. "That's my car there. End of the block."

When he'd left the police station earlier, the street had been lined with parked cars. Now there was only hers.

He pulled up behind the small tan vehicle. "I can prove it to you."

She'd released her seat belt and was gathering up the long strap of her bag. "Prove what?"

"That it isn't terrifying at all. I'll take you up sometime." He didn't stop to think about the complications of that particular offer. Yeah, renting the plane would be pricey for a guy on Jay Cross's salary, but he could explain it away.

She gave a laugh that was full of disbelief. "My brothers are always telling me my head is in the clouds, but I think I'll keep my feet firmly on the ground." She hopped down out of the truck. "Thanks for the ride." She closed the truck door and quickly hurried around to the driver's side of her car.

He watched her toss her bag through the opened
window. Then she opened the door and got behind the
wheel.

And just sat there.

He waited, his curiosity mounting even more when
she got out a few seconds later and walked back to the
truck. She stopped next to his door. "You don't have to
wait for me."

"Blame it on my upbringing. A guy just doesn't drive
away until the girl is safe inside."

"I *was* safe inside and you didn't drive away."

"Safe inside a car that wasn't locked to begin with
doesn't exactly count."

She showed him the cell phone in her hand. "I have
a few calls to make. So, you know, feel free to go." She
jerked her chin toward the building next to them. "I'm
sure you've got better things to do than sit parked in
front of the police station while I make them."

He'd been glad as hell to be finished with Teas earlier, but the more words that came out of Arabella's lips,
the less he cared about parking in front of the man's
office now. "You're not living in your car, are you?"

She looked genuinely shocked. "What on earth
makes you ask that?"

He shrugged. He wasn't about to tell her how often
he'd had to choose between rent money and gas money.
Rent was a roof over his head. Gas meant the means to
get to his next gig. "No reason. Make your calls. It's a
nice evening. I'll wait."

"There's no reason—"

"I'm not leaving until you leave, too, Arabella."

She huffed out a breath. "You know, I think you're as bad as my brothers."

"I don't look at you and think *sister*," he said dryly. "Trust me on that one."

Her gaze grazed against his then danced away. "My battery is dead," she admitted abruptly. She waved her phone again. "But I'm going to call someone and take care of it."

The level of his relief was almost laughable. "Someone's already here." He gestured. "Go wait on the sidewalk. I'll pull around in front of you and give you a jump."

She looked like she wanted to argue, but went over to the sidewalk and he moved the truck around until the vehicles were nose to nose. He turned off his engine and pulled out the jumper cables that were stored in a coil behind his seat. Five minutes later, her car was running and he returned the cables to their spot while she got behind the wheel of her car.

He dusted off his hands and looked through her window. "How far do you have to go?"

"I'm staying with Brady. Not even a couple miles from here."

"But you didn't call him for help with the battery?"

She looked resigned. "Do you have older brothers?"

He shook his head.

"Then you don't know what it feels like to grow up with big brothers constantly thinking you can't take care of yourself."

Lack of personal experience didn't mean he was incapable of understanding her feelings. "Can I see your phone?"

She narrowed her eyes at him, but passed the phone to him through the opened window.

He entered his number and handed the phone back. "If it doesn't start in the morning, you can call me." He knew what sort of hours Brady Fortune worked at the hotel. "We can get a new battery installed if it needs one and your brother never even needs to know."

"You'd do that?" She pressed her chin against her arm that was hung over the door and peered up at him. "Why?"

"Told you." He brushed his thumb lightly over her arm. Just a quick graze. One that satisfied his need for contact and one that gave him the added perk of seeing her eyes dilate for just a moment. "I hope you'll stick around awhile."

Her car engine was humming smoothly when he walked back to his truck and got inside.

She was watching him through the windshield, looking a little bemused, a little wary, and a whole lot of beautiful.

Then she smiled, shook her head a little, and put her car in gear.

He watched her drive away until she was out of sight.

Only then, wearing a smile of his own, did he pull out onto the road and finally head home.

And if there was a part of him that hoped her battery would be dead in the morning, he wasn't going to apologize for it.

* * *

"Auntie Bella." A small solid body bounced onto the foot of her bed. "You're late for breakfast!"

Arabella peeled open her eyes and tried to avoid the slathering tongue of the small dog who'd followed Toby onto the bed. "Murphy, stop." She squinted at her nephew. "Says who?"

"I do." Brady spoke from the doorway. His hair was wet from the shower and he still had a towel around his neck above his robe. "You've been here a week. You know the drill. Routine is what keeps the masses sane here."

"Routine for the *boys*," Harper said, also from the hallway. She, too, had wet hair and a towel around her neck. "Morning, Arabella!" She peered around Brady. "Toby, come on. Leave your auntie alone. Murphy, get off the bed." She snapped her fingers and the dog hopped down. He'd been a rescue and with a few exceptions was generally well behaved.

Arabella closed the notebook she'd fallen asleep writing in the night before and moved it to the nightstand before swinging her legs off the narrow mattress. "Yeah. Leave your auntie alone." She reached over to tickle her nephew's skinny ribs. He rolled with laughter, and unlike Murphy, made no attempt at all to get off the bed *or* to leave her alone.

She didn't mind.

She scooped him up by the waist as she got out of bed and carried him like a sack of potatoes toward the door, being sure to lightly knock his swinging feet against a few objects along the way.

He laughed even harder and for some reason found it particularly hilarious to try to muffle that laughter.

Arabella stopped in front of her brother and his fiancée. She looked from their twin wet heads and towels. "Conserving water again? Very…ecologically minded of you."

Harper snickered and padded along the hallway, disappearing behind the master bedroom door.

"Have to do something to offset the hour-long soaks you take," Brady countered. He slanted his head, studying the boy slung sideways over the hip of her striped pajamas. "Might want to see a doctor about that human appendage you've developed out of your side."

"Might have to," she agreed, managing to work her fingertip against Toby's ticklish ribs. "And once I find a real job, you won't have to complain about my so-called hogging of the shower." She bumped into her brother as she lopsidedly left the bedroom with the awkward, wriggling appendage.

"What's that supposed to mean?" Brady followed on her heels.

"It means I can't very well crash here forever." She reached the staircase and set Toby down. "Bet you can't finish your oatmeal before I finish brushing my teeth," she whispered in his ear.

Predictably, he was down the stairs like a shot.

She straightened again and arched slightly, working out the ache of carrying him that way. Both boys had grown noticeably in the last five months.

"And where do you think you're going to crash?" Brady followed her again, this time back to the bathroom, where he stood in the doorway as if she were still five instead of twenty-five.

She widened her eyes dramatically. "Somewhere wild and crazy like my *own* place?"

He looked askance. "You can't live on your own."

She propped her fists on her hips. "And why not?"

"Because you've *never* lived on your own."

"Then it's about time, don't you think?"

"No, I don't think!"

She made a face at him and shut the bathroom door in his face. And made a point of noisily locking it.

"Bella!" He banged once on the door.

She rolled her eyes at her reflection in the mirror over the sink and turned on the faucets until the water rushed loudly in the pipes.

Eventually she heard the creak of his footsteps moving away and her shoulders slumped with relief.

For all of Brady's insistence that he was nothing like their father, sometimes he showed a dismaying similarity to him.

Despite her brother's claims that she was a bathroom hog, she sped through her morning routine like usual. Because she *was* aware of the fact that she was taking up the bathroom in an already busy household. Plus, she'd learned her first morning there that the hot water ran out halfway through shampooing her hair if she dallied too long.

Also, there was that bet with Toby.

Her hair was streaming wet down the back of her T-shirt when she got downstairs a short while later.

Sitting at the kitchen table, Toby was still scooping

up oatmeal. Tyler was drawing on a paper with a crayon, his cereal already finished. Arabella filled a mug with coffee and sat down across from them before reaching for a slice of toast from the stack sitting on a plate in the center of the table.

Without being asked, Harper passed her a small jar of jam and Arabella smeared some on her toast. She took a bite of the deliciousness and chased it with hot coffee.

She looked from Harper to the boys and back again. "So what's on your schedule today?"

"We are going out to spend the day with Laurel and Larkin at the ranch. She's offered to start teaching the boys how to ride horses." Harper sipped her own coffee. "You can come, too, if you're free."

Arabella thought about her car battery and actually found herself hoping that it'd be dead. Just so she'd have an excuse to use Jay's number that was stored in her cell phone. She'd only been out once to Laurel and Adam's place located in the guesthouse at Callum's Fame & Fortune Ranch. "Sounds like fun, but Petunia's expecting me."

"Even on a Saturday?" Brady asked, entering the room. His robe and towel had been replaced by jeans and a necktie that hung loose over his dress shirt.

"Yes, even on a Saturday," Arabella said a little waspishly. The flower shop was open until noon. "*You're* the concierge at Hotel Fortune. *You're* working on a Saturday."

"Sadly," Harper said lightly. She rose and took the ends of Brady's tie and deftly crossed one end over the other. "He's going to miss out on all the fun."

Arabella had a vision of Jay helping Toby tie his shoes the day they'd met.

She felt suddenly flushed and looked down at her toast, willing the heat to fade.

"I'll leave the saddle-sore fun to you," Brady said. "When you need a massage as a result, that'll be fun for me."

Arabella felt an urgent need to wash out her ears. She was glad her brother was ridiculously happy with Harper, but still…

"Maybe neither of you can make it out there for the riding lesson," Harper said, "but we'll be having a cookout later this afternoon. You can come for that, at least. About three o'clock. Brady, you'll be off for the day by then. I'll expect you both."

"Yes, ma'am," Brady drawled. "Any more orders?"

"None for the moment," Harper said with a laugh.

Arabella tuned out their flirting as she slathered more jam on her toast and looked over to focus on Tyler's drawing. There was a sun on one corner of the page and a brown blob with a long tail in the other corner. Murphy, obviously. And in between, four people. "Impressive. Is that you and Toby?" She pointed at the two smaller figures with shocks of dark hair standing next to the two taller figures.

"No, that's the new babies," he said, without missing a stroke of his crayon. "That's me. That's Toby." He added slashes of bright red across Toby's chest, obviously mimicking the red-and-white stripes of the shirt his twin was presently wearing.

Arabella cast her brother and future sister-in-law a sideways look. "New babies, huh?"

Harper's cheeks went red. "Don't look at me!"

Arabella raised her eyebrows and decided studying her coffee was safer than interpreting the look passing between Brady and Harper. Soon enough, though, her brother was off to the hotel and after reminding Arabella to turn on the radio before she left, too, Harper and the twins were off to their day of riding lessons.

Music soothed not only the savage beast, but it soothed Murphy, too. Even though Brady had put in a doggie door so the animal could go in and out of the house at will, without the radio playing Murphy got up to all sorts of mischief when he was left alone.

Since Arabella had already sacrificed one pair of shoes to the dog when she'd forgotten to leave the music on, it wasn't a mistake she intended to repeat and she turned on the radio as soon as the door closed behind Harper and the boys.

Fortunately, at least the dog wasn't picky about what type of music and with Adele singing in the background, Arabella rinsed the dishes that were left in the sink. Then she loaded the dishwasher and wiped up the table while the DJ warned her listeners that it was going to be a record-breaker of a hot day.

She refilled the dog's water bowl and with her heart feeling jittery inside her chest, she went out to her car.

The engine started just fine.

And the little jitters jittered no more.

She had no reason to call Jay at all.

Feeling decidedly disgruntled, she drove to the flower shop.

Petunia was on the phone when Arabella walked inside. She was obviously taking an order and Arabella walked around her at the counter to go in back where two large worktables were covered with the makings of several bouquets.

She checked the delivery schedule; her first one of the day wasn't for another few hours. Petunia was still busy on the phone, so Arabella began sweeping up the bits of stems and leaves that surrounded the work area. She'd moved on to polishing the glass of the refrigerated cases when Petunia finally entered the workroom.

"Ever wrapped a hand-tied bridal bouquet?"

Arabella glanced over her shoulder. Petunia was holding up one of the lush bouquets, an inquiring look on her face.

Arabella shook her head. "Have only carried more than my fair share of bridesmaid bouquets."

"Close enough." Petunia gestured with the flowers in her hand. "Gerrie called in sick this morning."

Arabella gave a final swipe over the glass. "What do you need me to do?"

Petunia pulled a box of ribbons from beneath the worktable and set it near Arabella. "Need to have all of these bouquets wrapped. Bride wants the ivory ribbon." She withdrew the tail of one of the spools of ribbon inside the box. With enviable ease, she spun the bouquet, deftly encasing the fat bundle of stems in lovely ribbon that she fastened with a pearl-topped pin at the top. "Easy peasy." She handed the finished bouquet to Arabella. "Have twelve of them to do."

"Twelve! For one wedding?" Not even Tammy Jo was having twelve bridesmaids for her fairy-tale wedding.

Petunia shrugged. "Even here in Rambling Rose, some brides are prone to overdoing it." Her lips twitched. "What should I tell them? No, I don't want the business?" She gestured at the ribbons. "Let's see how you do. It's not rocket science."

"Which is also fortunate," Arabella murmured as she gingerly plucked the end of the ribbon and tried to emulate Petunia's work, albeit much more slowly. When she reached the top of the stems, Petunia cut the ribbon and showed her once more how to fold it back on itself so none of the raw edge showed, and pin it in place.

Then Petunia peered through her glasses at Arabella's work and nodded in satisfaction. "I'll have you making corsages and boutonnieres in no time."

She obviously recognized Arabella's horror, because she laughed. "I'm kidding, girl. I know you're looking for a permanent job. But today I am very glad to have you. My father usually fills in for Todd and even though the man is a regular MacGyver, he'd be all thumbs when it comes to this sort of thing." She moved down the table to continue working on the rest of the order. "Heard there's an opening for a cashier over at the grocery on Main."

"No offense to all of the grocery cashiers of the world, but if I'm going to stand on my feet all day, I'd rather be surrounded by the beautiful flowers here than scanning canned beans and heads of lettuce."

Petunia chuckled. "Pay's probably better at the grocery." She plucked a spray of greenery from the stems lying on the table in front of her and after a brief study, snipped off a trio of leaves. "Don't know why you haven't applied over at Hotel Fortune. Goodness knows you've got the connections there."

Arabella chewed the inside of her lip, not wanting to admit that working at the hotel—where Jay worked— had of course figured prominently in her dream world.

Reality, though, was that she had no experience in hospitality whatsoever.

"You know that one of the goals of the hotel was to fill as many positions with locals as possible." She studied her bouquet, trying to decide if the ribbon looked straight or not.

"You're a local now, too."

She unwound the ribbon and started again. "I appreciate the sentiment, but we both know that's not really true."

"Haven't you moved permanently to Rambling Rose?"

"Well, yes, but—"

"Makes you qualify in my mind, girl." Petunia's hands were fairly flying as she plucked a flower here, a bit of leaf there, and fastened them all together into something small and lovely. "Besides which, my nephew Jason works over there and he says they've been having trouble filling all the positions."

Arabella chewed her lip again, stifling the automatic urge to confirm that point. But the things that Brady spoke about over the dinner table at home probably weren't things that he wanted her broadcasting. So she stayed silent and reached for the scissors.

"No wonder, really," Petunia mused.

Arabella couldn't help herself. "Why is that?"

Petunia placed her finished corsage onto a bed of crimped tissue slices filling the bottom of a clear plastic container. "Well, the place seems cursed, doesn't it?"

Arabella's shoulders stiffened. "No."

Her boss must have recognized Arabella's offense because she looked up from her work again. "I'm not saying it *is*," she said quickly. "Or even that I agree. But there's no denying the accidents that have occurred there. That balcony collapsing?" Tsking softly, she snapped the plastic lid in place and set the corsage in a shallow box alongside several others, then immediately began selecting another flower. "My husband insisted Jason find a job somewhere else. At the time, I thought he was overreacting, but he can't very well control what Jason does."

A lot of people had overreacted to the balcony collapse, Arabella thought, her own father included. But it had been a fluke. A terrible accident that mercifully hadn't caused any more injuries than a broken leg for the woman who now managed the hotel.

"Jason listens way more to my father, anyway," Petunia went on, though Arabella was barely listening. "The two of them are thick as thieves. And my dad's been all for Jason working at the hotel." She glanced at Arabella over the rims of her glasses. "You're doing a good job. Going to have to give you a raise."

She was clearly joking and Arabella smiled obediently as she reached for the next bouquet. "All of this stuff is for the 10:00 a.m. delivery?" There were so many left to do and the clock was ticking along.

"It is. Don't look so worried," Petunia assured. "Everything will be ready in time. What kind of career *do* you want to have?"

Arabella let out a laugh that was a little short on humor. "I don't think in terms of a career," she admitted not quite truthfully.

"College?"

"Some." She focused hard on starting the ribbon off at the right spot, even though the task didn't take all that much focus. "It wasn't really for me." More to the point, her average grades hadn't been good enough to garner scholarships and there'd never been any hope of her parents footing the expense for college. She'd quickly learned that spending her paycheck on classes that she wasn't really interested in anyway was a lot less palatable than spending her paycheck on things that *did* interest her.

"Me, either. My father was less than pleased at the time. He's a military vet. He figured either you went to college or you went into the service. No middle ground. Oh, my Lord, the battles that went on between my mom and him. I think that was the last straw in their marriage." Petunia selected another small bit of leaves that would have looked like trimmings to be swept up had it been on the floor instead of the work surface and added it to the corsage taking shape between her fingers. "But I was straight out of high school and wasn't going to listen to anyone, least of all my dad. It wasn't until I was quite a bit older and realized I needed to learn how to run this business I loved that I went back for classes that seemed a lot more relevant."

The bell over the front door jangled then and Petunia went out to deal with the customer.

After giving up on her community college experience, Arabella had taken classes that seemed a lot more relevant to her, too. The only problem was that nobody else appreciated that relevance at all.

And she had no successful business, like Petunia's Posies, to show for herself.

As far as her folks were concerned, creative writing classes were pointless unless you planned to make a living teaching it. Thinking that she might be able to make a career out of it otherwise was just a pipe dream.

And so she continued spending her days in one deadly dull office after another, simply because she could type fast and follow instructions reasonably well, and spent her nights falling asleep over the unfinished stories in her notebooks.

She'd finished three more bouquets by the time Petunia finished with the customer, and by the time Arabella needed to load up her vehicle for the day's deliveries, Petunia's confidence that the wedding flowers would be ready was rewarded.

With the clipboard of delivery addresses sitting beside Arabella on her front seat, she set off.

The church was locked up tight when she arrived and she had to hunt around to find someone possessing keys to open up so she could place all the flowers in the sanctuary per her instructions. After that, she was off to the other side of town to deliver a dozen roses to a woman who took one look at the card included and dropped the long-stemmed beauties to the doorstep, where she ground her heel on them until they were pulp.

Then, taking in Arabella's horrified fascination, smiled and tipped her a twenty.

Arabella returned to her car and the potted plant that was her final delivery for the day. She didn't recognize the street at all, so she plugged the address into her phone's GPS and set off.

Twenty minutes later, she'd left the outskirts of Rambling Rose behind and was beginning to wonder why the GPS-lady was sending her down a dirt road. There was nothing on either side of the road. No cows grazed in the green fields. In fact, whatever was growing in the fields looked more like weeds to her than actual crops.

She was almost ready to stop and call the number on the order slip for better directions when a white two-story farmhouse surrounded by rosebushes came into view. Unlike the unkempt fields, the rosebushes were entirely orderly and filled with roses just as red as the ones that had ended up beneath the woman's heel.

The message on this card said "For my favorite granny" and the potted plant accompanying it would surely have a happier fate.

Arabella parked in front of the house, carried the plant up to the front door and used the eagle-shaped door knocker since there didn't seem to be a doorbell. She soon heard footsteps and was already smiling when the door pulled open.

But instead of a delighted granny named Louella standing on the other side of the door, it was Jay Cross.

And Arabella was pretty sure *she* was the one who looked delighted.

Chapter Four

"I wondered when you were going to get here."

"You did?" Arabella felt breathless looking up into Jay's smiling green gaze. "Why?"

"I was hoping the plant would be here before my grandmother got done at Mariana's Market."

Arabella rather stupidly remembered the fern in her arms. "*You* ordered this?"

He leaned his shoulder against the doorjamb. His dimple deepened. "I did."

"Special occasion?"

"Definitely."

He didn't elaborate and she handed him the plant. "Well, I hope she enjoys it. Tell her that Petunia says it wants filtered light and moist soil so…" She trailed off as his smile widened. "What?"

"Appreciate the instructions, but my grandmother can grow anything. You should see her garden out back." He straightened. "In fact, come on in. I'll show you."

Certain her smile was engulfing her entire being, she stepped past him into the cooler shadows of the foyer. He reached out, his arm brushing her shoulder, and her breath caught in her chest.

Then the door closed with a soft click and she realized he'd been only reaching around her to shut it.

Feeling as mature as a giggly girl, she stepped aside and glanced around.

The short foyer fed to a staircase on the left and an airy kitchen and living area on the right. Straight ahead, she could see through to tall, narrow windows at the back of the house. They overlooked another porch similar to the one at the front of the house. Beyond the porch were row upon row of fat, green bushes.

Obviously the garden Jay mentioned.

But the plants weren't relegated only to the outdoors.

As she followed Jay deeper into the house, she saw houseplants thriving in nearly every corner and crevice.

He set the plant she'd delivered on the wooden dining table as they passed it. At the shop, she'd thought the fern was one of the larger ones they had, but here, amongst all these others that his grandmother was already growing, it seemed positively tiny.

"You weren't kidding," Arabella commented. "Your grandmother must really love plants." Whatever the special occasion was, the plant that Jay had ordered barely stood out in comparison.

"That she does." He pushed open a door and the old-fashioned metal blinds hanging over the window on the upper half swayed. "She adamantly refuses to leave her garden, much to my mom's dismay."

He, on the other hand, didn't sound dismayed at all. "Why is that?"

"Mom figures my grandmother is too old to live here by herself, even though she's lived in this house since she married my grandfather when she was eighteen years old." He stopped on the covered porch and spread his arms. "She's spent seventy years here and she keeps up with all of this, but Mom still worries." He dropped his arms. "Come on."

His hand closed around hers as if it were perfectly natural and she nearly tripped over her own feet as they went down the porch steps. "I'm guessing *you* don't worry?"

He laughed softly. "Louella O'Brien defies worry." He tugged her around the end of one row and stopped next to a raised bed positively bursting with ripening strawberries. He plucked a bright red one and held it in front of her lips. "Taste."

She blinked, still too surprised by his presence there, much less his hand still clasping hers, to do anything at all.

His brows drew together and he pulled the strawberry away again. "Wait. You're not allergic, are you?"

"No," she said faintly.

"That's good. Nobody's berries taste better than my grandmother's." He held the fat berry closer to her lips. So close she could smell the sweet aroma. "Taste."

Feeling caught in his gaze, she obediently opened her mouth and bit into the fruit. Sweet juice exploded in her mouth and she chewed more quickly, laughing a little as she wiped her lips. It really was the sweetest strawberry she'd ever tasted. She swallowed. "Is her secret growing the plants in sugar?"

"You'd think." He grinned and popped the other half of the large strawberry into his mouth.

Arabella's stomach hollowed. Feeling hotter than the sunny day warranted, she pulled her hand free and walked alongside the raised bed, pretending to study the plants. What she saw were a lot of great fat leaves and a massive amount of strawberries. Surely more than one person—even one family—could consume. "What does she do with it all?"

"Makes jam." He'd plucked several more berries and handed her one as they moved down the row. "She sells jars of it at Mariana's Market. Lou's Luscious Jams."

"That's the jam that Harper buys. I had it on my toast this morning!"

"Then you know why it's so popular." He popped another strawberry in his mouth and grabbed her hand again as they continued walking along the rows. "Only one who comes even remotely close competition-wise is Mabel's Marmalades." They passed a three-sided potting shed that was as big as the bedroom Arabella occupied at her brother's house. On the other side of the shed were rows and rows of trees. The shade they cast was welcoming.

"Peach trees?"

"With fruit almost as good as the strawberries." He

lifted their joined hands and pointed his finger beyond the trees. "That's my place."

He was pointing at a small stone barn situated on the bank of a narrow stream. Beyond that was a green pasture surrounded by a white-rail fence where several horses grazed near a three-sided shelter.

It was all so picturesque that every little romantic cell in her body quivered in delight. "You live in a converted barn? Can I see inside?" She heard her own eagerness and was vaguely embarrassed by it.

But there was nothing in his expression that suggested she ought to be embarrassed. "If you won't judge me for my housecleaning."

She crossed her heart with her finger. "Promise."

His hand tightened on hers again and he headed toward the barn. But they hadn't emerged from beneath the shade of the peach orchard when the coughing rumble of an engine cut through the quiet.

"Sounds like my grandmother is back." He about-faced and started back through the trees.

Arabella couldn't really complain. Not when he was still holding her hand the way he was.

They rounded the potting shed again and passed the strawberry beds and were halfway up the rows of big green bushes when a thin woman with dark gray-and-silver hair appeared on the back porch. She looked a lot younger than Jay had indicated and in her hands was the plant that Arabella had delivered.

"Favorite granny?" Louella O'Brien had a sturdy drawl and an equally sturdy tone. "Your *only* granny, you mean." She balanced the plant on the porch rail and waited until they reached the steps. "If this is another attempt at bribing me to call your mama—"

"It's just a plant," Jay assured lightly. "So don't get your hairnet in a knot." He let go of Arabella's hand and dashed up the steps, leaning down to drop a kiss on the woman's tanned, lined cheek. "The plant was just an excuse, anyway."

"I thought it was a special occasion." The words escaped Arabella without thought and she saw the raised-brow look that Jay's grandmother sent him.

"It is." He beckoned Arabella closer. "Gran, this is Arabella Fortune. She delivered the newest addition to your indoor jungle. Arabella, my grandmother, Louella O'Brien."

Arabella hurried forward, extending her hand. "I'm pleased to meet you, Mrs. O'Brien."

Jay's grandmother's hand grasped hers in return. Not only were her fingers longer than Arabella's, they were more darkly tanned and much more calloused. "Another one of those Fortunes, hmm?"

Arabella's gaze collided with the amusement in Jay's. "I don't know about that," she demurred. "But…related. I just moved here from New York."

His eyes glinted. "You've decided to stay, then?"

She felt like steam might be radiating from her skin, but she kept her eyes from shying away. "The odds are beginning to look up."

His grandmother cleared her throat noisily.

Arabella flushed and belatedly released the woman's hand. She pushed her fingers into her back pockets and glanced over her shoulder. "Jay was showing me your garden, Mrs. O'Brien. It's amazing."

"Yes, it is," Louella agreed matter-of-factly. "Do you garden?"

Arabella shook her head. "I couldn't even keep the succulent a friend gave me last year alive."

"No matter what people think, succulents can be touchy. Come out here tomorrow. I'm making cuttings and a new batch of jam."

"Arabella has a job, Gran. At Petunia's—"

"Posies," Louella finished. "I can read well enough." She flicked the embossed card that was tucked among the potted plant's glossy leaves. "And I happen to be well aware that Petunia's shop isn't open on Sundays." She gave Arabella a look. "Churchgoer?"

Only if one counted Christmases and Easters. "Umm—"

"Ten sharp," Louella said, as if that settled it. "Jay? A word?"

Something in his gaze flickered, but he nodded. "Be right back," he told Arabella before following his grandmother inside the house.

They closed the door after them, which only increased Arabella's sudden sense of awkwardness. She stepped off the porch again, reaching out to steady the plant that was propped on the flat rail when it wobbled.

"An excuse or a special occasion," she murmured, placing it more squarely on the rail. "What are you really?"

The plant provided no answer and she turned away, moving back over to the first row of bushes. She glanced over her shoulder, but the door to the house was still closed.

Maybe Jay's grandmother was warning him not to get involved with one of those Fortunes.

The sun was getting higher in the sky and hotter and the faint buzz of insects seemed like summer music. Maybe when she found a real job and started looking for a place of her own, she should look for one that had space for a tiny garden. Growing something outdoors might be easier than keeping a container succulent happy on a windowsill in her bedroom.

She glanced back at the house. Door still closed.

She told herself there wasn't any reason to be concerned. If Jay's grandmother were warning him not to get involved with one of those Fortunes, then why would she have invited Arabella to come back the next day for cuttings?

From between the slats of the window blinds, Jay watched Arabella disappear into the shade of the potting shed. "She's just a friend, Gran," he insisted for the third time and his grandmother made a third, disbelieving snort in response.

"I've been able to read your mind since you were knee-high to a grasshopper." Louella set two glasses on the round serving tray she'd pulled from a cabinet. "I can read it now, too." She opened the refrigerator and pulled out a glass jug of homemade lemonade. "You're interested in that girl."

He spread his hands, exasperated. "So what if I am?"

"Goin' to tell her the truth, then?" She added the jug to the tray and turned back to the fridge.

Jay felt a faint pain start up inside his head. He'd been on the verge of telling Arabella the truth in January when they'd first met. But a lot of time had passed since then. Time for him to get even more settled into the routine of Jay Cross. Time for him to get further away from the man he'd been. But the further away he remained, the more interest kept growing to flush him out. "Eventually."

His grandmother gave him a look as she pulled a tray of ice from the freezer.

"Probably," he amended.

She said nothing. Just filled the two glasses with the ice, her lips compressed.

"Maybe," he tried again.

"I *knew* you were waffling!" She peeled the plastic lid off an old metal coffee can and removed several cookies from inside. She spread them on a flowered plate and added it to the serving tray along with a few of her fabric napkins that she kept in a drawer.

"And you don't approve."

She slid her finger between two slats in the window blind the same way he had and peered through the narrow slit. "She's a pretty girl."

Arabella was a lot more than pretty, but he wasn't going to argue the point.

"Not like that other one." The slats snapped together again.

He didn't have to ask who she meant. Louella had never pretended to like his ex-girlfriend. And Tina had never pretended to like Louella. The only thing Tina liked about Jay's background was that he came from Texas.

In her opinion it gave him a sort of credibility.

Not that he'd recognized that at the beginning. In the beginning, he'd been totally taken in by her.

"You ought to be happy about that," Jay said aloud. "Arabella being different than Tina."

"I am."

"Then what's the problem?"

His grandmother picked up the laden tray and pushed it into his hands. "You're a smart boy," she said irritably. "So be smart. Start as you mean to go on."

"She's not even certain she's going to stay in Rambling Rose." The words were as much for himself as they were for his grandmother. A reminder that jumping in with both feet was fine when you were eight and standing on the precipice of a cool swimming hole on a hot day.

But his life was a lot more complicated now than it had once been. More complicated even than it had been in January. Staying two steps ahead of the man he'd been was getting harder by the day.

"Are *you* staying in Rambling Rose?" she asked pointedly.

He sighed noisily. She knew he didn't have an answer. "You know I'm working tomorrow," he told her. "But you invited her to be free labor for you."

"She'll learn a little about gardening and a little about jam-making. It's a fair trade. Don't worry. I won't tell her who you really are, *Jett*."

"I'm *really* Jay Cross," he said flatly.

She gave him a steady look. "We'll see 'bout that, won't we?" She pulled open the door. "It's hot out there. Go have lemonade and cookies with your girl."

"Don't think I miss the significance, Granny."

Her eyebrows rose. "Can't imagine what you mean."

He made a face and passed her through the doorway.

He found Arabella in the potting shed. She was sitting on a stool at the scarred metal workbench, paging through one of his grandmother's binders that were stored on one of the many shelves above the bench.

"Did you know she keeps notes on what she plants?" She glanced at him. "The dates and what the weather's like and all sorts of little details?"

"As a matter of fact, I did know." He set the tray next to the binder. "She has binders going back for decades. Before I was born, even. How else do you think she developed her sugar-soil recipe?" He filled both glasses with lemonade and handed her one. "Better drink it all. She squeezes the lemons by hand, too."

Arabella's eyes danced. "Did she mill her own flour for those cookies, too?"

He grinned. "Anything's possible." He lightly tapped his glass against hers. "Cheers."

She took a quick sip of lemonade, made a soft, appreciative "mmm" sound that slid down the base of his spine and took a longer drink. "Delicious."

He had to force himself to look away from the way her lower lip glistened. "Best lemonade in the county." He chugged down half his own glass, feeling parched in a way that lemonade would never quench. "She has a box of blue ribbons from the county fair that goes back about as far as the binders do."

Arabella picked up one of the golden cookies. "Chocolate chip?" She didn't wait for his nod before she broke off a little piece and popped it in her mouth. She made that same throaty "mmm" sound. "How many blue ribbons did she win for her cookies?"

"No idea," Jay admitted. "But she did win my grandfather with them."

Arabella looked even more delighted. "Really?"

If her eyes hadn't held such vivid interest, he would have wished that he'd kept his mouth shut. "They met when she was just seventeen. Her father wouldn't let her go out with him because he was eight years older. But her mother, who was a piano teacher, said he could come to their house on Sunday afternoons for piano lessons. After which, my grandmother would serve him her homemade lemonade and chocolate chip cookies. He always claimed that it was the lemonade and cookies that kept him coming back. They eloped a week after she turned eighteen."

Arabella propped her chin on her hand. "That's the sweetest story. Is she your mom's mom or your dad's?"

"Mom's. She was their only child. Lonely only, as my mother says."

"Are you a lonely only, too?"

A crumble of cookie caught in his throat. He coughed slightly and nodded.

"Do your parents live here in Rambling Rose also?"

"Houston. That's where I grew up. My dad's a math teacher. Mom's a piano teacher."

"I remember you mentioned that the day we met. Like your great-grandmother."

He nodded. "But I spent a lot of summers here with my grandparents." Until he'd turned fifteen and decided he was too old for such nonsense. It had taken him another ten years before he'd begun to appreciate the error of his ways. Fortunately, his grandmother hadn't held that against him too much when he'd needed a bolt-hole.

"And now you live here with her."

"No, I *live* in the barn," he corrected dryly. "Which she tolerates only because I feed the horses she refuses to give up and my presence here keeps my mother relatively quiet on the subject of moving Gran to Houston. In case it's not apparent by her choice to live way the hell out here, my grandmother likes her privacy." Something that also suited him very well these days.

Arabella shook her head. "I'll bet she loves having you here. You, who surprises her with potted plants."

"One plant." He rotated his glass in the pool of condensation that had formed around the base. "And it was just so you'd have to deliver it," he admitted.

Her eyebrows pulled together. The corners of her lips curved again. "You're joking."

"You didn't call me this morning to tell me your battery was dead. What else was I supposed to do?"

She looked down at the tray between them. Her lashes were dark and long and looked entirely natural. "So the plant really was an excuse?"

"For a special occasion."

She wrinkled her nose and looked at him. "Special occasion being…?"

He was barely aware that he'd leaned down on his arms on the workbench, putting him at her level. "Getting to see you again."

Her eyes softened. "Jay."

"Arabella." He couldn't help himself. He touched the ponytail hanging over her shoulder. The red strands might look fiery, but they slid through his fingers cool and silky.

"I think you'd better kiss me," she murmured and her cheeks turned rosy.

"Yeah?" His voice dropped also.

"If you don't, then I'll know this is just a dream."

"And if I do?"

She moistened her lips. "Then I'll know this is just a dream."

He smiled slightly. He brushed the silky end of her ponytail against her cheek and leaned closer. "Dream, Bella," he whispered, and slowly pressed his lips to hers.

He felt her quick inhale and his own quick rush. Tasted the brightness of lemonade, the sweetness of strawberry.

He slid his fingers from her ponytail to the back of her neck and urged her closer.

Her fingers splayed against his chest. She murmured something against his lips. He barely heard. His head was full of sound. Full of pulse beats and bells.

She murmured again. This time not against his lips.

He frowned, feeling entirely thwarted. "What?"

She pulled back yet another inch. Her fingertips pushed instead of urged closer. "Do you want to answer that?"

It made sense then. His cell phone was ringing.

He exhaled his annoyance and pulled the offending device from his back pocket. The number showing on the screen wasn't familiar, but the area code was. He declined the call, the ringing went quiet and he shoved the phone into his pocket again.

"Nobody important?"

He shook his head, but some piece of conscience in him prickled.

Start as you mean to go on.

When had he stopped believing in that?

"Bella. Arabella—"

"I like when you call me Bella." Her hand had found a place against his chest again, her fingertips grazing his neck.

The urge to pull her out of the potting shed and beyond the peach orchard to his barn was painful.

He closed his hand around hers, moving it away from his chest. "Then you'll always be Bella to me." He kissed her fingertips. "But I—" He broke off with a curse when his phone rang insistently again. He didn't need to look at the screen to know it would be the same caller. Just as he hadn't needed to recognize the number to know it would be the same caller.

Despite their long alliance, Michael Devane had cut Jay loose the year before without a speck of regret.

Then everything changed and Jay had been dodging Michael ever since. When there was money on the line, the other man was like a bulldog.

He pulled out his phone again, turned it off and left it facedown on the bench.

But even though he wanted to start up right where he'd left off—namely the pouty curve of Arabella's lower lip—that damn piece of conscience prickled harder than ever. So instead, he raked his fingers through his ruthlessly short hair and refilled his glass of lemonade. "Damn, it's getting hot out, isn't it?"

She looked vaguely confused. "The heat isn't so bad, but the humidity is worse than I'm used to." She freed her ponytail, only to bundle her hair up into a knot on the top of her head and secure the tie around it again. "I actually ought to be going. I have a thing I have to go to this afternoon." She closed the binder and stretched up to replace it on the shelf. Her shirt rode up above the waistband of her jeans, briefly revealing a narrow strip of creamy skin.

He looked away and chugged another quarter glass of lemonade. "A thing?"

"Barbecue. My brother's fiancée is expecting me." She went back down on her heels and tugged the bottom of her shirt. "You know, if you don't want me to come tomorrow, you can just tell me."

His mind had been occupied with fantasies of exploring that soft-looking skin. To see whether the sprinkle of light freckles across her nose were repeated anywhere else. "Why wouldn't I want you to come?"

"I don't know." She tugged at her shirt again, but this time he knew it wasn't an unconscious act but an indicator of uncertainty. "Just thought I should make sure. She's *your* grandmother. Maybe she doesn't really expect me to take her up—"

"You haven't spent enough time with her yet," Jay

said wryly. "She doesn't say things she doesn't mean."
Which was why he trusted that she wouldn't tell all to
Arabella just because she figured Jay ought to. "You
didn't decline her invitation. She's going to expect you
tomorrow. And she's going to put you to work, so you
might as well come prepared."

"And you? Is she putting you to work, too?"

"She would if I didn't have to be on duty at the hotel.
Can't tell you how many hours of weeding she's gotten
out of me since I moved into the barn."

She looked crestfallen. "You have to work at the
hotel tomorrow?"

Her disappointment was ego-boosting to say the
least. "Afraid so." He tucked his finger beneath her
chin. "Which means I'll have to think of some way to
make it up to you."

"Really?" It was practically a squeak and she
blushed. "Really?" she repeated in a much lower register and with a lot more aplomb.

Everything about her charmed him. "Really." He
wrapped the remaining cookies in one of the napkins
and handed them to her. "Gran'll figure I screwed up
if all of the cookies aren't gone."

Their fingers brushed as she took the napkin from
him. "Can't have that."

He walked her back to her car, going around the
house rather than through it. But his attempt at avoid-
ing his grandmother was futile, since she was outside at
the front of the house anyway, tending her rosebushes.

She peered from beneath the brim of her ancient
straw hat. "Leaving already?"

"Arabella has a family thing to get to," Jay answered, knowing that was one thing that would quell his grandmother's well-intentioned nosiness.

"I do," Arabella confirmed. "Thank you for the cookies and lemonade, Mrs. O'Brien. They were delicious."

"Pleased to hear it," his grandmother said. "Nothing more satisfying when everyone's feeling warm."

Arabella obviously took the words at face value, but Jay was glad his grandmother's straw brim shaded her undoubtedly crafty expression.

He opened Arabella's car door for her and closed it again once she was behind the wheel. When she turned the key, the engine started immediately.

She smiled wryly. "Guess the battery thing must have been a fluke."

"Fluke. Divine intervention. Either way, I'm grateful."

Her smile widened as she put the car in gear. "You don't happen to be Irish, do you?"

"Are you kidding?" He took a step back when her tires began to slowly crunch over the drive. "Gran's name is O'Brien."

"That doesn't necessarily mean you're Irish. But if you are, it at least explains the gift you have for blarney!" Then she was driving away, leaving behind the sound of her laughter.

He stood there, long after her car was out of sight and the dust she'd kicked up was finally settled.

"Didn't tell her, did you." It wasn't a question.

He exhaled sharply and turned to face his grandmother. "Do you ever get tired of being right all the time?"

"It's a burden I've learned to bear," she deadpanned.

Then she wielded her snips with deliberation and a dying rose fell to the ground.

Chapter Five

"...*And that's 'Giving It All Up' by the newest sensation—*"

The radio went silent as Arabella turned off her engine. She stared through her windshield at the front facade of Hotel Fortune and wondered for about the hundredth time if she was really doing this.

Applying for a job at Hotel Fortune.

Any job.

Three days ago, Todd Bellamy had returned from his family vacation and three days ago, her job at Petunia's Posies had ended.

She also hadn't heard one word from Jay Cross. Not even after she'd spent several hours working in his grandmother's garden more than a week ago.

Which, considering the way he'd kissed her in the

potting shed, left her once again mired in a swamp of uncertainty. Was he interested in her or wasn't he?

You're the one who asked him to kiss you.

She swatted away the thought like an annoying fly. But like any respectable annoying fly, it just kept returning to the picnic.

She couldn't even be certain whether or not her decision to actually seek a job at Hotel Fortune was because of Jay or in spite of him.

She got out of the car, slamming her car door harder than necessary, and straightened her shoulders as she marched through the entrance of the hotel.

She hadn't been there since January. The only noticeable change to the Spanish Mission–style lobby since then were the flowers in the massive arrangement on the table positioned beneath a skylight centered in the soaring ceiling.

She stopped at the reception desk. "I have an appointment in human resources?"

The attendant was a young man who didn't even look old enough to shave. "Third floor. Just follow the signs."

"Thanks." She headed for the elevators. There were very few people about. Only one middle-aged couple sat in the massive leather chairs in one corner of the lobby near the door. They had small suitcases sitting on the terra-cotta tiled floor next to them. Probably waiting for transportation. Another couple exited the elevator when the doors opened and Arabella stepped into the empty car and punched the third-floor button.

As the doors closed, she couldn't help remembering

the small elevator that Jay had shown her the day of Larkin's party when she'd taken the twins outside to play.

"Stop thinking about Jay Cross," she said under her breath. The soft bell chimed at the second floor and the doors slid open to reveal an empty corridor.

Arabella poked her head out of the car and seeing nobody standing by, ducked back inside and poked the close button a few times to hasten it along. She wouldn't be cutting the time so closely for her appointment with the human resources department if she hadn't had to change her outfit at the last minute thanks to Murphy's muddy paws.

But the doors stubbornly refused to close at all. Not even pressing the third-floor button again garnered any results.

Huffing in frustration, she left the elevator and pressed the call button for its mate, but that button didn't even light up and after another minute waiting for it to respond, she huffed again and headed down the corridor looking for signs for the stairwell.

As she went, she passed the entrance for Roja's banquet room. The door was open and she glanced inside as she hurried past. Round tables—currently naked of tablecloths—were situated around the room. Then she remembered the stairwell they'd used in January and quickly found it around another corner. The heavy door clanged shut behind her and her heels rang out as she raced up the cement steps. She reached the landing where a door was marked with a black numeral 3.

She'd been on dozens of interviews in her life. She shouldn't be so nervous now, yet she was. She drew in a deep breath and smoothed her hand down the side of her skirt before grasping the door handle and pushing it down.

The handle moved.

The door did not.

"No way." She twisted the lever up. Twisted it down. But it remained locked. Cursing under her breath, she hurried back down the stairs, the whole way to the first floor, and burst breathlessly out of the door, inordinately relieved that it hadn't been locked as well.

The stairwell hadn't been particularly confining. Just a basic square tower filled with concrete steps and a bunch of doors that didn't open, but she still felt shaky from nerves.

She smoothed her ponytail and hurried back to the lobby, passing a trio of people now waiting for the elevators along the way.

"One of them was stuck on the second floor," she told them as she walked by, heading once more back to the reception desk.

The same young guy was there.

"That was fast," he said as she stopped in front of him.

"Only because I couldn't get up to the third floor." She inhaled yet another deep, calming breath. "The stairwell doors are all locked on the inside."

"It's a security thing," he said. "Unless you're a guest with your room key, you can't enter other floors except the main floor. Of course the fire department can override the locks in an emergency. The elevators—"

"—decided to hang out permanently on the second

floor," she interrupted, wanting to cut to the chase. "One of them, anyway." Who knew about the other elevator.

"Oh, yeah." He nodded as if just now remembering. "That's been a problem lately."

Arabella wanted to ask him why something hadn't been *done* about that problem lately. "What about the service elevator?"

"Sorry but that's for staff only."

"Which I won't have a chance to even *be* if I can't get up to the human resource department. Can't you just give me a room key or something so I can get through the stairwell door?"

He frowned as if the idea of it caused him physical pain.

Arabella leaned closer and lowered her voice conspiratorially. "Isn't it a bit of a hazard having only one way to get from one floor to another?"

"Is there a problem, Jason?"

Jason got a definite deer-in-the-headlights look when a brunette with a serious expression on her face stopped next to the reception desk. "No problems, Ms. Williams."

"You're Grace," Arabella said, realizing it even before she saw the discreet name badge on the other woman's lapel. Grace Williams. General Manager.

The woman's expression was friendly but Arabella thought she detected a sense of reserve in her eyes.

"I do have the distinct pleasure of being GM," Grace said, holding out her hand. "And you—"

"Arabella Fortune." She pumped the manager's hand. "I'm Br—"

"Brady's sister!" Warmth entered Grace's eyes. "I'm so pleased to meet you. Your brother has told me all about you."

Arabella couldn't help making a face. "When it comes to big brothers, that isn't always a good thing."

Grace laughed lightly. "He sings your praises," she assured. "Are you here to see him?"

"Actually, no," Arabella admitted. Brady didn't even know what she was up to that afternoon. She cast a look toward the elevators. Two members of the waiting trio had given up and disappeared, leaving only the third standing there still staring at the unmoving illuminations above the doors. "I have an appointment with Sybil in human resources. Starts—" she glanced at her nonexistent wristwatch "—about ten minutes ago."

"You're applying?" Far from being concerned over Arabella's tardiness, Grace just looked delighted. "Your brother didn't say a word about that."

"He doesn't really know," Arabella admitted. Even though he'd teased her unmercifully about going to work at the hotel when she'd first broached the subject of moving to Rambling Rose. "I didn't want anyone thinking that I was hoping for special favors or something."

"Trust me," Grace assured. "I understand that completely."

Arabella remembered then that Grace was involved with Wiley Fortune, who was one of *those* Fortunes. Considering he was one of Arabella's cousins, she ought to have more than a vague recollection of meeting him at Larkin's party.

But the truth was that she'd been far more interested in the server named Jay than she had been with anyone else.

"Which position are you applying for?"

Arabella spread her hands. "I'm not picky. I just want a paycheck so I don't have to keep sponging off my brother."

"Well, then." Grace extended one arm in the direction of the elevators. "I have a meeting on four. I'll go up with you."

"Um—"

Grace's eyebrows rose slightly. "Yes, Jason?"

"One of the elevators is stuck on the second floor," Arabella provided because the poor guy looked like he was about ready to choke on his bobbing Adam's apple. "And the other one seems stuck somewhere also."

Arabella heard the faint sigh that Grace exhaled. But her expression was calm and still smiling as she looked at Arabella. "Excuse me for just a second while I take care of that."

Arabella wasn't going to argue. Certainly not with the woman who was not only Brady's boss, but boss of the whole place. She waited until Grace had disappeared through a doorway behind the reception desk and looked toward Jason again. "Make up your mind about that key yet?"

Jason cast a quick look over his shoulder toward the doorway. "I think she meant for you to wait for her."

Arabella actually had that same impression. But she

hadn't been able to resist asking him the question. "How long have you worked here, Jason?" She felt sure he was the nephew Petunia had mentioned.

He stood rather stiffly behind the reception desk and after her question he straightened his blue tie. "Since they first opened," he said proudly. "Two weeks ago I got promoted here to the desk."

Grace reappeared. "Maintenance is taking care of the elevators and I buzzed Sybil to let her know why you were delayed. Jason, until the elevators are fixed, be sure to direct anyone needing them to the service bay. One of the girls from housekeeping can escort them to their floor."

He nodded. "Yes'm. Um. Ma'am."

Grace's smile gentled. "And one more thing, Jason. *Relax.* You're doing fine." Then she turned to Arabella again. "Shall we?" She led the way out of the lobby.

There was no sign of the broken leg she'd sustained when the balcony had collapsed and following her, Arabella couldn't help but admire the confidence in Grace's bearing.

Maybe someday she'd exude some of that herself.

They used the same service elevator that Jay had used back in January and in minutes, Arabella found herself sitting in front of Sybil's desk.

"Take good care of her." Grace's voice was light as she departed for her meeting. "If she's anything like her brother, we don't want her getting away."

Left alone with Sybil, Arabella smiled a little awkwardly. "I'm nothing like my brother," she warned.

"You're a Fortune," Sybil said, sliding a blank job

application and a pen across the desk toward Arabella. "That's the only qualification you'll need."

Arabella picked up the pen and hesitated. "There's nothing magical about my last name."

"Says the person who possesses it." Sybil's voice wasn't unkind. But it *was* matter-of-fact.

"I don't expect to be given preference over another applicant just because I'm related to—"

Sybil cut her off with a wave of her hand. "You won't be. Right now, we have more open positions than we do applicants. Just fill out the top section. Name, address, social security number. That stuff. Then sign the bottom. We're running background checks on new hires, so assuming all that checks out, we've got positions available in everything from maintenance to housekeeping to front office to accounting. What sort of experience do you have?"

Arabella quickly filled in the boxes on the application and added her signature at the bottom. "Most recently, I was an administrative assistant at a plastics manufacturer before I moved to Rambling Rose." It was true, but Arabella had always considered the title a glorified one considering the scope of her clerical duties. She slid the application back across to Sybil. "I've also worked back office at a dental practice, had the ubiquitous phone bank job when I was still in school. Retail work—um, a department store as well as a small independent book—" She broke off when Sybil waved her hand again.

"When can you start?"

"Immediately."

Sybil made a note on the application and slid it into one of her desk drawers. She rose and rounded her desk. "The trainee program was designed with Rambling Rose locals in mind but we'll start you there for now. Come with me and we'll get you set up with a name badge and such. I'll get a copy of your ID while we're at it. And then I'll give you the tour."

Getting a job couldn't possibly be this easy. Feeling bemused, Arabella followed the older woman out of her small office. "What about the background check?"

Sybil cast her a sideways look. "You're going to pass it, aren't you?"

"Well, yes." Unless occasionally skipping to the last page of a book counted, there was nothing remotely scandalous in Arabella's background. Still, it hardly seemed prudent to just trust a person's word on that score, even if one's surname *was* Fortune.

"Then there's no reason why you can't start tomorrow— provisionally, of course."

They stopped in the security office and Sybil made introductions, then went off to get her copies of Arabella's proof of ID, while she had her photograph taken and a name badge made up right there on the spot.

"The badge is an access key. Encoded with your security rights. So don't lose it and don't let anyone else use it," she was instructed when she received the badge.

Then Sybil returned, and feeling like she was pretending to be something she wasn't, Arabella fastened the badge on her blouse and hurriedly caught up with Sybil's ground-eating stride as she started off on the tour.

She introduced Arabella to every department head

and supervisor until Arabella's head felt like it was spinning. The only person they didn't see was Brady, and that was undoubtedly because Sybil knew he was Arabella's brother.

The dizzying tour ended once more in Sybil's third-floor office. She poured herself a cup of coffee from a communal pot and sat on the edge of her desk again. "Any questions?"

Tons. Arabella smiled with more confidence than she felt. "Only two. What time do I start tomorrow and who should I be reporting to when I get here?"

Sybil looked pleased. "Eight sharp and check in at the front desk. I'll leave further instructions for you there."

"Thank you." Arabella shook the woman's hand. "I appreciate the opportunity."

"Hope you'll still feel that way after tomorrow," Sybil said humorously. She moved around her desk to sit once more and taking her cue, Arabella departed.

Arabella didn't need to use her new badge to call the service elevator because an older woman with bright blond hair in a big bun on her head was already entering.

She held the door and smiled as Arabella joined her. "New here?"

Arabella nodded, fingering the sparkling new badge. "As of an hour ago, actually."

"Well, congratulations!" The woman punched the button for the second floor and after a questioning look at Arabella, hit the first floor button, too. "I'm Mariana. I help run Roja here."

"Mariana! You run the flea market, too, don't you?" Arabella pumped the woman's hand with genuine pleasure when the other woman nodded. "That's where Jay's grandmother sells her jams."

Mariana looked delighted. "You know Jay Cross? I remember when he was just a skinny little rug rat. He's sure grown into a handsome man."

Arabella flushed. "We've met," she allowed. "Brady talks a lot about you. He says the boys love going out there because of all the food trucks. Yours is the original one, right?"

Mariana laughed even more merrily as she nodded. "Food trucks have come a long way these days from our humble roach-coach beginnings." She touched the badge on her own buxom breast. "Some might say the same thing about me." The elevator lurched slightly and the door opened. "Come by Roja soon and tell me how you're settling in." She left the elevator, stepping around the tall ladder just outside of the car. "Hey there, Jetpack," she said on her way. "Were your ears burning?"

When Jay maneuvered the ladder into the elevator, she wanted to disappear through the padded walls. She'd known the chances of running into him around the hotel were good. But she hadn't really thought it would happen like this.

He looked equally surprised to see her. "Bella. You're—"

"On staff here." She flicked her name badge and tried not to get drawn in by his emerald eyes as the elevator doors closed yet again.

"I see that." He shifted the ladder until it was leaning against the padded wall. "What department?"

She shrugged. "No idea. I'm starting off in the trainee program tomorrow."

"Same as me, then." He smiled. "Be prepared to try your hand at everything from cleaning toilets to delivering room service."

"And hefting ladders, evidently."

"I was helping maintenance with the elevators." He hooked his arm over one of the rungs and his fingers hung loosely on her side of the ladder. If she moved even half a foot, they'd brush against her.

She pressed her back harder against the padding as if to warn herself not to move toward those callused fingertips. "You've been here for how long now? Six months?"

"Little past that."

"Is it common to stay in the trainee program that long?"

"Is that your way of suggesting I'm doomed to be a perpetual trainee?" His teeth flashed. "When I joined the program, they said it was designed to last about a year. After which, theoretically, the person should be ready to move into one of the junior management positions."

"What sort of management—" She broke off when the elevator doors slid open.

She hadn't even been aware that the car had stopped moving.

Still holding the ladder propped against his shoulder,

Jay shifted sideways until his back was pressed against the edge of the door. "After you."

She detached herself from the padded wall and quickly stepped out of the elevator. It meant passing him even more closely and she only realized she'd been holding her breath when it escaped after she'd put half the width of the corridor between them. Whether or not he'd ignored her for more than a week, walking away without saying some sort of goodbye felt rude.

"Well." She pressed her palms together. "Guess I'll see you around." She turned to leave only to bump hard against the corner of one of the empty rolling racks stored against the wall. Feeling like an idiot, she steadied the cart as she moved around it.

"Bella, wait."

It was painful the way her nerve endings tingled so swiftly where he was concerned. She took another sidestep, waving her arm. "I can see you're busy and I need to get going."

"Bella—"

Her neck prickled. "Arabella, actually. Only my family calls me that."

His gaze flickered. "I should have called you this week."

Something inside her head sort of popped. "Then why didn't you?" The words flew out. Cheeks on fire, she backed up again and banged into yet another rack. "Never mind. Don't answer that."

"It's not you, it's—"

Good grief, she was going to cry at this rate. "Yeah, I know. Sorry if I don't want to hear another *it's not you, it's me* story. No sweat, you know. You don't have to explain a thing. We don't even really know each other."

I think you should know that...

She clamped down hard on that thought, cutting it off at the head.

"Tell your grandmother thanks again from me. The jam she sent me home with is already gone thanks to my brother and his family." Afraid of what she might do or say if she let him get a word in edgewise, she quickly turned and mercifully avoided running into another one of the racks as she hurried away.

It was only divine mercy that kept her feet moving in the proper direction, because she honestly wasn't sure how she ended up back in the lobby. The couple with the luggage was gone now and a curvy girl in a black T-shirt and trousers was dusting the leather chairs they'd occupied.

Arabella managed a smile as she sailed past her and out the door. She felt a little compunction for not looking in on Brady, but told herself he would have been busy, anyway.

Clouds had formed overhead while she'd been inside the hotel, and the air felt heavy and humid. Her car provided no relief, either, and she was grateful to get back to Brady's place.

The house was empty—a momentary condition, she felt sure—and with Murphy trailing after her every step, she changed out of her skirt and blouse and into cutoffs and a spaghetti tank and went down to the kitchen.

"And that's another deep cut called 'Lonely Only' from Carr's first album that was released nearly ten—"

Arabella snapped off the droning voice on the radio and opened her arms. Murphy nimbly jumped up into them. She rubbed his ears. "Did you behave?"

He licked her neck, which wasn't much of an answer, but was pretty delightful, anyway. She gave him a treat and he jumped out of her arms and darted through the dog door.

Harper and Brady had taken to leaving notes on the refrigerator for each other in an attempt to keep up with the increasing busyness of their lives. Brady's schedule. Harper's menu plans for the coming few days. Another note in Harper's neat handwriting that said simply *Love you.*

The sweet, ordinary things of an ordinary life. Arabella sighed as she traced Harper's little note.

How nice it would be to have someone with whom to share that sort of ordinariness.

Predictably, Jay filled her thoughts and she determinedly shrugged him off along with the clouds inside her mind as she pulled open the refrigerator door.

The least she could do was get dinner started and according to Harper's note, the menu du jour was hamburgers on the grill and salad.

She had the salad and burger patties waiting in the fridge and was poking at the fiery coals in the grill in the backyard when she heard the rumble tumble of the twins inside the house behind her. Several minutes passed, though, before Harper came outside, Murphy on her heels. She was wearing a T-shirt and shorts.

"Look at you," Harper greeted her delightedly. "When the boys' checkups at the clinic went later than

I expected, I figured I'd be resorting to PB&J for their supper if I wanted to get them to bed at a reasonable hour."

"Just waiting for the coals to get hot." Arabella hung the poker on the side of the kettle-shaped grill and fit the domed lid in place. She eyed the kiddie pool that Harper was manhandling through the doorway. "Need help?"

"I've got it." Proof was in the pudding. The hard plastic pool popped out of Harper's hands and rolled on its side off the edge of the patio, flopped down onto the grass. Murphy went nuts, immediately hopping inside it to sniff every blue plastic crevice. "Picked it up at the store on the way home. This humidity is killing, isn't it?" Harper didn't wait for an answer as she grabbed the end of the coiled garden hose. "Murphy, come."

The dog flopped on his belly and woofed.

Harper shook her head, resigned. "Get wet, then." She dropped the end of the hose into the pool and turned on the water.

Predictably, Murphy yelped. He disliked water as much as he disliked being left alone in a silent house. "Coward," Harper accused when the dog bolted inside, leaving the dog door swinging wildly.

With the pool filling, she flopped down onto the deck chair beside Arabella. "So, how's the job hunt?"

"I start at the hotel tomorrow."

Harper's eyebrows rose. "I knew you were putting applications in everywhere, but Brady didn't tell me you were applying there, too."

"He didn't know. They put me in the trainee program."

"Well, that's great!" Harper beamed.

"What's great?" Brady stepped out onto the patio. He was loosening the tie that Arabella still found hard to believe he wore to work every day.

She'd never thought her brother was particularly a suit-and-tie sort of guy. But as the hotel concierge, he was living up to the task as well as the look.

Harper tilted her face for his kiss. "Arabella's gotten into the trainee program at Hotel Fortune. She starts tomorrow!"

Brady gave her a sideways look. "Wondered how long it'd take you to get around applying there."

She lifted her chin. "Why's that?"

"'Cause that's where your crush works."

She stared him down, refusing to react. When it came to her brothers, she had that down to a fine art.

When it came to Jay Cross?

Pure and utter failure.

"I have no idea what you're talking about," she said with just the right amount of boredom. She got up and turned off the hose because the pool was almost over-flowing. Then she lifted the lid on the grill to check the coals and the twins and the dog raced out to join them.

Clad in only their swim trunks, the boys sent water splashing over Arabella when they jumped pell-mell into the pool.

"Guys!" Harper chided as she reached down to calm the dog who'd scrambled under her chair. "Don't splash Auntie Bella."

Arabella just laughed, though, because the cold water dripping down her front did feel refreshing.

"I need to grab towels," Harper said, heading to the door. "Brady, can you help?"

As a ploy to get her fiancé alone for a moment it was pretty transparent and Arabella didn't bother hiding her amusement.

"Bring the burgers, too," Arabella called after them because the charcoal in the bottom of the kettle had turned a perfect ashy shade around the edges. She put the lid back in place to keep in the heat and with one leap, jumped squarely into the center of the pool, splashing the boys much more thoroughly than they'd splashed her.

They rolled with giggles and before long, the pool was nearly empty thanks to the waves of water they splashed back and forth at Arabella. She was soaked to the skin when she dragged the hose back over to fill up the small play pool again. "I ought to pour bubble bath in there with you. Would save time later tonight!"

"That it would," Harper agreed, finally returning with a stack of folded bath towels in her arms. Brady followed. He carried the tray of burger patties and concentrated on the task of removing the plastic wrap covering the tray with unusual ferocity.

Harper handed Arabella one of the towels and set the rest a safe distance away. Arabella easily recognized the linens from her mom's supply. They were the "good" towels patterned with a hideous pink crest on one side from her mom's royal-watching phase several years ago.

Evidently, their mom had sent Brady off to Texas with more provisions than she'd provided Arabella. She seriously doubted Brady would have chosen to steal the towels.

"Earth to Arabella."

She looked up. "What?"

Harper was grinning. "Delivery for you inside."

Arabella frowned. She wasn't expecting anything. But she quickly mopped her wet legs and feet before going through the kitchen to the front room of the house.

Jay was sitting on the couch.

No wonder Harper had been grinning.

Arabella bunched the towel against her midriff but it didn't do diddly to squash the swirling squiggle inside her. "What are you doing here?" It was much more a demand than a welcome.

"Delivery." He reached into a paper bag at his feet and pulled out three jars of his grandmother's jam. He set them on the coffee table.

"That wasn't necessary."

"Maybe not." He pushed to his feet and her swirling squiggle squiggled faster. "But an explanation is." He stepped around the coffee table and only through sheer willpower was she able to keep her feet rooted where they stood when he reached out to lift a hank of wet, tangled hair from her shoulder.

Then she just shivered and was glad that she had the towel to clutch in front of her.

"It's been a complicated week."

She would *not* let herself be curious about the reasons why. Particularly when she wasn't convinced his words were anything more than an excuse. Though why he'd feel a need to make an excuse at all was beyond her comprehension.

His hand moved and she couldn't help her faint jerk, but he'd merely released her hair and was pushing his fingertips into his pockets.

Not reaching for her at all.

She finally took a step, turning away slightly. She tucked one end of the towel beneath her rear and perched gingerly on the arm of the sofa. She pressed the other end of the towel against her wet hair.

He paced to the end of the couch, stepping around the colorful tower of building blocks that the boys had built the night before. It was a miracle that Murphy hadn't knocked it down by now.

"My whole life is…was…complicated," he said in the void of her continued silence.

I think you should know that…

…my life is complicated.

Well, that at least fit. She lowered her hand to her lap. "What's so complicated about it?" Did he have a wife in the wings somewhere? A passel of children he'd run out on? "You work at a hotel in a town where nothing seems complicated."

His frowning gaze roved over her and she shivered again. She was too light on the curve-quality to go winning any wet T-shirt contests but she was nevertheless excruciatingly aware of how thin and wet her tank top was. And just how much it showed.

It was probably her imagination that his eyes seemed to catch for a moment on her chest, but her nipples tightened even more, anyway. "I'm getting the upholstery wet." She hopped off the couch. "I need to get another towel. You can find your way out." She bolted for the stairs, miraculously not falling over her feet in the process.

Once upstairs, she didn't retrieve another towel, though. She left her wet clothes in a heap on top of her empty laundry basket, dried off enough with the now-damp towel to pull a loose-fitting T-shirt dress over her head, and went back to the stairs.

She could see the living room was empty by the time she was halfway down the staircase. Well, good. He'd left.

She didn't want to hear more excuses anyway, right?

Twisting her hair into a wet rope over her shoulder—no, her shoulders were *not* slumping—she padded barefoot through the kitchen and back out to the patio.

"See, Jay?" Harper's voice greeted her. "I told you she wouldn't be long." She was setting out paper plates on the picnic table and she smiled at Arabella. "Jay's agreed to join us for dinner. Isn't that nice? We're ending up with a proper summer cookout here."

Chapter Six

*N*ice.

Arabella's teeth clenched but she summoned a smile. "Aren't we the lucky ones?" She started to turn right back around to escape. "I'll get the salad."

"Already have it," Harper told her.

Sure enough, the salad bowl was sitting in front of Jay.

"I'll get the drinks then," she said, annoyed that she sounded a little desperate. "Can't have a summer cookout without libations. Milk for the boys, I know. Beer for everyone else?"

But Harper shook her head. "I'll just have milk, too." Her voice was casual. Too casual.

Arabella eyed her soon-to-be sister-in-law's down-bent head for a moment, then looked at her brother. Brady was focused on the burgers. Too focused.

The suspicion she'd been harboring since the twins had drawn that picture over a week ago warred with her consternation over Jay and won. So victoriously won, in fact, that in her effort to contain a broad smile, her gaze collided with Jay's. He, too, seemed to be struggling not to smile, though surely he couldn't understand *her* reason.

Warmth engulfed her and only being jostled by two wet, slippery little boys as they chased their ball under the table near Arabella's feet was enough to break the trance. Bad enough that Murphy was already under the table, too.

"Come on, guys. Get out from under there and finish drying off." She grabbed two towels and lightly flipped the ends under the table.

Tyler popped out and giggled madly when she dropped the towel over his head. "Can we have the radio?"

Toby popped out, too, and caught his towel midair. "Yeah, I wanna floss!"

Jay laughed. "Where'd you learn to do that dance?"

"Harper taught us."

At the sound of her name, Harper finally looked up. "Sorry, what was that?"

Arabella bit back another smile. She was convinced that Harper was pregnant. "The boys say you taught them how to do the floss. Which means we definitely need some music out here."

"Get that new Bluetooth speaker that Brady brought home the other day," Harper called after her as she went inside the house. "It's on the washing machine."

When Arabella went back outside a few minutes later with the beverages and the speaker, she was equally convinced that her brother knew about the pregnancy and was reeling. There was no other way to explain his uncommon silence, the tinge of pallor on his face and the totally abject adoration in his eyes when he looked at Harper.

She opened her streaming service on her phone, connected to the speaker and music from her favorite radio station back home in New York filled the patio as though she'd just hooked up a huge sound system. "Don't you love technology?" She had to raise her voice above the robust volume.

Jay's smile seemed to twist slightly. "Sometimes."

Brady finally looked away from Harper. "Geez, Bella. Neighbors?"

She made a face but turned down the volume. "This is *so* much better than Murphy's radio."

"The dog has a radio?"

Arabella didn't look at Jay. "Don't they all?"

"Only thing that keeps Murphy out of mischief when we're all gone is to leave the radio playing," Harper explained. "Don't ask how many pairs of shoes we sacrificed before we figured out the solution, though." She patted her lap and the dog hopped up. "Yes, you're still a good boy," she crooned, then broke into giggles because the boys were jumping around doing their surprisingly coordinated version of the floss, swinging their hips one way while their arms went the other.

"Auntie Bella," Toby called. "Come and dance."

She shook her head. "No, thanks. I'm not that co-ordinated!"

"I doubt that," Jay said.

"Go on," Harper encouraged. "You can do it."

"You're the one who taught them," Arabella reminded.

"Come on." Jay stood and held out his hand. "It's not that difficult."

Arabella eyed his hand, not wanting to be as tempted as she was.

Fortunately, Brady announced just then that the burgers were ready, which solved that. The ravenous boys sat up at the table, and with the exception of Jay sitting next to Arabella and the conversational gaps that kept happening whenever Brady and Harper looked at each other, it was just another normal night in the Radcliffe/Fortune household.

Arabella supposed it wasn't surprising that they weren't announcing anything—verbally, that was. Not with an outsider present in the form of Jay. On the other hand, she wanted to whoop and jump around the same way her nephews had been doing and hug her brother silly because nobody deserved that panicked look of awe and devotion more than he did.

After hamburgers, though, Harper and Brady disappeared inside for a few minutes, leaving Arabella and Jay alone with the boys, who'd gone back to racing around the yard with their boundless energy. The only difference now was that they'd progressed from dancing to brandishing twigs as if they were light sabers.

She rolled her empty beer bottle between her palms

in time to the beat coming from the speaker and eyed Jay from the corner of her eye. "So. Complicated week."

"Right." He sat forward and clasped his own empty bottle, his hands close to hers. "That."

He didn't say anything else, though, and she looked at him fully. Waiting. With a pained expression, he sat back again.

Frustration wore at her edges, helped along by the earworm song she detested that came on the radio just then. Again. Even from her beloved Buffalo station. "I hate that song," she muttered.

His beer bottle clattered onto its side and he righted it. "It *is* pretty annoying."

"Right? I mean the singer's got a nice enough voice but that song is played *way* too often." She fiddled with her phone and found another station, then took the empty bottles into the kitchen to toss in the recycling bin. Her brother and Harper were still MIA, so she grabbed a bag of marshmallows and went back outside. "Boys! Bring your light sabers over here."

Even though the sun was starting to set, they plainly saw the bag that she held and made a beeline from across the yard.

She checked the ends of their sticks for signs of obvious mud and, finding none, impaled a marshmallow on each one. "Hold it over the grill," she told them. "There's still enough heat from the coals to toast them. But stand right here." She positioned them as far from the kettle as possible. "Murphy, get back." She snapped her fingers and pointed behind her.

The dog interpreted that as "climb into my seat."

She let it pass and focused on her nephews. "All right, guys, no closer than right here or you might get burned. Remember when Toby burned his finger on the stove?"

They wore twin frowns of concentration mingled with wariness and she returned to her seat. The dog looked up at her, one maple-colored ear cocked forward hopefully.

Resigned, she scooped him up and sat down with him on her lap, holding the marshmallow bag out of his range.

"Cute dog."

"If you like a crooked-eared mongrel," she allowed, nuzzling the dog's head. "I guess he's okay." If she were brave, she'd tell Jay to either start talking or just leave. Instead, she shook the marshmallow bag. "Want one? I can get another stick for you. Or a proper long-handled fork if you're squeamish."

"I'm not squeamish, but I'll pass."

"Suit yourself." She plucked a marshmallow from the bag and shoved it in her mouth. She didn't need to toast a marshmallow to love a marshmallow. She leaned forward to toss the bag on the table and adjusted the volume on the speaker again.

"What kind of music *do* you like?" Jay gestured at the speaker. "It's obviously not Jett Carr."

Harper walked out onto the patio. "Isn't he that singer everyone is looking for?"

Brady was on her heels and he spotted the bag of marshmallows and aimed for it as quickly as Toby and Tyler had done. "Publicity stunt." He grabbed a handful and dragged his chair over to the boys. They were still waiting for their marshmallows to turn at least the faintest tinge of gold and they immediately climbed onto his knees. "Gotta be a publicity stunt."

Harper stood behind him, her hands on his shoulders. "Don't be so cynical." She kissed the top of his head. "When those marshmallows finish toasting, it's off to bed with you boys."

"What's cynical?" Brady jabbed the coals with the poker, spurring them along. "The guy puts out a music video that supposedly goes viral just when he seems to disappear off the planet? Too coincidental if you ask me. He's probably sipping margaritas sitting on some beach in the Bahamas, raking in the money."

Jay snorted. "There're more singers scraping by than sitting around raking in money."

"Says the hotel trainee," Arabella drawled. "What *did* you do before you started there? Aside from getting your private pilot's license, I mean."

He reached for the marshmallow bag, evidently unable to resist the lure, after all. "I wasn't flying drugs back and forth across the border if that's what you're wondering."

"He used to work at an insurance company in California," Brady said, then spread his hands when they all looked at him. "I checked his personnel file," he said defensively.

Jay was frowning. "What for?"

"I know exactly what for!" Arabella jabbed her finger in the air at Brady. Because he was an overprotective big brother who wanted to know more about "her crush," as he called it. "You had *no* business doing that."

"I had every business," Brady countered unapologetically. His gaze skated over Jay. "You were hired early on at the hotel. Before the balcony collapse. After that, they started doing deeper background checks on the employees."

"But the balcony was an accident!" Arabella wanted to throttle Brady.

Her brother's expression didn't change. "Tell the insurance company covering the hotel that." He looked at Jay again. "Security's reviewed the files for all of the original employees at this point, so don't take it personally."

"You're not security," Arabella said through her teeth. "You're the *concierge*."

Jay waved his hand. His frown was gone. "He's right. No reason to take it personally. At Hotel Fortune, everyone pitches in where they're needed."

Arabella shook her head. "Stop making excuses for my brother, Jay. As usual, he's sticking his nose in where it doesn't belong."

"My marshmallow's on fire," Tyler suddenly wailed.

"It's fine," Harper assured calmly and showed him how to blow it out.

"But now it's black!"

"That's the best way," Jay told him. "Crispy and burnt a little on the outside and—"

"—gooey on the inside," Arabella finished. "That's my favorite way to eat toasted marshmallows." She addressed her nephew but from the corner of her eye, she saw Jay's dimple flash.

Somewhat mollified, Tyler subsided, leaning back against Brady's chest while he waited for the gooey marshmallow to cool enough to eat. Toby, on the other hand, had already eaten his marshmallow before it got to such an inflamed state and he was climbing onto Harper's lap now that she'd pulled up a chair alongside Brady's.

The afternoon of water play, sunshine and food had worked its magic and the twins were clearly getting sleepy. Even Murphy had abandoned her lap to curl around Brady's feet.

Arabella studied the picture they all made together. A family already. And now, she felt sure, with new babies on the way as well.

She exhaled, feeling her annoyance with Brady dribble away. Most of it, at least.

"It's getting late." Jay pushed away from the table and stood. "And I should leave you folks to your evening."

"You don't have to run off," Harper protested.

"I've got horses to feed and I usually check in on my grandmother every evening about now," he said, even though Arabella felt sure he did no such thing. If anyone did any "checking in" where Louella was concerned, it was probably Louella herself checking on Jay. "Thank you for the dinner, though." His gaze rested on Arabella. "I can't remember when I've enjoyed myself more."

Feeling a little like a slightly scorched marshmallow, Arabella followed him through the house to the front door. "Thank your grandmother again for the jam." The jars were still sitting on the coffee table in the living room. "I'm going to have to hide one away in my bedroom to keep it safe."

"You know where there's more." He stepped out onto the porch.

She suddenly didn't want him to go. "Insurance office. Really?"

He smiled slightly. "Really."

She wrinkled her nose. "That's as bad as a plastics manufacturer. That was my last job in New York."

"Surprised you were able to tear yourself away," he said dryly. "And insurance is boring only until you find yourself in need of it."

"Sounds like a slogan but I'll concede that point."

His smile widened. He suddenly lowered his head slightly toward hers. "Is your brother's fiancée pregnant?"

She gaped, and hearing a noise behind them in the kitchen, joined him on the porch so she could pull the door closed behind her. "You got that, too?" She pressed her hands over her mouth until she got control over her chortling. Then she grabbed his shirtfront urgently. "You can't say anything, though."

He covered her hands with his. "I promise."

Just that easily, her knees went weak. Thanks to her own riotous imagination, the last week and a half had been an emotional roller coaster where he was concerned.

Which meant she needed to stop overreacting at

his slightest touch and start acting like the adult she claimed to be.

She only needed to figure out how to think straight for more than ten seconds at a time whenever he touched her.

Simple enough, right?

"What's going on inside that beautiful head of yours?"

She froze. "What do you mean?"

His eyes roved over her face. His thumb brushed against the back of her hand. "I can practically see the wheels turning."

She made a face and shook her head. Her fingers finally listened to the frantic signals from her brain to release his shirt and she pulled her hands from beneath his. "The sunset," she lied. "Reminds me that I should get in there." She tilted her head toward the door behind her. "Make sure I'm set for tomorrow. Big day and all." She rubbed her hands together with false excitement. "Trainee program and such."

"You might like it."

"I'll like it fine as long as it pays my way out of the twin bed I sleep in upstairs here."

"Twin bed?"

She realized too late that was a topic better left alone. "It's a small bedroom." She fumbled behind her back for the door handle. "Maybe I'll see you around the hotel."

"Pretty sure you will."

"Well." She got the door open. "G'night."

"Arabella."

Her nerves went tight again. "Hmm?"

"It was a complicated week because of old business from California."

Her mouth dried. Business? Or relationship? "Insurance business?"

His lips compressed. "Not exactly."

Her stomach sank. Relationship then. Despite her little mental lecture about overreacting and overactive imaginations, she was as certain of that as she was about Harper being pregnant. "Are you married?"

His eyebrows yanked together. "*That's* what you're worried about?"

She didn't like feeling foolish any more than the next person did and she lifted her chin. "That's not an answer."

"No, I am *not* married," he said emphatically.

She felt a little like Tyler, then. Somewhat mollified. Somewhat reassured. But not entirely convinced. "People have lied about that before."

"You were involved with someone who was married?"

"Well, not once I learned the truth!" She cleared her throat and lowered her voice again. "It was just one date. We didn't—" Her words freeze-dried on her tongue when he curled his palms over her shoulders.

"Arabella." He exhaled and she felt the press of his fingertips through her knit dress. "One of these days, I hope you'll want to be Bella to me again."

Her knees went weak all over again.

"I am *not* married," he said softly. "Never have been married." His fingers squeezed her shoulders slightly. "The stuff from California is just…old…stuff.

An inconvenience. And it doesn't have anything to do with us."

Forget freeze-dried. Her mouth was suddenly watering and she swallowed hard. "Us? Is there an *us*?"

His fingers slipped her hair behind her ear before trailing along her jaw. "I think there could be." His thumb reached her chin. Rested right below her lower lip. "Don't you?"

The entirety of five months of fantasizing couldn't match that single moment standing on her brother's porch while the sunset beamed red and gold and orange behind Jay. "Yes," she breathed.

"Then let's just go one day at a time and see where it takes us. Hmm?"

She nodded jerkily. Every fiber of her soul wanted him to kiss her. But she'd asked for his kiss the last time and then he'd gone a whole week and then some before speaking to her. And then only because they'd run into each other at the hotel.

She didn't have the guts to ask again.

Not even when he ran his thumb slowly over her lip.

Her knees were already mush. The rest of her bones followed suit.

As if he knew it, he smiled slightly. "G'night, Arabella."

Then he turned and walked away.

Thankfully, the front door was hard and substantial. It held her up when she leaned weakly against it while she watched him climb into his truck parked at the curb. A moment later, his taillights were disappearing down the street.

"Call me Bella," she whispered soundlessly.

Then the door opened behind her and she fell back, knocking straight into Brady.

"What the hell're you doing?" He set her back onto her feet.

"Thinking that I can't wait to have a place of my own!"

"Not that again. You can't afford a place of your own."

"Not yet, but I will. And I'd think you'd be glad about that." She poked him in the chest. "Seeing how you're going to need the room I'm using."

"What for?"

She went around him toward the staircase. "Who for, would be more the point, wouldn't it?"

"Bella—"

"Don't worry." She started up the stairs. "I won't say a word more about it until the two of you are ready to announce it. But—" She shot him a look. "I just have to say one thing first."

"Just *one*?"

She let the sarcasm pass and smiled broadly. "You're already a heck of a dad, Brady. I can't wait to see you with a baby, too."

He frowned suddenly and seemed to find the newel post at the base of the staircase inordinately interesting. "What if I screw it up?"

She went back down a couple steps until she was at his eye-level. "Then you'll adjust and do it better. But you won't screw it up."

"How do you know?"

"Because I see Tyler and Toby." She gave him a quick, hard hug. "Gord and his wife knew what they were doing when they named you in their will as the boys' guardian."

"I can't imagine life without them now," Brady admitted huskily. "I wouldn't have moved to Rambling Rose if not for them. Would never have met Harper." He sniffed and gave an awkward laugh that just reminded her why he had always been her favorite brother. "Rambling Rose seems pretty lucky for those of the Fortune persuasion."

Arabella smiled and gave him another hug. "That's what I'm counting on, big brother."

Then, before he could make too big a deal out of that, she turned and hurried up the stairs.

"All right, then." Sybil smiled at Arabella the next morning. Instead of leaving instructions at the front desk for her, she'd met Arabella there in person and escorted her to housekeeping. "I'll leave you in Hallie's capable hands to get you started. She's an excellent floor supervisor so you couldn't have a better trainer. We'll check in again—officially—next week." Nursing her coffee cup, she walked out of the office.

Hallie, who'd turned out to be the same girl that Arabella had seen cleaning in the lobby the day before, cast a measuring look over Arabella before hunting through a shelving unit stacked high with folded shirts wrapped in plastic. She pulled one out and handed it to Arabella. "You can try it on in the night supervisor's office." She waved at a darkened doorway. "It's empty. Jordan quit a week ago and they haven't replaced her yet."

"Am I going to be fired if I admit I don't know what the night supervisor even does?"

Hallie laughed. "Night supervisor's responsible for all the public area cleaning that's done while everyone else is supposed to be sleeping and makes sure that all guest requests are answered after regular hours."

While she'd explained, Arabella had unzipped the plastic pouch and pulled out the T-shirt. It was black with the stylized Hotel Fortune logo embroidered in turquoise on the cap sleeve. "What about pants?" she asked as she headed toward the office.

"Those black jeans you're wearing are fine. Basically anything black is allowed except leggings." Hallie covered a yawn. "I'm going to grab a coffee. You want one?"

"I've already had two. Thanks, though." She stepped into the office and found the light switch on the wall before closing the door.

Arabella whipped her own blouse off her head and pulled on the T-shirt. It was identical to the one that Hallie wore, though Hallie's clung to her generous curves and Arabella's hung loosely from her shoulders.

She left the office again and went to the lockers lining one wall adjacent to the control desk where an unsmiling woman sat in front of a computer with a phone headset on her head. Her name was Beulah, which would have probably wiped a smile off of Arabella's face, too.

She'd already been assigned one of the lockers and

she stored her blouse inside along with her book bag and lunch box that she'd crammed inside earlier. Hallie still hadn't returned, so she pocketed her locker key and wandered over to the bulletin board that was covered with as many little scraps of paper as it was with large employment posters.

She peered closer at one of the scraps—Roommate Wanted—and made a mental note to check the board again in a few weeks when she had her first paycheck in the bank.

Two other young women, both wearing the turquoise-accented T-shirts, came in. They stopped in front of Beulah and signed in, then waited for the woman to give them their assignments for the morning.

Hallie returned then and she, too, stopped in front of Beulah. A few seconds later, she had a printed sheet in hand and came back over to Arabella. "You learn quick to stay on the right side of Beulah," she said under her breath as she led Arabella out of the office. "She handles the scheduling for all the room attendants. Get on her bad side and she'll either assign you enough rooms to kill an elephant or else so few that you'll be looking for a second and third job just to make it through to payday."

She led the way to the service elevator and they went down to the second floor. There, Hallie unlocked a door near the service elevator and rolled out one of the large carts stored inside. She showed Arabella the chart on the sheet that Beulah had given her, which indicated the rooms that had been occupied the night before and of those, which ones had already been vacated. "She coordinates with the front desk and will update us throughout the shift as more rooms are vacated. These ones that are circled—" she pointed out the rooms "—are stayovers. Multiple night stays, so it's up to us to keep an eye out for them. If the guest takes the newspaper we leave outside the door overnight, we know they're awake, for instance. If we see them leave for breakfast or for the pool, that sort of thing, we can turn the room while they're gone."

"How long does that take?"

"It's a little faster than a total turn. But on average thirty minutes or so for a standard guest room, which is what all of yours are today." As Hallie talked, she was busy counting out linens and supplies and adding them to the cart. "But it also depends on the state of the room. Some guests are complete and utter slobs and it takes longer." She held up the box of disposable gloves. "Get used to these things," she said dryly.

Arabella smiled weakly.

Once Hallie judged the cart ready, they were off.

For the next four hours, Arabella reached and stretched and squatted and crawled around, all for the purpose of leaving each room Fortune-Hotel perfect. Linens were changed. Every surface—from bathroom toilets to wall switch plates—was left polished and sanitized.

By the time they took their lunch break, Arabella felt like she'd been training for a marathon. "I never knew cleaning could be so hard," she moaned after collapsing onto one of the molded plastic chairs at the round table Hallie commandeered. "I've never wanted a foot massage as badly as I do right now." She had to content herself with curling and uncurling her toes inside her tennis shoes. For one, they were in a cafeteria so removing them was probably in poor taste. For another, if she took off her shoes, she wasn't entirely certain she'd be capable of putting them on again. "How long have you been doing this?"

Hallie set a glossy magazine on the table, followed by a can of soda. "Six years." She popped the top of the soda and unwrapped her sandwich. "I was working at a resort in Austin before I came here."

"What made you want to come to Rambling Rose?"

"What else?" Hallie looked wry. "A guy, naturally. Of course, two months after I'd already signed an apartment lease here in Rambling Rose, the creep gives me the 'it's not you, it's me' speech and heads off to Chicago with an old girlfriend."

"That stinks."

Hallie shrugged. "What're you going to do?" She winked. "Stink happens."

Arabella groaned humorously. "Terrible."

"Blame all the toilets I've cleaned in the last six years. I just hope things start picking up around this place."

"What do you mean?"

Hallie shrugged again. "The owners put on a good front, but the vacancy rate's still pretty high, even for Rambling Rose." She chewed her sandwich and flipped open her magazine. "What about you? What brought you to town?"

I think you should know that...

...there may be an "us."

"Family," Arabella said instead. "Three of my brothers had already moved here." She wasn't hiding the fact that she bore the Fortune name, but since Sybil hadn't introduced them using their full names, it just hadn't come up yet.

Hallie's dark eyes danced. "Any of 'em available?"

Arabella chuckled. "Only the two still living in Buffalo."

"Bummer. I haven't had a decent date in three months." Hallie nodded toward Arabella's barely-touched salad. "You're gonna get even skinnier if you keep bringing rabbit food like that and then don't even eat it. We're back on in ten minutes."

Arabella was starving, but the energy that it took to lift a fork seemed immense. "How many more rooms will we have?"

"Seven. We should have gotten six done this morning, but—"

"—I'm too slow," Arabella finished. She'd never thought it was that complicated to clean mirrors but she'd ended up leaving fingerprints that necessitated re-cleaning more often than not. And she was supposed to be ready to go out on her own without Hallie's help the following day.

"Get yourself a pair of these." Hallie held up the earbuds that were presently hanging loose around her neck. "You'll work faster when there's music going. Don't ask me why, but it always works."

"It better. Or I'll be lucky if I'm not fired on my second day."

"You're in the trainee program," Hallie said dryly.

"Once you're in the trainee program, you don't get fired."

"I'm only in the trainee program because they didn't know where else to put me. Is that something you wanted to do?"

Hallie shook her head. "Being a floor supervisor is enough for me." She was responsible for inspecting all the cleaned rooms before releasing them again to the front desk for use with another guest. "I'm not interested in getting into management. Too many reports to fill out. It's more fun sticking to room cleaning."

Arabella made a face. "I don't know about that."

"I even met a couple of celebrities in Austin who stayed at the resort." Hallie flipped her magazine around to show Arabella an image of a ridiculously handsome man with dark eyes and short dark hair. "This guy? Grayson?" She air-quoted the name. "He used to be big in rodeo. Now his Grayson Gear clothes are everywhere. I have a pair of his jeans. Do wonders for my butt. Anyway, he stayed at our resort a couple of times when I first started working there. All the gossip magazines said he was a real player, but I thought he was super nice. And he tipped great."

Arabella held her tongue. Hallie didn't realize that Grayson was one of "those Fortunes" any more than she knew Arabella shared the name, too. Adam and Kane had met him several years ago at that wedding in Paseo that her father was still complaining about. She knew Grayson had two identical brothers, but that was the extent of it. She hadn't met any of them herself. "Who else famous have you met?"

"Matt McIntyre. He's on a daytime soap." Hallie's eyes lowered to half-mast. "Sexy," she drawled. "But total slob." She closed her magazine and tapped an inset photo on the cover of a man with long dark hair. "Wouldn't mind cleaning *his* hotel room. He's so hot I'm not sure I'd even care if he *were* a slob."

Where in the World is Jett? was the photo's caption.

Arabella turned the magazine to get a better look. "You think he's hot? You can't even see what he really looks like. Not with those sunglasses and that beard."

"Seriously? He's got the bad-boy look nailed down."

Arabella shrugged. "My mom always says she wonders what guys are hiding behind their beards. I guess it's stuck with me." Jay's clean-shaven face danced in her mind.

"My mom says the same thing. But seriously, have you seen his music video? There's a reason why that video put his name on the map." Hallie fanned herself when Arabella shook her head. "Whether you like facial hair or not, you are missing out. Whenever I get depressed over my lack of a love life, I pull out my phone—" she did just that, pulling her cell phone out of her pocket to wave in the air "—and watch me some hottie Jett Carr crooning about his lost love and I am all good again."

Arabella couldn't help but laugh. "I'll keep that in mind." She steeled herself against her protesting muscles and stood. They packed up their lunch boxes and reported back to duty. Hallie went to inspect some of the other rooms also under her watch while Arabella went to the floor pantry and retrieved the cart. She replenished the linens and carefully began backing it through the doorway.

"How's the first day going?"

She jumped and turned around.

Jay was leaning against the wall watching her.

She forgot all about her sore feet and muscles. "It's going great." She waved her hand, taking in his appearance. "Back on food and beverage again?"

"Shows, does it?" He grinned. "Some corporate thing going on this afternoon. Using the banquet room and a couple breakout rooms. I'm on water and coffee detail. Tough gig."

She laughed softly. "Did you ever have to do a stint in housekeeping?"

"Yep." He straightened away from the wall. "After the first day, I sent flowers to my mother and grandmother for all the years they spent cleaning up after me."

She laughed again and finished pulling the cart into the hall. "I'd better get to it. I'm already behind schedule."

He glanced around the piled-high cart, then leaned closer to her. "Hot tub in the fitness center does wonders for helping with the aches and pains." His murmur next to her ear sent shivers dancing down her spine.

She turned her head slightly toward him. His green eyes mesmerized. "Fitness center is for guests."

"It closes at nine." His smile turned wicked. "And I have a connection who can get us in." Then he kissed her lightly and straightened away from her just in time to avoid being caught by Grace Williams, who stepped out of the service elevator.

"Good afternoon, Jay. Arabella. How's the first day going?"

Arabella couldn't have wiped away the smile on her face if she'd tried. "Better than I ever dreamed."

Chapter Seven

She met Jay outside the hotel that evening promptly at half-past nine.

Prompt, because she'd waited in her car around the corner to the hotel for fifteen minutes so she wouldn't look too eager.

Even though she was, in fact, very eager.

"Ready?"

She nodded and felt even more breathless when he took her hand in his and led her around the side of the hotel to the door they'd used that day in January. Although she knew the balcony had been rebuilt since then, Arabella couldn't help looking up at it a little warily as they passed it.

Jay noticed. "It's been inspected a couple dozen times over by now." He knocked twice on the door.

"I know." Even the bushes that had been growing beneath the balcony had been replaced. "Kane and Brady have both talked about it."

The door opened and Mariana peeked out.

Arabella eyed the woman with surprise, but Mariana just gave a quick look around as Jay pulled Arabella through the door and into the fitness center.

"Thanks, Mariana." Jay kissed the older woman's cheek. "You're a peach."

"Sweet and juicy," Mariana quipped, giving a broad wink. "Just be sure to get out of here before the night crew comes in to clean at eleven." Then whistling tunelessly, she hurried out of sight.

There really was no need for Jay to hold Arabella's hand as they made their way through the well-equipped room. Dim lights lit the perimeter, illuminating the way well enough.

But Arabella didn't tug her hand free and Jay didn't let go of it either, not until they reached the opposite end of the space and he pointed at the sign on the door. Women's Lockers. "You have your suit?"

She patted her trusty book bag. "Even brought a towel of my own. Just in case."

"Hot tub is through there." Jay pointed to an archway. "Meet you there."

Her eagerness reached such a peak she was possibly in danger of passing out. She nodded and hurried into the women's locker room and reminded herself to breathe again. She quickly changed into her swimsuit and pulled her hair up into a high ponytail. Then she wrapped the towel she'd stolen from Brady's around her waist, bundled her sundress and undies into her book bag and slung the strap over her shoulder.

Heart pounding, she peered around the edge of the locker room door, and squealed out loud when Jay moved. She pressed her hand to her chest and slipped through the doorway. "For a second there, I thought we'd been caught!"

His teeth flashed. "Nothing like the fear of getting caught to keep things exciting."

She swallowed hard, not certain how to take that particular innuendo.

He'd changed out of his jeans into a pair of black-and-gray board shorts, and his white shirt hung unbuttoned over his chest. It was nearly impossible to keep her eyes from straying to the strip of flesh showing. It seemed as rude as guys who just stared at a girl's chest. Or in her case, her lack of one. "What if we *do* get caught?"

"Don't know," he admitted. "Hasn't happened yet. Pretty sure *you'd* be safe, though."

Yet.

He'd done this before. Of course he had. "Why would I be safe?"

He winked. "You've got the right name."

"But it wouldn't save me from embarrassing Brady."

"Want to sneak back out?"

Arabella didn't hesitate. Not even figuring she wasn't the first girl he'd brought there was enough to sway her. "No."

His smile widened. "Good." He closed his hand over her elbow and drew her toward the archway.

The in-ground hot tub was oval shaped and large enough to accommodate at least a dozen people. It was surrounded by several mesh lounge chairs and several potted plants that looked real. The ceiling overhead was vaulted and with the lights low the way they were, gave the impression of being open-air even though it really wasn't.

Jay let go of her and shrugged off his shirt, pitching it at one of the chairs as he passed it on his way to the control panel. A second later, the hot tub lit up from an underwater light and the surface began churning. He joined her where she was still hovering near the chair. She'd hung her bag off the back of it and glanced around, because wondering if there were security cameras felt safer than getting caught ogling his bare torso.

She didn't see any cameras but maybe they were just more discreetly placed here than they were in the rest of the hotel. "How many times *have* you done this?"

"Twice before." He'd been wearing tennis shoes with no socks and he toed them off before stepping to the edge of the churning water. "Stepped wrong a while back and sprained my ankle." He stood on one foot and rotated the other. "Whirlpool helped." He stepped down onto the first step and the water swirled around his calf.

"I sprained my wrist once and the doctors put me in a sling for more than a week," she said absently. He was slim but that only made the V from waist to broad shoulder even sharper. And slim, she realized, didn't mean undefined. He was practically a textbook study in musculature and sinew. He had a small tattoo near his shoulder blade that she couldn't quite make out.

"Didn't bother with a doc. Not the first time I've sprained something. I know the drill."

He glanced over his shoulder at her, catching her in the act of squinting at him. His eyebrow rose. "Ready to take the plunge?"

She could have fanned herself in the same way that Hallie had done during lunch.

There was nothing seductive about her utilitarian tankini. The only thing it had going for it was the jaunty blue-and-white stripes of the halter top that supposedly gave the impression of curves where there were none. Feeling as self-conscious as if she were stripping down to her undies, she pulled the towel from around her hips and dropped it on the chair. He hadn't brought one, she realized. "Is it hot?"

His lips tilted. "Very." His gaze never left her face as she gingerly dipped her toe in the water. "The water's pretty warm, too."

She hoped he'd blame her flush on the steam rising from the churning water.

His smile widened and he took another step down into the water. "Come on. I remember what a workout it is cleaning rooms. Fitness industry's missing out on a whole trend if you ask me."

She glanced over her shoulder. It was a fine time to start having reservations. "Are you sure we're not going to get caught?" No matter what he thought, having the last name Fortune didn't mean they had a pass on following the rules of the hotel.

"You *are* getting cold feet."

"No, I'm not!" She made a face because it was so

obvious to them both that she was. "No," she said more firmly.

"I've known Mariana since I was a kid. She's not going to tell a soul about this," he said calmly. "And the only cameras down here are in the hallways that head to the lobby in one direction and Roja in the other. I've done my research on that score. I know where they're all located."

"The advantage of working in every department, I guess."

"Something like that. And nobody should be here until the cleaning crew." He held out his hand. "You heard Mariana. Time's tickin', sweetheart. So what's it going to be?"

She looked at his palm extended to her. Even in the dim light she could see the ridge of calluses across his fingertips.

She swallowed hard and quickly placed her hand in his. His fingers closed around hers, steadying her as she stepped down into the water.

It was like being encased in comfort and she wasn't entirely sure if that was owed to Jay's hand clasping hers or the steaming, churning pool. Either way, she couldn't stop a heartfelt groan. Nearly all of her nervousness floated away. Magical. "Oh, yessss."

"Had a feeling you'd like it." Jay didn't let go of her hand until she stood waist deep in the water. Then he moved toward one end of the oval and sat, stretching out his arms on the travertine coping behind him. The water bubbled around his shoulders. "Jets are stronger over here." He patted the curved tile.

She walked toward him and the tub got deeper toward the center of it, but never so deep that she couldn't reach the bottom and still keep her chin above water. He'd said he'd used the hot tub because of a sprained ankle, but she still couldn't help wondering if he'd been alone or not.

It was the only fly in this heavenly ointment.

She sat down near him, keeping a circumspect arm's length between them, and pretended not to see the way his lips twitched. Unlike him, though, she slumped down as far as she could in the water until the bubbles flitted over her chin, tickling her nose as they popped and spit. "I haven't had a bath since I left Buffalo," she said. "Well, *showers* obviously," she qualified hastily.

"No tub at your brother's place?"

"Yes, but it's usually filled with the twins' bath toys. And the hot water only goes so far."

"Gran has a big old claw-foot thing in the middle of her peach orchard."

Arabella turned slightly toward him and felt the thrum of water pound against her side. She arched slightly, relishing the massage. "What does she grow in it?"

"Bubbles?" His eyes smiled. "She takes baths in it. Heats the hot water in a big old barrel on wheels with a propane burner that my grandfather rigged up when I was still a kid. Sort of like those things that people use these days to fry a turkey. Only a helluva lot bigger."

She bent her elbow on the coping and propped her head on her fingertips. "Have to admit, I have a hard time envisioning that."

His chuckle was low and deep and as much a physical pleasure as the hot, bubbling water was. "Wish I had a hard time envisioning it," he said. "Accidentally discovered her using it once when I was a teenager. Couldn't bring myself to visit her again for a few years. Love my grandmother. Did not want to see her lolling around in a bathtub in the middle of a peach orchard."

She laughed softly and sank deeper in the water again. Her ponytail dragged in the water, floating like a coiled rope between them. "Your grandmother's amazing."

"Always has been. Just took me getting old enough to appreciate it."

"Is your mom like her? I know you said she'd rather your grandmother move to Houston, but—" She broke off. He was already shaking his head.

"Mom is nothing like her mom. But that's okay." He shrugged. "I'm nothing like my dad. Doesn't mean there's a lack of love because of it."

"Preferred selling insurance over teaching math, hmm?"

"I didn't sell insurance." He lowered his arms into the water and his fingers toyed with her ponytail. "I was working on becoming an actuary."

She twisted a little more, centering the waterjet against a fresh ache. "Doesn't that entail like *all* math?"

"Math. Statistics." He suddenly rotated until his legs floated straight out toward the middle of the hot tub and his arms were stretched out, hands cupping the coping as he faced her.

"Not so different than your dad, then."

He ducked his chin in the water almost to his nose and in the dim light, his green eyes looked dark above the water. She could still see the laughter in them, though. Especially since the arm's-length distance between them had somehow been reduced by half.

He lifted his chin. "I hated it. Spent all that time studying actuarial science in school and went straight into the field, only to detest every minute of it. The second I could afford to, I got out of it."

"What'd you really want to do? Be a pilot?"

He bent his arms, pulling himself closer to the edge. Closer to her.

Still floating. But closer.

"Not necessarily."

"And now you're here. Hotel Trainee Cross."

"So are you, Hotel Trainee Fortune. At least it offers a lot of variety." His expression shifted and she couldn't help wondering if he even realized it. "Expectations are straightforward," he said flatly. "Honest day's wage for an honest day's work. Nobody trying to make you into something you're not."

"Plus an illicit hot tub session now and then."

His face lightened again just as she'd hoped, and his hands inched closer to her shoulders. "Illicit." His deep drawl gave the word an added nuance.

She sucked in a breath that was too redolent of chlorine to be particularly helpful. She turned until her spine was in front of the jet again and suddenly found Jay floating directly in front of her, his hands on either side of her shoulders.

"That's a great word." His gaze roved over her face,

seeming to rest on her mouth. He drifted closer. "Evocative," he murmured, just loud enough to be heard over the bubbles and jets.

"I…like words." She moistened her lips that, impossibly, felt dry despite the water all around them.

"They have a power," he agreed. He ducked his chin in the water again and closed the distance even more.

She felt him kiss the point of her shoulder and then the curve of her neck. Her head fell back, resting against the tile. She watched him from beneath her lashes. "Who else have you snuck in here like this?"

A quick line came and went between his dark eyebrows as if the question surprised him. "Only you."

She wanted to believe him more than she wanted her next breath. The jetted water seemed to be pushing her spine away from the wall until her legs floated upward and glanced against his. Lightly. Tantalizingly.

He let go of the wall with one hand and lowered it to the seat beside her.

Then he kissed the point of her collarbone and her head fell back a little more, only this time the tiled wall wasn't behind her. It was just swirling water that seemed to bear her torso upward toward his.

Or maybe that was his hand, now splayed flat against the small of her back beneath the tank-length top of her swimsuit. They were both floating now, anchored only by his one hand on the edge of the pool.

His legs slid against hers and she trembled when her abdomen brushed against the hard barrier of his chest. His head dipped again into the water and she felt his mouth brush her skin right at the deepest V of her halter top. He raised his head again. "Yes or no?"

She realized his hand was at the tie behind her neck. "Yes, please," she exhaled the words.

His lips curved and she felt a faint tug. Then the jaunty blue-and-white stripe started to float away from her shoulders. She was in no danger of losing the top altogether. The tie merely held up the bra portion. And regardless of her insecurities where her slight figure was concerned, when his head dipped back into the water to catch a rigid nipple between his lips, some portion of her reeling sensibilities decided they were just about right for this particular moment.

For this particular man.

Borne on his arm and the swirling water, Arabella stared blindly up at the skylike ceiling and slid her hands through his wet hair. Feeling him dip and taste, dip and kiss, dip and delight.

Her legs tangled with his and her ponytail swirled around them and she hovered there in a suspension of pleasure, oblivious to everything except him.

I think you should know that...

He jerked his head up suddenly and swore. With a splash, his hand grabbed hers and her feet hit the bottom of the pool.

"Wha—"

"Someone's out there," he said under his breath. He was practically propelling her right out of the hot tub and she stubbed her toe on the step as she gained her footing and yanked at her top.

In one fell swoop, he grabbed up his shirt and her

towel and their shoes while she snatched the strap of
her book bag, upending the lightweight chair in the process. The racket it made echoed against the travertine
and Jay didn't even stop at the control panel to kill the
hot tub jets. Their feet slapped wetly on first tile, then
soundlessly on carpet as he pulled her around a corner
and into an alcove next to a large metal ice machine.

"Who was it?"

"Sshh." He cupped her head against his chest and
edged deeper into the alcove. There wasn't a lot of space
for their bodies and it was so dark she couldn't see. Only
a slight gleam of light reflected over the stainless steel
of the ice machine.

Adrenaline rushing through her veins, she slid her
arms around him and huddled close despite the bundle of shirt and towel caught between them. His heart
beat as fast as hers. She knew because she could feel it
pulsing against her cheek. When his hand drifted upward and grazed her bare breast, desire cramped hard
inside her. Until she realized he was just pulling up the
straps of her halter to tie it behind her neck once more.

She pressed her forehead against him and suddenly
wanted to laugh. And not being able to do so exacer-
bated the need to.

When the ice machine suddenly vibrated loudly and
belched out a fresh batch of cubes somewhere in its
metal innards, a muffled snort escaped, despite her best
efforts to contain it.

She felt his chest rumble with silent laughter, too.
His head dipped and his lips brushed her ear. "Sshh."

She clung to him even more tightly, plastering her

mouth against the bulge of his biceps. His rumbling silent laughter increased and he twisted slightly, picking her up at the waist and pressing her back against the narrow wall behind her. "Sshh," he murmured again and then kissed her.

She forgot about laughing, then.

She twined her arms more tightly around his shoulders and her calf knocked into the ice machine as she mindlessly wrapped her legs around his hips.

His weight against her was heady. The rub of his tongue against hers delicious. When his head lifted too soon, she slid her fingers into his hair and pulled his head back. "Don't go," she said against his mouth.

He let out a sound, equally muffled. Half exultant. Half frustrated.

All perfect to her ears.

He dragged his mouth from hers, running it along her cheek. "It's the cleaning crew," he whispered. "Hear the vacuum?"

She hadn't. Not above her pounding pulse and the ice maker and the rush of music inside her head whenever his mouth touched her.

"Stay here." He disentangled himself from her. "There's a security camera in the hall around that corner. So stay *here*." He edged out from their hiding hole.

If there was a camera, why was he leaving?

She didn't have a chance to voice the question, because he was already gone.

She exhaled deeply and unwound her book bag strap from her forearm where it had twisted around without her notice. She slid it over her head crosswise then stuffed his shirt inside. She was cautiously feeling around the floor with her foot for the towel that she'd dropped when he returned.

He grabbed her arm. "We've got to be fast." He pulled her back around the way they'd come, then he pushed her head down while they dashed—bent nearly in half—through the weight-lifting section of the fitness center. The lights were all turned on now, clearly illuminating them if they were noticed. His route made little sense to her, but there was no time to argue. Not with the way he dragged her along after him.

On the other side of the room, one person was using the big vacuum, another was polishing surfaces and a third wielded some sort of wand that emitted a fine cloud over the workout equipment.

None of them so much as glanced their way, not even when Jay pushed open the same one-way door they'd used to enter.

They slipped through, and he held on to the edge of the door with his fingertips, gingerly letting it close with a soft *snick*.

As soon as it was closed, Arabella dropped her bag on the ground and started laughing. "I can't believe they didn't see us!"

Jay's laughter was deep and rich, too. His hand curled around the back of her neck and he pressed a fast kiss to her lips. "So much for a therapeutic soak." He grabbed her hand. "The pool's free game, though. What do you say?"

"I dropped my towel. And you don't even have one."

In answer, he grabbed the strap of her bag and pulled

her around the side of the hotel to where the pool was located. "Good grief," he said as he hefted the bag. "What're you carrying in here?"

"Notebooks."

"Full of what?" He curled his arm as if he was weightlifting. "Feels like you're carting around a couple of my grandmother's garden binders."

"Nothing so productive." She rubbed her nose, feeling suddenly self-conscious. "Just stuff I...write."

"Journals?"

Sure. That was close enough. She made a sound he took for agreement.

"Dear Diary." Beneath the swag of lights crisscrossing high atop the pool area, Jay's eyes crinkled at the corners. "Tonight, I nearly got caught by—"

She reached up and pressed her hand over his mouth. "Stop!"

She felt his smile against her palm and her stomach swooped. She should have felt chilly in her damp swimming suit. Instead, she felt warm from the inside out.

She pulled her hand away and turned to face the pool again.

Even at that hour there were a half-dozen people in the water playing a noisy game of water volleyball. A few more guests lounged on the chaises surrounding it. They all had drinks in their hands, served up from the bar situated next to a small dais where a trio of musicians played live music. On the other side of the musicians sat another table with pale blue hotel towels stacked on it.

Jay gestured. "See? Towels."

He was impossible to resist even when he was being impossible. When he was grinning at her the way he was now? It was a lost cause altogether. "Why would the hot tub be reserved only for guests but the pool isn't?"

He shrugged. "The hot tub accommodates twenty people and the pool handles a lot more? I don't know. Ask your brothers. They're more likely to know the answer to that than me."

She made a face. "If my brothers find out I'm here with you swimming, you're going to regret all of this."

His lips twitched. "Pretty sure I'm not."

I think you should know that...

...I'm the perfect guy for you.

His confidence was intoxicating. "Swimming pool it is." She stepped off the paved pathway and cut across the grass diagonally toward the nearest chaise lounge. She dropped her bag on it and kicked off her sandals and slid into the water.

In comparison to the night air, it felt warm and welcoming. Not quite at the level that the hot tub had, but it was still wonderful.

She expected Jay to follow her in, and when he didn't, she slicked her hair out of her eyes and looked back at him. "Well?"

He was no longer smiling. Instead he was staring fixedly toward the bar where a tall man was watching them.

Then the man walked toward Jay and she saw the glint of a badge on his belt.

That's when she placed him. He was the officer at the municipal building.

Not officer. Detective. Detective Teas.

"Cross," he said as he stopped in front of Jay.

"I've already answered all your questions," Jay said flatly. "I don't know what else you want from me."

"I'm not here to question you again," the detective said. "Not yet, anyway."

Arabella frowned. She was barely aware of the way Jay and the police detective had drawn the attention of the guests nearest them as she started up the steps. The night air no longer felt hot and balmy, the water no longer soft and warm.

Jay's face tightened even more. He looked hard and nearly unrecognizable. "Then what—"

The detective raised his hand. "There's been an incident. With your grandmother."

Water splashed as Arabella scrambled out of the pool. She slid her hand into Jay's.

He didn't spare her a glance, but his fingers closed tightly around hers. "What kind of incident?"

The detective looked suddenly uncomfortable. "She and Mabel Forsythe got into it over at Provisions. Afraid they were both hauled in for—" He broke off, grimacing.

Arabella hugged Jay's arm to her. "For what?"

"Public brawling," the detective finally said, looking pained. "She's gonna need you to bail her out."

Chapter Eight

"Well? Anything you have to say for yourself?" Jay peered through the bars of the cell. It was empty except for his grandmother. An identical cell next to it held Mabel Forsythe.

Both women sat on the hard benches that lined the perimeter of each cell. They had their backs to one another and their arms folded across their chests.

At his grandmother's stoic silence, he sighed and rubbed his fingers through his hair. "If Mom finds out about this—"

"She'd better not," his grandmother warned. "I keep your secrets, you better be prepared to keep mine." She suddenly looked over her shoulder at the woman sitting behind her. "And if I hear you've been spreading tales, Mabel Forsythe, I'll hunt you down and finish what we started."

Mabel looked fit to spit.

"She didn't mean that, Mrs. Forsythe," Jay soothed.

"The hell I didn't!"

He eyed her. "Threats aren't going to help the situation here, Granny. If you want me to post bail—" he'd already done it, but she didn't need to know that "—then you're going to have to explain yourself."

She harrumphed and folded her arms again, looking prepared to sit there until kingdom came.

If his grandmother wouldn't talk, then maybe Mabel would.

He moved past his grandmother's cell—just *thinking* those words made something inside his head clang painfully—and stopped in front of Mabel. "What about you, Mrs. Forsythe? Do you want to explain what went on over at Provisions tonight?" Teas had already told him that Mabel's daughter-in-law was driving in from Dallas to post bail, but she would be hours getting there yet. "I might be willing to look at paying your bail if—"

"You'd damn well better not," Louella said furiously. "You'll have your grandpa rolling over in his grave if you spend one red cent on that woman."

That woman had risen to her feet, too, wrapping her arthritic fingers around the cell bars as if she were prepared to push them apart Samson-style. "Herb would still be alive if he'd married me instead of you."

"You miserable—" Louella reached through the bars and yanked on Mabel's hair, pulling the glossy brown coif askew to reveal the sparse white hair beneath.

"Ladies!" Detective Teas strode into the holding area and his bark echoed around the cement walls. "And believe me. Right now I'm using that term generously." He glared at the women. "Keep it up and I'll keep you both here all night. Is that what you want?"

"What I *want* is for her to admit she stole my strawberry jam recipe fifty years ago!" Mabel tugged her wig into place with a sharp jerk. "Just like she stole Herbert twenty years before that."

"Herb never gave you the time of day and you know it, Mabel. And that recipe was my mother's before it was mine. I have it written down in her handwriting in my recipe card box."

"Lies."

"And *you* can't cook your way out of a pot of stone soup! That's why your Donny, God rest his poor soul, kept coming over to eat dinner with Herb and me!"

Teas sent Jay a weary look. "They've been at it like this since we brought them in." He unlocked Louella's cell and pulled open the door. "Sooner you get her out of here, the sooner we'll all have a little peace and quiet." He beckoned. "Come on now, Mrs. O'Brien."

His grandmother gave Mabel a goading smirk as she sauntered out of her cell. "I'm sure your daughter-in-law will be here soon. We all know how *fond* she is of you." She glanced up at Jay as they followed the detective out of the holding area. "Only reason Donny Jr. moved to Dallas was because Charlene refused to live in the same town as his mama." She didn't bother keeping her voice down and Mabel obviously heard, because her shrieks followed them until the heavy door to the holding area clanged shut behind them.

"Here." Teas handed Jay a sheaf of papers. "Judge has ordered your grandma and Mrs. Forsythe to keep one hundred yards away from each other until their hearing's scheduled." He focused on Louella. "Ma'am, you understand that if either one of you breaks that order, you're both gonna end up in a cell for a mite longer than a couple hours?"

"Might be worth it," Louella grumbled, "just to make her suffer."

"You'd suffer, too," Jay pointed out. He gestured toward Arabella, where she sat on a bench looking worried. "Now go over there and say hello to Arabella. She's the one who drove me here."

"I don't appreciate being spoken to as if I'm five," his grandmother said thinly.

"Then don't act as if you're five," he returned.

Her lips compressed and she turned away from him, marching across the room to Arabella.

Jay blew out a breath and looked back at the detective. Even though he'd spent the last few weeks loathing the other man, he knew that Teas could've made this situation a lot more difficult. He extended his hand. "Thank you for your help tonight."

Teas looked resigned. He shook Jay's hand. Firmly. But briefly. "First time I've ever arrested two women of their...ah..."

"Maturity?"

"Afraid maturity wasn't one of the things on display." He tucked his hands in the pockets of his jacket. "Do your best to make sure she follows the judge's order," he advised.

"I will." Jay started to turn away, but looked back at the detective. "How *did* you know where I was tonight, anyway?" He hadn't seen his grandmother since morning. She hadn't known where he'd be, any more than he'd known she was going to have dinner at Provisions with her supposed friend Mabel Forsythe.

"You're not going to like the answer." Teas glanced past him.

Arabella and Jay's grandmother were sitting together now. Jay wasn't sure if the fact that they looked deep in discussion worried him more or less than whatever Teas was going to answer. "Regardless. I still want the answer."

Teas capitulated with a small shrug. "We've had you under surveillance since the day I brought you in for questioning."

Of all the things Teas could have said, that was the last thing Jay expected.

His jaw tightened until it ached. "Surveillance," he said through his teeth when he could finally form a word that didn't involve the furious outrage bubbling inside him. "You're wasting a helluva lot of time and taxpayer dollars."

Teas pursed his lips. "Not so sure 'bout that. You're hiding something, Mr. Cross. There're just too many gaps in your timeline for my taste. And I'm the kind of detective who tends to follow up on that sort of thing."

Jay pinched the bridge of his nose. "My private business has nothing to do with Hotel Fortune's misfortunes."

The detective was unswayed. "Sounds like the name of a bad song, Mr. Cross."

Jay returned the man's stare. If the cop was looking for a reaction, he'd wait a long while.

And then he felt Arabella touch his arm. "Jay."

He finally looked away from Teas.

"It's really late," she murmured softly. "I think your grandmother's exhausted."

He exhaled sharply. Of course she was exhausted. Once Jay and Arabella had arrived at the station, it had taken a few more hours before the bail had been processed. And now, it was nearly 3:00 a.m.

He didn't exchange another word with Teas as he went to collect his grandmother from the bench. Exhausted she might be, but the only evidence of it was in her eyes. He still took her arm as they left the municipal building.

Arabella led the way, glancing over her shoulder periodically as if she were nervous.

Police stations probably had that effect on most law-abiding citizens.

She'd changed out of her swimsuit into a swingy yellow sundress before they'd driven to the station. Jay, on the other hand, was wearing the wrinkled shirt she'd pulled from her canvas purse and a pair of old cowboy boots he'd fortunately had stored in his truck.

God only knew where he'd managed to drop his tennis shoes during their escape from the fitness center.

The end result, though, was that Arabella looked like

a ray of sunshine and he looked like an advertisement for Menswear Don't.

At least the only ones following him around these days were the cops who didn't care what he looked like so long as they kept trying to link him to the balcony collapse.

"I didn't tell Detective Teas to find you," his grandmother said as they left the building through the front doors. "So don't blame me that you had to come to my rescue."

"And what were you planning to do if I *hadn't* shown up?"

"I have friends. I could have arranged the bail and you'd have never been the wiser."

Jay snorted. "Worked out well for you, didn't it, then?" And it meant he needed to thank the detective for yet one more thing, he thought blackly.

"Don't take that tone with me," Louella said.

He scrubbed his hand down his face as they stopped next to Arabella's sedan.

His grandmother looked confused. "Where's your truck?"

Jay's eyes met Arabella's over the roof of the car as she unlocked the driver's-side door. And despite everything—the frustration of not being able to kiss her as long as he'd wanted, the shock of his grandmother's arrest and the fury of knowing the cops had been following him and he hadn't even noticed—he couldn't help smiling.

"Dead battery," he said.

* * *

"Well?" Brady tossed a towel patterned with a distinctively ugly pink crest on his desk and gave Arabella a look. "Anything you have to say for yourself?"

She rubbed the pain in her temple and held back a yawn with no small amount of effort.

After getting Jay and his grandmother out to their place and driving back into Rambling Rose, it had been nearly four in the morning when she'd finally crept into her twin-size bed at Brady's house. She'd been so tired, she hadn't even spent her usual hour writing. "Like what?"

Brady had made no secret that he was annoyed with her. That had been plainly obvious when he'd summoned her to his office in the middle of her cleaning shift.

"Like the fact that this—" Brady shook the towel in her face "—was found next to the ice machine on the first floor last night by the night crew."

"It's just a towel, Brady."

"It's a towel from my own damn linen closet, Bella. And I sure didn't leave it there."

"Actually, it's a towel from *Mom's* linen closet. Do you remember when she ordered them? How appalled Dad was that she'd spent hard-earned money on a set of towels just because they had a royal crest on them?"

His expression told her plainly that he appreciated neither her irony nor the little trip down memory lane.

"Okay, fine," she huffed. "I was using the hot tub after hours last night, okay?"

"Alone?"

"Of course I was alone," she bluffed. "Every muscle in my body hurt after cleaning all day and—"

He thumped a pair of men's tennis shoes on his desk. "These were with the towel. Your feet suddenly grow about four sizes?"

Arabella pressed her lips together.

"How'd you get into the fitness center?"

"Does it matter?"

Brady grimaced. He sat back in his chair and tugged at his tie as though it was suddenly choking him. "Yes, it matters."

"Why? Look, we weren't doing anything terrible." Not entirely. "Jay just—"

Brady swore. "Jay *Cross*?"

She shoved out of her chair because sitting in front of Brady's desk the way she was felt a little too similar to being called in front of the principal. And those elementary school days were long past. "So what if it was?"

"You snuck in the house at four this morning!"

She jabbed her finger in his direction. "Stop acting like Dad."

"Stop acting like an irresponsible teenager, then!"

She gaped at him, feeling stung. "I'm a grown woman, Brady. If I choose to stay out all night with a guy it is my business. Not yours."

He rose and planted his hands flat on his desk. "It's my business when it's under my roof."

She slapped her hands on the desk, too, going practically nose to nose. "Well, we know the solution to that, don't we?"

"Ahem."

They both looked over to see Grace Williams standing in the doorway to Brady's office.

As furious as Brady was with Arabella, she was somewhat surprised to see amusement in the other woman's eyes.

"Brady, the camera crew is here to get started on filming the new commercial. Would you mind getting them set up? I'm afraid I have to deal with that other matter." Her eyebrows rose slightly as if she were speaking in code meant only for Arabella's brother.

Brady looked at Arabella. "We're not finished with this discussion," he warned.

"Damn straight we're not," she muttered under her breath after he and Grace had left the office again.

Arabella plucked Jay's tennis shoes from the desk and left, too.

She knew that he wasn't on duty that day. A happy coincidence for him since he needed to deal with getting his truck battery changed. Unlike hers, his hadn't responded to charging, which was why she'd ended up driving him to the police station the night before.

On one hand, she was grateful that Jay had seemed glad to accept her help. On the other hand, she was left with more questions about him than ever before.

What had Teas said when he'd appeared at the pool? *I'm not here to question you again. Not yet, anyway.* Question Jay about what?

Even if there'd been an opportunity to ask him what the police detective had meant, Arabella hadn't been brave enough to voice it.

She could go toe to toe with Brady all day long and

Complete the survey below and return it today to receive up to 4 FREE BOOKS and FREE GIFTS guaranteed!

twice on Sundays if she had to. But ask Jay one simple question?

I think you should know that...

...I'm wanted by the police.

She shook her head sharply. "Ridiculous," she muttered and reached out to wave her badge over the service elevator call button.

"The first sign of genius is talking to yourself."

Startled, Arabella dropped the shoes as she whirled to see Mariana walking toward her.

"I'm sorry, hon." Mariana's brows pulled together as she bent over to pick up the shoes. "Didn't mean to scare you all to bits and pieces." She handed her the tennis shoes.

"Thanks." Arabella hugged them to the front of her black T-shirt. "And you didn't. I was just, uh, just preoccupied."

Mariana tilted her head slightly as if listening for sounds of the elevator's movement. "These days, everyone here seems preoccupied."

"Why is that?" Arabella flushed at the urgency in her tone.

"Oh." Mariana waved a dismissive hand. "Nothing seriously bad has happened here in the last few months. Instead, we just have these little annoyances that keep happening." She obviously read Arabella's obliviousness. "You know. The elevators breaking down so often. The glitches in the reservation system and the security system that's registering doors as locked when they're not and vice versa."

Arabella wondered if the security system was Grace's "other matter" that needed her attending.

"Leaves a person waiting for the other shoe to fall." Mariana's gaze drifted to the tennis shoes Arabella was clutching. "No pun intended."

The service elevator rumbled softly and a moment later the door opened. Arabella gestured for Mariana to go first.

"Thank you, dear." Mariana waited until Arabella was inside the car, too, and pushed the button for the second floor. "Now, tell me how you and the Jet-pack are doing."

"Jet-pack?"

"Jay," Mariana said, as if it were obvious. "That's what his grandpa always called Jay when he was visiting. Boy had so much energy it was like he was pumped up on jet fuel. Lord, the way he'd run around out at the market. Mischievous as hell. Always wanting to sweep up inside my food truck just so he could snitch a lemon tart when I wasn't looking." She grinned. "Used to figure he'd end up flying jets. Instead, he heads off to California when he was just a young pup and was gone for so long—" The doors opened again and she stepped out. "Goes to show you never can tell," she said just before the doors started sliding closed.

Arabella hurriedly blocked them with her shoulder. "Mariana—"

The older woman paused midstep. Beyond her, Arabella could see servers loading carts in preparation for the latest event being held in the banquet room.

Aware that she was holding up Mariana from her

duties, Arabella just shoved out the words. "Do you let Jay into the fitness center often?"

"You're the only one he's ever brought with him." Mariana answered the question that Arabella *hadn't* asked. "That's how I can tell you're someone special."

The tight little fist inside Arabella's stomach that she'd almost forgotten suddenly eased. "Really?"

Mariana's eyes softened. She dashed her fingers in a cross over her chest. "Promise." Then she winked and hurried away, her big bright bun bouncing on the top of her head.

Arabella shifted and the doors finished closing.

She didn't have time to go up to the fourth floor to store Jay's shoes in her locker there, so she just tucked them in a bag on her cart after she'd pulled it from the floor pantry. With her headphones tucked in her ears, she pulled the assignment chart she'd gotten from Beulah that morning out of her back pocket.

I think you should know that...

...you're someone really special.

Hallie shook her head for the third time in as many rooms. "Sorry." She dashed her finger along the wooden cabinet that housed the flat-screen television. "This needs a better polish."

That entire afternoon—ever since she'd left Brady's office with Jay's shoes—Hallie had been critical of Arabella's work.

"I'll polish it again," she said and pulled out a fresh cloth. "Hallie—"

The other girl's lips were pursed as she raised an eyebrow.

"Did I do something to upset you? Besides my sub-par cleaning, I mean?" She tried a wry smile but it was met with a stony stare.

"What could possibly upset me?"

She waved her dust cloth a little helplessly. "I don't know. That's why I'm asking. I thought...well, yesterday, I thought you and I might become friends."

"I don't need friends who hide the truth about themselves from me." Hallie looked back at the clipboard she used to mark off her inspections before releasing a room back to the front desk. "You'd better pick up the pace. You're an hour behind." She walked out of the room, leaving Arabella gaping.

She hurriedly applied the cloth to the offending wood, then darted out of the room after Hallie. There were only two rooms rented on this end of the floor so far, and Arabella knew the occupants were down at the pool where the marketing people were still working on filming. "It's done," she yelled, "and what truth am I supposed to have hidden?"

Hallie turned on her heel and marched back along the carpeted corridor. "Acting like you're one of us when you're really one of them!"

Arabella frowned. "I have no idea what you are even talking about."

"Really? And here I thought you Fortunes were all supposed to be so brilliant."

Fortunes.

It dawned on Arabella then. She'd completely forgotten about her last name. "Hallie, I'm not one of *those* Fortunes." Hearing it, she couldn't help but cringe. "I mean, I'm no different than you! I have to work for a living. Criminy, I can't even afford to move out of the twin bedroom I'm living in at my brother's yet because I'm so broke!"

But Hallie was obviously unconvinced. "I'd say *whatever*," she drawled, "except I wouldn't want to lose my job for being disrespectful."

Arabella let out an impatient snort. "I'm not—"

"I'll check back in an hour." Hallie cut her off. "Front desk needs these rooms available. They've all been blocked for a wedding tomorrow." Then she spun on her heel again and walked away.

Arabella flopped her arms at her sides. "What's a name matter, anyway?"

But Hallie wasn't listening and with a sigh, Arabella reentered the room. She stuffed her squishy headphones into her ears.

"...all up and gonna be someone new..."

The familiar words snuck into her head and she cursed. "I'd like to be someone new, too, buddy," she told the deep voice singing in her ear. "Someone without the last name of Fortune!"

Then she attacked the dusting with renewed vengeance.

She was finally pushing her cart back into the floor pantry nearly an hour later when an alarm suddenly sounded and she nearly jumped out of her skin.

She'd never heard that specific noise at the hotel before, but that didn't mean she didn't recognize a fire alarm when she heard one.

She slammed the pantry door closed on the cart and darted around the corner to the service elevator, only to remember that the elevators automatically shut down and returned to the first floor when the fire alarms activated. She'd polished the signs affixed to the backs of the room doors that explained that very point often enough by now to be able to quote the entire list of safety rules.

She hit the stairwell, where footsteps were already echoing throughout the cement tower and started down, hurrying even faster to help the woman ahead of her who was trying to manage a toddler and a baby and not get trampled by the people coming down behind them.

"Let me help," she said and swept the wailing toddler up in her arms.

The mother's eyes were wide and tearful and they took in Arabella's T-shirt with the hotel logo. "There's not *really* a fire is there?"

"Even if there is, it's all going to be fine." She spoke with a calmness she didn't really feel. "I'm Arabella." Her voice vibrated from the impact of her shoes hitting the steps. "What's your name?"

"Sierra." The mother clasped her baby closer as they reached the second-floor landing and started down the last stretch. "That's Mia you're carrying."

At the sound of her name, Mia wailed even harder, and knocked her elbow hard into Arabella's face as she strained to reach her mommy.

Pain exploded in her face and Arabella yanked her head back.

Blinking hard, she slowed only slightly, using the railing to help guide her while she blinked the stars from her vision.

In seconds, they'd reached the bottom of the stairs and they darted out into the corridor where Brady stood. His tie was loosened and it was only because Arabella knew him so well that she could see the agitation in his eyes despite the calm way he was directing people toward the exits.

"There's no need to run," he said in a loud voice. "Please proceed calmly to the exit—" He broke off for a moment, his expression tightening when he spotted Arabella carrying the little girl past him.

But she didn't slow. Her face was throbbing from the impact of Mia's elbow and she nearly ran right into Petunia in the lobby. The florist was carting a box of bouquets as if her life depended on it. An older man with gray hair was with her, carrying a second box.

"Leave the flowers," Arabella said sharply and pushed them both to the front door.

As soon as they were through, Arabella chased after Mia's mother. The young woman had broken into a trot right along with the dozens of other guests who were also more than a little anxious to get away from the building.

Finally, Sierra stopped, though, and sank down onto the grass and Arabella caught up to her. She gratefully surrendered the wailing toddler to her mama's arms and gingerly cupped her hand over her aching face.

Sierra was looking at her oddly. "Are you all right?"

She nodded. "I'll come back and check on you as soon as I can."

"You don't have to—"

"I want to." She cleared her throat and channeling Mariana a bit, gave Mia a quick wink before she turned to work her way back to the front entrance.

It felt oddly similar to the day the balcony collapsed, only this time Arabella didn't have her dad dragging her away. This time there was no ominous cloud of debris wafting through the air. Her nose was stuffy but not from the smell of smoke. She knew better than to trust that meant there wasn't any fire somewhere.

Alarms didn't go off all on their own, did they?

Not unless it was another one of those glitches that Mariana mentioned.

Gingerly pressing her fingertips against the pain beneath both of her eyes, Arabella looked around, wondering how best she could help. She spotted Grace Williams talking to Sybil and Beulah. They were obviously taking count of guests.

Hallie and a few of the other room attendants were pacing around with servers from Roja. They were handing out water bottles to guests and staff alike.

The three-person film crew who'd been taking footage all over the hotel were panning their cameras over the melee as three fire engines turned in to the property.

If this was all just a glitch, it was turning out to be a whopper of one.

"There you are." Jay suddenly appeared next to her. He was breathing hard, as if he'd just run a half-marathon. "I've been looking every—" He broke off with an oath and caught her face between his hands. "You're hurt!"

Before she had time to blink, he lifted her right off her feet.

Chapter Nine

"Jay!" Arabella's hands were patting his chest, but Jay barely noticed. He was too busy looking for a safe place to take her until he could get her some medical attention.

There were people everywhere and the hotel alarm was still blaring.

"Maybe this place *is* cursed," he muttered, finally stepping right over a retaining wall so he could get to the chaises surrounding the pool.

"It's not cursed," she said thickly. "Oh, criminy—" She was holding up her bloody hand as if she'd never seen it before.

"You're going to be fine," he promised even though he had a pit in the bottom of his stomach that made him want to punch something. Instead, he kicked the corner of one of the chaises and it spun on its legs so that he could lower Arabella onto it. His hand shook as he carefully brushed her hair out of her blue eyes. "I'm going to get some help and you're going to be just fine."

"I *am* fine," she insisted. Her voice sounded thick and she kept trying to sit up despite his efforts to keep her still. "I got elbowed in the face is all." She looked annoyed. "I didn't know my nose was bleeding."

"Someone elbowed you?" There were no pool towels conveniently stacked next to the vacant bar now and Jay yanked his shirt over his head and tried staunching the flow of blood with it.

"Not intentionally!" She scrabbled at his hand and the bunched shirt. "Jay, I can hardly breathe here."

He swore and moved his shirt away.

She inhaled through her mouth with obvious relief and closed her eyes for a moment. "I used to get bloody noses all the time when I was a kid. You'd think I'd remember how they felt." She looked at the shirt, stained crimson. "Oh, geez. That's going to be hard to wash out."

Half a choked laugh escaped. He sank down on his knees beside the chaise. "The last thing I'm worried about is a stained shirt." He unwound the bundle enough to find a shirttail and used it to gently dab her cheek. "I never thought the sight of blood bothered me until I saw it covering half your face."

"Half my—" She groaned, then winced sharply and yanked back when his careful dabbing got too close to her nose. "What does a broken nose feel like?"

"Don't know. I've never had one. Who elbowed you?"

"Just a scared liddle girl. She didn' know." She gave a cautious sniff, only to lean over with a choked cough which sent droplets of blood spattering everywhere. "Ohmigod," she groaned.

"We'll get it cleaned up."

"Yeah, by someone who'll have to wear a hazmat suit or something." She raised the back of the chaise, grimaced when she saw the smear she left, and then leaned back against it. She took the bundled shirt from him and held it beneath her nose as she tilted her head back. Her eyes were blue crescents beneath her lashes. "Where'd you cubb frob, anyway?"

They both went still when the strident fire alarm cut off midwail.

"Texas," he said a moment later.

She raised an eyebrow.

"It's where I come from."

She gave a groaning sort of laugh. "Keep your day job," she advised. She slid her fingers through his. "Stadd-up comedy may nod be in your future."

He smiled and kissed her knuckles.

She made a soft sound that finished the job of melting the remnants of panic inside his gut.

"Reminds me of January," she murmured.

"Me, too." Even though there really wasn't room, he slid onto the chaise beside her, careful not to tip it onto its side before he could get his weight centered with hers. "Are you going to disappear on me this time, too?"

She nuzzled her head against his chest. "I didn't want to disappear. You were the best thing about that trip."

He pressed his lips to her temple. "Not the bread?"

He felt her soft laugh. "Nod the bread."

The alarm might have been shut off, but that hadn't stopped any of the emergency responders.

Fire engines were in position, parked strategically around the hotel entrance. Police cruisers had arrived, too, and several officers were busy pushing the crowds back even farther while two more stretched caution tape across the divide.

"What were you going to tell me that night?"

"When?"

Her palm flattened against his abdomen and she pushed herself up a little so she could look at him.

"In January. At the birthday party." Her eyes shied away from his. "You were going to tell me something, but then we heard the balcony start to go and—" She sat up even more, which—unfortunately—was enough to upset the chaise and it tipped them right over the side.

They landed in a heap barely a foot from the edge of the pool. Jay's shoulder hit hard, but at least he reacted quickly enough to turn so that Arabella landed on him versus the unforgiving travertine.

Her shoulders were shaking. "What else?" She lifted her head and he realized she was laughing. "What else can possibly happen?"

He ran his hand up her slender back as they both sat and disentangled the legs of the chaise from their own. "What else?" he echoed, watching Detective Teas duck beneath the caution tape and head toward the hotel.

* * *

It took two hours before the fire chief announced that the alarm was false. Word spread through the crowd waiting outside a lot faster.

There wasn't a single guest remaining in the hot afternoon sun by the time the police cars departed. The fire crews were slower to leave. Before they left, one of the EMTs mopped up Arabella's face and taped her nose. "Looks like a simple break," he told her. "Check with your doctor, though, if it starts bleeding again or the pain gets worse instead of better."

Nicole and Mariana opened the doors of Roja, offering complimentary meals. Standard rooms were upgraded. Additional free nights were doled out.

In short, Hotel Fortune did everything it could to appease their guests who'd been so inconvenienced by the false alarm.

They still lost half of them before morning.

Arabella learned that from Beulah when she checked in the next day for her room assignments.

"Broken?" Beulah peered over her half glasses at Arabella's face.

She nodded. Just as the EMT the day before had warned, she'd woken up with bruises beneath both eyes.

"You look like you've done a round with my ex-husband." It was the first time Arabella had heard anything approaching compassion in the other woman's voice. "Had my share of black eyes just like those."

"That's horrible. I'm so sorry, Beulah."

"So's he." Her tone went right back to its usual terseness. "Pig's still doing time for it." She pulled something from her drawer and tossed it on the counter. "Shake it up and it'll stay cold for a couple hours. It'll help the swelling."

Arabella's eyes suddenly stung. "Thanks, Beulah."

As if she regretted her momentary lapse, Beulah's lips pinched together and she turned back to her computer.

Arabella pocketed the thin pack and left the office to start her day.

Fortunately, it progressed better than the day before. Hallie still wasn't the chatty, friendly soul she'd been initially, but at least she was satisfied enough with Arabella's work to release her rooms the first time around. By the time her lunch break rolled around, she was actually on schedule with the rooms. Which was amazing, because she'd even taken a few minutes in between them to press the cold pack against her tender face.

She knew Jay was working the wedding—that, at least hadn't been canceled—so she wasn't surprised when the whole day passed without running into him even once. Nor did she see his truck in the parking lot when she clocked out at the end of the day.

It was Friday. She wasn't scheduled to work again until Monday. The time until she might see him again stretched out disappointingly.

Until she got home and Harper handed her a jar of brilliant red jam. A small note had been taped to the top of it. "Found it on the front porch after the boys and I got back from taking Murphy for a walk."

Feeling weak inside, Arabella unfolded the note.

Mariana's Market. Tomorrow. Six a.m.

He'd included a simple sketched map as well.

She clasped the note to her breast and practically floated up the stairs.

"I know that look," Harper called after her.

But Arabella didn't respond. She was hearing another voice in her head.

I think you should know that...

...you're the only girl for me.

By morning, the bruises under Arabella's eyes were nearly purple. No amount of cosmetics could disguise them so she gave up trying. She wove her hair into a long braid, pulled on her favorite ball cap that matched her short denim sundress and followed Jay's map to Mariana's Market.

She got there well before 6:00 a.m., but even at the early hour, there were already dozens of vehicles parked in the big lot where venders had set up shop. There didn't seem to be a particular order to the way they were arranged and Jay's map hadn't gone beyond how to get to the location of the market itself, so she just began wandering up and down the nearest rows.

She hadn't really had any expectations about the market. She knew about the jams, of course. Louella's and Mabel's. Knew, too, that Petunia had a booth there at least once a month.

She was nevertheless surprised by the variety of wares that were on display.

She bought a hand-sewn scarf to send to her mother, knowing she'd love it, a vintage record album for her father and a jaunty doggie sweater for Murphy. Admittedly, the dog wouldn't need it for months and months, but how could she resist when "nothing but a hound dog" was embroidered across the back?

Humming under her breath along with the tinny sound of music coming from nowhere in particular, she reached the row of food trucks and spotted Mariana's right away. She wasn't all that surprised that there was a line of people standing outside the window and she couldn't help but wonder how Mariana managed to keep up with all of this as well as help run Roja. But there she was, her bright blond head visible from inside the truck.

Close by the truck a row of tables shaded by green-and-white market umbrellas marched up the center of the aisle. One table was already occupied by a group of old men playing cards.

When she reached the center of the market she noticed an orderliness to the booths that had been absent on the outer rows and after buying a coffee from one of them, she browsed happily among the bins of shining red tomatoes and melons as big as basketballs. She added a basket of deep red cherries to the mesh bag she'd gotten along with the doggie sweater and turned up the next row. A sign for Lou's Luscious Jams hung at the top of an empty booth straight ahead of her. It was more than a tent. Less than a shack. And the long table in front of it was nearly covered with the jars of jam that Jay was unpacking from a big crate.

She hesitated there because watching him stack his grandmother's wares felt so very sweet. He was wearing faded blue jeans, a plain blue shirt and an off-white cowboy hat. The only other time she'd seen him wear the hat was the day she'd run into him at the police station.

It was only a few weeks ago but it felt so much longer.

Then, as if he'd sensed her, his head lifted and his green eyes met hers. A slow smile crossed his face.

I think you should know that...

"I want to see your smile for the rest of my days," she murmured.

He straightened and thumbed his hat back an inch before gesturing at the table. "You just going to stand there talking to yourself, or come and help me?"

She raised her voice. "Maybe I'm enjoying the scenery." She took a sip of coffee. It really was an excellent cup. Almost as excellent as the view of him.

He craned his head, looking behind him, then along the row of booths. "What scenery?"

She laughed and walked the rest of the way to the booth. "False modesty, Jet-pack."

He shot her a close look. "Who told you about that?"

"Mariana."

He seemed to relax. "What else has she been telling you?"

"That you used to steal her lemon tarts."

"I swept in exchange for every single one," he defended. He lifted the coffee out of her hand and set it on the table behind him. "I do have a serious question for you, though."

"I don't know how to make lemon tarts."

His dimple deepened and he slid his hands around

her waist, linking them behind her. "That's not the question."

She couldn't help leaning into him. "Oh?"

"How's your nose feel?"

She groaned a little. "Thank you for the reminder. I'd almost forgotten that I look like a raccoon."

"Yeah, but you're a cute raccoon. The nose?"

She wrinkled it. "Honestly, it doesn't even hurt anymore."

"Good. That means I can do this." He leaned down and brushed his mouth slowly, gently across hers. "All mornings should start with a kiss from a beautiful raccoon," he murmured and kissed her again.

And she fell a little more in love with him.

"You going to stand there kissing the lady or set up shop?"

Jay finally lifted his head. "How you doin', Norman?"

"Fair." A tall, spare man with gray hair and a tanned face stopped in front of the table and though Arabella recognized him from the day before at the hotel when he'd been with Petunia carrying flowers, he obviously did not recognize Arabella. Not if the polite nod he gave her was any indication. "Lou's not sick or something, I hope. Can count on one hand the number of times she hasn't been out here bright and early on Saturday morning."

"She's fine," Jay assured him. "Offered to let me take over this morning so I'd have a chance to impress my girl."

He spoke lightly, but Arabella's heart still swelled.

"Women'll do that to ya," Norman agreed.

Arabella stuck out her hand. "Arabella Fortune, Mr. ah—"

"Just Norman," he said and shook her hand with all the enthusiasm of her nephews when they were afraid of getting cooties. "One of those Fortunes, you say."

Norman's smile was nonexistent but Arabella managed to keep hers in place. "*A* Fortune. I just moved here from New York."

He looked like he thought she ought to have stayed there.

He turned his back on her and gestured at the array of jam jars. "I'll take five jars."

Jay bagged up the jars and gave them to Norman in exchange for the cash that Norman passed over.

Norman didn't spare Arabella so much as a glance when he walked away a minute later.

"Friendly guy," she murmured under her breath.

"He usually is." Jay watched the departing man. "According to my grandmother, he's been having some trouble keeping his medicine straight. Gets forgetful. But he's still a staple out here at the market. Every weekend. Either playing chess near Mariana's truck or helping out at Petunia's flower stand when she's here."

"Selling flowers?"

"He's her dad."

"Ah. Okay." The missing dots connected. "Petunia mentioned him when I was working at her shop. No wonder he was helping with the flowers yesterday. Where's her stand?"

"Doesn't look like she's going to be there today." He

pointed down the row. "Her space is empty. It's next to the yellow tent with the striped awning. That one's Mabel's."

As the minutes had been passing, more and more vendors had been showing up. Rolling up the sides of vinyl tents. Trotting out portable tables. Unloading carts of bric-a-brac and setting out handmade crafts and every other imaginable item. The booth with the striped awning, however, sat empty.

She dumped her purchases and her bag on the square of fake grass covering the dirt ground inside their booth and plucked several jars out of Jay's box. "You just stack these things around?"

"Yep. On the shelves, too."

Since Jay had the table itself well in hand, she began adding jars here and there on the milk-crate shelves in what she figured were artful sort of displays. "How *is* your grandmother?"

"Nursing her aggravation where Mabel's concerned."

"I still can't believe they were brawling over her jam recipe."

"Tell me about it," he muttered. "Gran and Mabel go way back."

"But that's why you're here? To work her booth because of the hundred-yard thing?" She knew the judge had ordered both women to keep away from each other by at least that much distance.

"You heard what I told Norm. I'm trying to impress my girl."

She bobbled the jars and barely managed to catch one before it rolled off the shelf.

"And because my grandmother didn't want to chance running into Mabel," he went on humorously.

It was no less than she'd expected, but her balloon of joy over the "my girl" term deflated slightly. "Considering how desolate Mabel's booth looks, I'm not sure she needed to worry about it. But I guess if·one of them doesn't work, it's fair for the other one not to as well."

"Yeah, except Gran's jams are going to sell, anyway, thanks to us." He cupped his hand behind her neck. "So why are you looking sad?"

She looked toward the yellow booth again. "Mabel's booth just looks forlorn to me. Nobody is helping her out like you're helping your grandmother."

He smiled and dropped a quick kiss on the tip of her nose.

"What was that for?"

"Because not everyone has a heart as sweet as yours."

She couldn't manage to form a word. Not with the way her chest felt all full up and her face felt all stretched in a smile.

She hadn't finished stacking the shelves when another customer came by the booth, quickly followed by two more. As the sun climbed higher in the sky, the aisles among the booths became more congested with shoppers and the supply of Louella's jams dwindled.

It wasn't even close to noon when they were gone completely and Arabella gathered up her purchases and slung the strap of her bag over her shoulder.

"Where do you think you're going so fast?"

"What else is there to do?" She swept her arm out, encompassing the empty table and shelves. He could say that she had a sweet heart, but working alongside him all morning had been sheer delight. He had a way with people that was entirely captivating. Male, female, young, old. Didn't matter. They all walked away with smiles on their faces as well as jars of jam in their hands. "Everything's sold."

He closed his hands around hers. "Yeah, but that doesn't mean the fun's over, does it? Come on." He drew her around the empty table that he pushed back onto the fake turf so that it no longer protruded out into the aisle where the shoppers walked. "You haven't lived until you've had one of Mariana's fry bread tacos."

He seemed to take it for granted that she would agree, and since she was more than happy to prolong the pleasure, she did.

Her book bag bounced between them as they wandered through the rest of the market and Jay took it from her to sling over his own shoulder. "This thing gets heavier every time I see you. What're you doing? Collecting rocks?"

"I told you." She poked her hand down into the depths and blindly pulled out a binder with a bright orange cover. "My notebooks." She let it fall back into the bag.

Instead of taking her hand, he dropped his arm around her shoulder and fresh heat flowed through her veins. "How many journals does a girl need?" He angled around a young couple pushing a baby stroller. "And why carry them with you all the time?"

"They're not really journals," she admitted. "They're... stories. Like...novels. Sort of. And I carry 'em around with me because I can't help myself. I had five nosy big brothers. If I didn't want them making fun of me, I learned not to leave them lying around. It's a habit I can't break." And then she braced herself.

But he didn't mock. Didn't laugh. "What are sort-of novels?"

She made a face. "Ones that I start but never finish?"

He lifted the bag as if judging its weight. "How many?"

"Six."

"That was a loose-leaf binder. You write in long-hand?"

"Yes."

"Why not a computer? A laptop or a tablet? Would weigh a lot less than all those binders."

"Yeah, but there's something satisfying about a pen on paper."

He grinned. "What do you do when you want to change what you've written? Wouldn't pencil be better?"

"Probably, but I think better with a pen." She shrugged self-consciously. "It's just my thing."

He squeezed her shoulders. "Your process is your process. What do you write about? What kind of novels?"

"Just…stuff." She could feel the look he gave her and stopped to examine a table filled with screen-printed T-shirts as if they were positively fascinating.

"Stuff, she says cagily," he said. "Now you've really got me curious." He leaned down until he was looking over her shoulder, his chin touching her shoulder. "What secrets are you keeping, Arabella Fortune?" His deep voice caressed her ear.

Her knees went to mush. "A couple mysteries," she admitted faintly. "Fantasies. A bunch of children's stories. And—" She slid a look toward him, feeling engulfed by the warmth in his green gaze so close to her own.

"And?"

"And a romance," she finished in a rush.

But again, he didn't laugh. Instead he just straightened with a smile. "That's quite a variety. Are those the genres you also like to read?"

"I like to read everything," she admitted.

"Looks like they do, too." He picked up one of the shirts so the printed front was visible. Two skeletons wearing sunglasses and holding books in their hands reclined on chaise lounges in the shade of a cactus. *It's a dry heat* was printed below them.

"We're having a special on tees today." A bubbly girl quickly moved from her chair deep in the shade of a market umbrella. "Buy one, get two free." She tugged proudly at the white T-shirt she was wearing that had the words *I'd give it all up for Jett Carr* splashed across her breasts. "Have a whole new batch of these in. We sold out of them last weekend." She turned around briefly to show them the back, which had a black-and-white image of the bearded singer's profile, and smiled brightly over her shoulder at Arabella. "What do you think?"

Arabella smiled ruefully and shook her head. "Pass."

Jay made a sound that sounded vaguely choked. "Not even cactus and bony readers?"

She gave them both an apologetic shrug. "Not in the market for T-shirts today, I'm afraid." She folded the skeleton shirt and placed it neatly atop the small stack of them. "Good luck with your sale, though."

Even before they moved away from the booth, they'd been replaced by two other shoppers—both women—who screeched a little excitedly over the Jett Carr shirt the seller was wearing.

Arabella shook her head. "I don't know what they find so exciting about that singer."

Jay laughed and kissed her on the head. "Me, either." He dropped his arm over her shoulder again and they fell into step once more. "How often do you write?"

He was still talking about her books. As if they were actually something to be taken seriously. "Most every night. Sometimes it's only a paragraph or two."

"Isn't that how books get written? A paragraph or two at a time?" He squeezed her shoulder. "Why d'you suppose you haven't finished any of them?"

"I guess because I get another idea that I think'll be better, and so I abandon what I'm doing and start all over again." The latest were the children's stories that she'd started working on when Brady had become guardian to Toby and Tyler.

"Do you have a favorite?"

"I've never thought about it." She did then, briefly, and shrugged. "I don't have one."

"Is that why you keep toting around even the ones that you abandoned in favor of the next greatest idea?"

"No, I keep toting them around because one day, maybe I'll finish one of them."

"Then they're not really abandoned, are they? They're just hanging out, waiting for some sunshine to start growing again."

He stopped and she realized they'd reached Mariana's food truck. The picnic tables that had been vacant earlier were all now occupied and the line at the window was even longer than it had been earlier. The tinny music that had been playing before was still going strong, though the volume had been turned up.

"Waiting for some sunshine." She looked up at him. "That sounds a lot better than that I can't bring myself to throw them away because it feels like admitting failure."

"Nothing creative is a failure."

A short laugh escaped. "Says the insurance actuary."

He grinned. "Former insurance actuary. I didn't last long."

"I thought you went into that straight out of college."

"I did." They'd reached the end of the line at Mariana's truck.

"What'd you do after that?"

He didn't answer and she looked up and followed his gaze toward the quaint carts filled with fruits and vegetables where Mariana was holding court, talking to a young woman with a mic while a brawny guy nearby wielded a television camera. "Looks to me like she's too busy to be making fry bread tacos."

"Looks that way to me, too." Jay turned to face her and settled his hat more firmly as he studied the line they'd joined. "No wonder it's not moving. What say we take a rain check on the fry bread until next weekend and raid my grandmother's kitchen instead? Sound good?"

So he expected to see her next weekend.

She beamed. "Sounds perfect."

Chapter Ten

Louella was not home when they arrived at her house.

Arabella had followed Jay in her car and when they walked in without even knocking, she could read his surprise when they found the place empty.

"Did she leave a note?" Her mother always left a note for her dad whenever she went out.

He glanced around, presumably at the obvious places. "Not that I can see." He dropped the fat envelope filled with the cash they'd taken in at the market into a kitchen drawer and pushed it shut again before opening the refrigerator door.

"Jay!" She couldn't help a protesting laugh. "We're not really going to raid her fridge when she's not even here, are we?"

He gave her a look as if she'd grown a second head.

"You think she makes all of this because she wants to eat all of it herself?" He removed a platter wrapped in plastic wrap and set it on the counter. "Cold fried chicken." He followed it up with another covered bowl. "Potato salad." Then a tall glass pitcher. "Fresh lemonade." He added it to the collection on the counter and then leaned over to open a lower cupboard. "She's been trying to put meat on my skinny ass my entire life."

"Please. You're perfect." The words escaped without thought and she flushed when he shot her a look over his shoulder, catching her right in the act of ogling his butt.

His smile turned wicked as he straightened with the wicker picnic basket he'd pulled out of the cupboard. "We could always compare yours and mine."

She flushed even more and injected some bravado into her eye roll. "How suave you are."

He chuckled soundlessly as he stacked the food inside the basket. Then he grabbed the lemonade pitcher and headed toward the rear door. "Come on."

She hurried around him to open the door since his hands were full and they went outside. She half expected him to stop and set everything on the patio table that overlooked the garden, but he kept walking. Around the beds of strawberries, past the shed and around through the peach orchard.

She saw the big tub of his grandmother's, nestled in a shaft of sunlight beaming through the trees, and her heart began skittering around inside her chest as they neared his stone barn and her feet dragged a little.

He noticed and gave her a curious look. "Something wrong?"

"Not…uh, not at all. I just, I just didn't realize you had a water wheel," she said quickly. Not entirely untruthfully. Because she *hadn't* realized it until now. Hadn't seen it, because she hadn't gotten so close to the barn the last time she'd been there.

But there it was. Positioned closely against the far side of the stone barn, dipping into the stream and producing a soothing, distinctly rhythmic creak as it turned.

But her sudden shot of nerves was caused only because it had dawned on her that she was finally seeing his place. That they were alone.

That *anything* could happen.

She wasn't a virgin. Before Tammy Jo had landed Ham, Arabella had been involved with him first. But that had still been a while ago. Was she really ready to take that step with Jay?

He was still waiting for her to catch up to him. "Barn used to be a flour mill."

She blinked. "Seriously? I was only joking when I asked if your grandmother milled her own flour for her chocolate chip cookies."

"She's probably capable, but she couldn't do it here. Not anymore. The mill was dismantled a long time ago. My grandfather was a farrier. He did a lot of his work here." He aimed toward a rough-looking door positioned closer to the short side of the barn and she was surprised that he stopped to pull a key out of his pocket to unlock it.

"Get a lot of break-ins out here in the middle of nowhere?"

He pocketed the key again. "You'd be surprised." He pushed open the door and waited for her to enter first.

She did, and what she saw inside made her jaw drop.

Whatever the stone building's previous uses had been, the interior now was plainly meant as living quarters for humans. The stone walls on the outside were the same on the inside, but the floors were gleaming wood. A galley-style kitchen was located on one narrow end. At the other side of the room, a couple of rough-hewn posts anchored a staircase leading to a loft area that filled only a limited portion of the magnificent space soaring up to the crisscrossing barn rafters.

She assumed the bedroom was upstairs, because between kitchen and stairs, it was all living space downstairs. A small dining table that looked like it was made of the same kind of wood as the posts sat behind a long leather couch that anchored one end of a large rectangular rug woven in mottled shades of gray. Opposite the couch were a wooden trunk serving as a coffee table and two chairs. Most surprising of all, though, was a gleaming black grand piano that stood near the stairs. It ought to have looked out of place, but it didn't.

In fact, everything looked magazine perfect in one of those modern-yet-rustic ways. Perfect, yet totally impersonal. There wasn't a single personal item in sight.

She turned in a circle, taking it all in. "Your grandmother must have spent a fortune doing all of this."

He set the pitcher and the picnic basket on the concrete kitchen island.

"Was she hoping to rent it out or something?" Arabella wandered nearer, stepping around the buttery-soft-looking couch. There were only a few narrow windows, but they spanned nearly the entire length of the space. Hung horizontally as they were, one above the other, they afforded a view of the horses and the pasture from every position within the barn.

"Or something." Jay opened a cupboard and pulled out a sleeve of red cups that he tossed onto the island. He followed it up with a package of paper plates. "Nothing but the finest china here. Makes doing the dishes a breeze."

She laughed as she undid the twist-tie and removed two plastic cups while he did the same with the plates. She filled them with ice from the dispenser in the door of the refrigerator.

The sound of the ice maker reminded her of the towel that Brady had found. "My brother knows I was in the fitness center the other night," she admitted abruptly.

His eyebrows rose. "How? I know we weren't caught on the security camera."

She told him about the towel as she reached for the pitcher of lemonade and began pouring. "And he knows I wasn't alone. Because not only was my towel there, but your tennis shoes were as well."

"You told him they were mine?"

"Of course not, but he's not an idiot. He knows I'm—" She took a long drink of the cold lemonade, swallowing it along with the rest of her sentence. "I mean he suspects there's something…you know. Going on. Between you and me." Why on earth couldn't she seem to stop her tongue?

A small smile flirted around the edges of Jay's lips. "Does that bother you?"

"No!"

"So then what's the problem?"

"The problem is that he knows we were there when we shouldn't have been. We broke the rules. I never break the rules," she muttered. "I should have known we'd get caught."

He pulled off the plastic wrap from the plate of fried chicken and set it in front of her. "The hotel would have to fire me before they could fire you, so I wouldn't sweat too much over it."

"I don't know how you can sound so calm."

He uncovered the bowl of potato salad and stuck a big mixing spoon into it. "I've weathered worse."

She wanted to ask him more, but instead, followed him to the table, where he set the food in the middle. Then, when he pulled out a chair for her, she forgot to be curious in favor of being quietly charmed. The only other time a man had done that had been with Ham.

Just once.

"What's so funny?"

Arabella looked at Jay. "Sorry?"

"You were smiling to yourself."

She chuckled. "It's nothing. Just remembering the last time someone pulled out my chair."

"A guy?" He eyed her over the rim of his red cup. "Do I need to be jealous?"

She'd always thought jealousy was an unattractive trait. Yet the notion that she could even inspire him to such an emotion was entirely novel. "You be the judge. He took me to the fanciest restaurant in town."

"Any guy can do that. Now this?" He gestured with a fried chicken drumstick. "Raiding grandma's fridge? Takes real thought. So what happened after the restaurant?"

She bit the inside of her lip, but there was no real way to keep her smile from growing. "He dumped me during the soup course."

For once, she was pretty sure she was the one to surprise *him*. "Were the two of you serious?"

"I thought so at the time." She picked a drumstick of her own and took a bite. Even cold, it was delicious. "He's getting married soon. Well, actually, maybe it's this weekend. Or last?" She shrugged. "I can't remember. Far as I'm concerned, he and Tammy Jo deserve each other." She took another bite. "Is *everything* your grandmother makes delicious?"

"Yeah. Tammy Jo the reason he ended things with you?"

"Is that the polite term for getting dumped?" She grinned. "And no. There were a few other girls before Tammy Jo. Knowing Ham, she'll be lucky if there aren't a few other girls once they're married, too."

"Doesn't sound like he left you with a broken heart."

"Mildly bruised." Another bite and her drumstick was demolished. She set the bone on the side of her plate and scooped up some potato salad. "What about you?"

"Mildly bruised."

If jealousy was unattractive, she was looking as pretty as a toad, right about now. "Long time ago?"

His dimple appeared and he lightly tapped the edge of his red cup against hers. "The present company I'm keeping makes it hard to remember."

"Better be careful," she warned with a lightness she didn't exactly feel. "Saying things like that, I might start to believe you."

His gaze held hers. "Would that be so bad?"

Her throat suddenly felt too tight for words. She pressed her lips together and shook her head.

He set down his cup and rose from his chair enough to lean across the table. "Come here."

She swallowed hard and just like he had, set down her cup. She rose and leaned toward him over the chicken and the salad until they were mere inches apart.

His voice was low. "Can I call you Bella yet?"

The sweet heat that had slid into her veins slipped into her heart. "Yes."

He leaned two inches closer.

So did she.

Then his lips touched hers and the knowledge was suddenly just there.

Filling her.

I could love this man.

Not just a crush. Not just infatuation.

Seriously love him. As in good times and bad. As in now and forever.

He pulled back slightly then. His eyes searched hers.

Even though she'd been certain she hadn't said the words aloud, she felt her cheeks warm. "What?"

"I'm really glad your battery died that day."

She smiled. "So am I."

"But—" His gaze dropped. "You're smashing the grub."

She looked down, too, then and realized she'd planted her hand right in the middle of the bowl of potato salad. "Oh, for crying out loud!"

He gave a bark of laughter and kissed her again. "Bathroom's upstairs."

Even though she had mayonnaise and bits of potato stuck beneath her fingernails, she was pretty sure she floated up the stairs.

The bathroom was as lovely as the rest of the place, with a separate tub and shower that both looked out over the top of the water wheel. She washed her hands and controlled the urge to peek into the medicine cabinet behind the mirror. Her dress had a gold zipper from the top of its scooped neckline to the hem that hit her midthigh. Feeling breathless, she lowered the zip a few inches. Then looked at her raccoon-reflection and yanked it back up where it belonged and left the room.

The wide bed occupying most of the loft was covered in a deep blue spread. A chest of drawers was situated beneath another one of the horizontal-style windows. A pair of cowboy boots lay haphazardly on a rug similar to the one downstairs and a guitar was propped in a corner with a couple shirts tossed carelessly across it.

At least there were signs of his occupancy. As well as the fact that he didn't put his clothes away any better than she did.

She was still smiling when she went back downstairs. He'd cleared the table. "Honey, I did the dishes."

She laughed. "What a hero."

"I try." His eyes crinkled. "What do you want to do now?"

Muss up your neatly made bed?

The words only sounded inside her head, though. "Show me the horses?"

He smiled slowly. "As much as I appreciate the outfit, you're not exactly dressed for riding."

"That's okay. I don't know how to ride, anyway."

He pressed his palm to his chest. "You're killing me. You're in Texas, sweetheart. That's something we'll have to rectify as soon as possible."

Any reason to spend time with him was okay with her. "That doesn't mean we can't go look at them now, does it?"

In answer, he took her hand in his and he led her back outside where it was even more hot and humid thanks to the clouds that had rolled in. They crossed the short bridge that arched over the stream and ducked between the rails of the white fence to cross the pasture toward the three light brown horses standing still on the far side of the field. They would have looked identical if not for the white markings on their faces.

Jay gave a soft whistle and the one with the smallest mark flicked its dark tail jauntily and trotted toward them, not stopping until it butted his head against Jay's upraised palm. "This is Loretta. Looking good for a thirty-year-old lady."

"Thirty!"

"Year older 'n me. I learned to ride on her. Almost before I could walk." He tugged Arabella closer and guided her fingers to the white mark. "She likes her star rubbed. Right there."

Arabella rubbed her fingertips against the smooth white hair and Loretta's liquid brown eyes turned in her direction. She felt strangely moved knowing that the old horse had borne a small, young Jay on her back. "I didn't realize horses lived so long."

"Some do." Jay ran his hand down the horse's gleaming shoulder. "She's pampered and healthy. Hopefully she's got a lot more years left in her."

As if in answer, Loretta butted her nose against his shoulder.

He laughed and stuck his hand in the pocket of his shirt and pulled out a peppermint. He barely managed to unwrap it before the horse nipped it out of his fingers.

By then, the other two horses had plodded forward, too. "Waylon," Jay said as he pointed out the one with a long narrow stripe down his nose, "and Willie." He dropped another candy in Arabella's hand. "Unwrap it and hold it flat in your palm."

She did as instructed and Willie's velvety lips rubbed against her palm as he took the peppermint. She giggled and scrubbed her palm down her side. "Tickles."

Jay chuckled. "Here." He unwrapped the third peppermint and handed it to her. "Waylon isn't quite as polite as Willie," he warned.

She eagerly presented her palm with the candy in the center and Waylon butted against Willie to get to it, and left a slobbery smear behind once he did.

"Definitely not as polite." Arabella wrinkled her

nose, laughing. "Your grandmother must really like country music. Considering their names, I mean."

Jay pulled out his shirttail and wiped her hand dry. "She's more of a Sinatra fan. My grandfather was the one who named them. They got Willie and Waylon as foals not long before he died." He patted his empty pocket for the benefit of the horses. "All gone, my friends."

Waylon and Willie bobbed their heads and plodded away.

Loretta remained, though, seeming content with the brush of Jay's hand on her back.

Arabella slowly stroked the horse's back, her hand following Jay's. "It's no wonder your grandmother doesn't want to give them up."

"She never will as long as I have something to say about it."

Her heart squeezed. "You're a good grandson."

His lips twisted slightly. "Not as good as I should have been." He looked over her head toward the barn but Arabella had the sense he was focused elsewhere.

She held her hand still on Loretta's back, knowing his hand would bump into hers. "Why?"

She wasn't sure he'd answer at first. But then his gaze shifted to her face. "I was so focused on my own life I couldn't even make time to get back to celebrate holidays. Birthdays. Then when everything went to hell—" He glanced up when thunder rumbled softly overhead.

She slid her fingers through his, keeping his hand on Loretta's back when he would have pulled away. "What went to hell?"

He frowned. "Arabella."

She winced, wishing for Bella again. "Does it have to do with Detective Teas?"

"Teas?" He frowned even more and his lips thinned. "He thinks I had something to do with the balcony collapse at the hotel."

It took a moment for his abrupt words to sink in. To make sense. "That's ridiculous!"

"I know it is, but why do you think so?"

She turned toward him and settled her palms on his chest. Even through his shirt, she could feel the solid warmth of him. "Because I know you."

He gathered her hands beneath his. His eyes searched hers with a sudden urgency that pulled at her. "What do you know?"

"I know you put your family first."

He started to shake his head and she curled her fingertips into his chest. Even Loretta cooperated, conveniently shifting her considerable size behind him so that he couldn't back away from Arabella. "Maybe you didn't always, but you do now. And now is what I know. I know you're a hard worker. You're loyal to the hotel." She took a step closer until their hands were caught between their bodies. "And I know how you make me feel."

Something else entered his green eyes. Something warm. Something heady. "And how is that?"

She stood on her toes and pulled his head down close enough to press her mouth to his. She put everything she had into that kiss. All of her emotion. All of her yearning. And when she finally went down off her toes again, her heart was hammering so hard inside her chest he couldn't fail to feel it. "Like that," she whispered huskily.

He drew a finger down her cheek. "You're too good for me."

She shook her head. Reached up and kissed him a second time. Went back down on her heels and had to hold on to him just to keep her legs from collapsing beneath her. "I've never wanted anyone the way I want you."

His jaw flexed. She knew he wanted her, too. She could feel it. Not just in the hardness of his body but in the heat of his eyes. In the tension of his hands as they roved down her back.

But still, he was holding back and her frustration rose in her throat.

She went up on her toes a third time. She stopped shy of kissing him, though. Need was a hot hollow cramping inside her. "Do I need to strip off my dress right here, Jay? I'm on the Pill. Perfectly safe, I promise you."

He groaned slightly. "Bella."

"I will," she warned—promised—huskily. "One zip is all it takes." To prove it, she reached between them to tug at the zipper.

"No." His hand caught hers, stopping her.

Her dismay never had a chance to get off the ground, though, because he suddenly reversed their positions until it was her back pressed against Loretta's stalwart side.

"I want to do it," he said gruffly. His fingers brushed against hers as he took over.

Her breath came hard in her chest as she stared up at him. Every nerve ending she possessed stood at high alert, sending frenzied little charges in accompaniment to her pounding heartbeat as he lowered the zipper tab with excruciating slowness. Her dress loosened tooth-by-tooth and she sucked in an aching breath when he took a step back and lowered to one knee as he continued pulling down the zipper. Right to the very bottom of her hem. Then he tugged one last time and the zipper separated altogether.

He exhaled audibly and his hands slid under the denim, settling first on her waist for a long moment before slowly sliding behind her back, drawing her toward him again.

She shuddered, drowning in desire. When he rested his forehead against her belly, she ran her fingers through his thick, dark hair. In that moment, there was something intimate and impossibly vulnerable about him. The slightly sunburned skin at the nape of his neck below his short hair. The long sweep of his spine, just visible beneath the gape of his shirt collar.

Loretta shifted then, pushing so hard against Arabella that she lost her balance and fell forward against Jay, taking him right with her down to the tall, sweet grass.

He caught Arabella against him, his eyes glinting. "Good old Loretta. Always has my back."

Arabella laughed softly as she tried to sit up, but Jay just caught her hips in his hands to keep her in place, sitting right there on top of him.

Then he pressed hard against her and her laughter

died. Her dress had slipped down one arm and was barely hanging on to her other shoulder. And even though she'd been the one threatening to strip, now that she was all but nude in front of him, she was acutely aware of how she must look. No bra. A pair of white bikini panties with pink sunglasses printed all over them.

She started to pull the dress together but he shook his head. "Don't." In fact, he curled his fingers in the dress fabric as if to make sure she couldn't.

Her skin tingled. She didn't think her nipples could get any tighter, but they did. Inside, however, she was simply liquefying.

"Undo your hair."

She moistened her lips and tried not to reveal how shaky she suddenly felt as she raised her hands to her ponytail and worked the thin band free. Her hair fell down around her shoulders.

"Do you know how many times I've thought about you?" His fingers flexed against her hips and his voice deepened even more. "Dreamed about you?"

Thunder murmured again but it didn't matter since she was suddenly incapable of speech, anyway.

"Months." His eyes were almost as green as the grass surrounding him. "And more months. And then there you were. In Rambling Rose. At the police station."

It dawned on her then. She pressed her palm flat against his abdomen and felt his muscles bunch. "Was that why you were so unfriendly? Were you there because of the balcony collapse?"

"I warned you that you're too good for me."

She was shaking her head even before he finished speaking. "I'm perfect for you and you know it."

His dimple appeared suddenly. "Now who's confident?"

She could only attribute her sudden wealth of self-assurance to him. Particularly when she slowly rocked her hips against his. "Does that feel perfect?"

His eyes darkened and the edge of his white teeth showed as he inhaled audibly. "Getting close to it." He deftly slid his hand between them, fingers curling unerringly beneath her panties to find her.

Then she was the one to catch her breath.

"Even closer," he murmured.

And then she couldn't think anything at all. All she could do was feel. His fingers on her. In her. Driving her right to the edge of insanity only to pull back and taunt her even more until she was so desperate that she mindlessly caught his hand in hers, pressing his fingers against her until finally, finally, the pressure inside her escaped.

His exultant groan worked through her as she collapsed in a heap against his chest. But even then there was little rest because he rolled until it was her back cradled in the lush grass. Her eyes staring up at the clouds overhead. He kissed her again. And again. On her lips. On her breasts. On her navel and her big toe and every point in between.

She wasn't even sure how he'd gotten rid of her panties, much less his own clothes, but it didn't matter because he was there, pressing inside her, filling her more perfectly than she could have ever imagined.

She wrapped her legs around him. Her arms around him. Took him into every cell of her soul, and when the ecstasy was almost more than she could withstand, his eyes met hers.

"Now." His voice was breathless. Raw. Beautiful. "Now, we're perfect."

She threw back her head, and together, they flew.

Chapter Eleven

The sweat on their bodies didn't even have a chance to cool when the sky suddenly opened.

Arabella jerked when the first big raindrop plopped squarely between her eyes. "What?"

Jay jerked and swore, too, because that first big plop was immediately followed by a couple million more.

Arabella could only sit there and giggle as he darted around, trying to gather up their bits of clothing that had decided to take flight thanks to the wind that sprang up as unexpectedly as the rain.

"Big help you are." He was laughing too as he hitched up his jeans and swiped his face at the same time.

She giggled even harder, trying vainly to rezip her dress.

"Oh, hell." He grabbed her hand. "Just come on."

And so they ran, half dressed, half not, back to his barn, where they left their clothes in a wet heap on the floor inside the door before chasing up the stairs, where Arabella was all too happy to muss up his neatly made bed but good.

After, they slept for a while. Then Jay brought up the rest of his grandmother's fried chicken and they polished it off lying right there on the bed as they watched the rain pour and pour and pour outside the horizontal windows.

He was facedown, stretched out diagonally across the wide bed. She was stretched out atop him and she idly traced the tattoo on his shoulder blade. She was no musician, but even she recognized the stylized image as intertwined music clefs. She reached out to point at the laundry-laden guitar in the corner and rather less-than-absently enjoyed the feel of his spine against her breast. So much so, that she wriggled slightly again, just to repeat the pleasure. "Do you play that?"

He didn't even bother to look where she was pointing. "Not anymore." He folded his arms beneath his cheek and closed his eyes.

She slid along his back, enjoying the feel of that, too, until she could hook her chin over his shoulder. His lashes were so long she was a little jealous. "Why not?"

His lips curved. He didn't open his eyes. "I'm not very good at it."

"What about the piano downstairs?"

"My mom was a teacher, remember?"

She kissed a bony protrusion in his shoulder. "Doesn't mean that she taught you how to play."

"She did."

"Is that what the tattoo is about? Ode to your mother?"

Jay glanced at the guitar. It was an old one. Back from the days when he'd first started out. "Isn't that what good Texan sons do? Get tats in honor of their mamas?" He reached his hand behind him and closed it unerringly over her thigh. It was warm. Sleek. And he recalled the sprinkle of freckles just above her knee. "Keep rubbing against me like you're doing and neither one of us is going to be able to walk for a week."

She, though, slid her hands over him as if she were luxuriating in the feel of his hairy arms as much as he luxuriated in the feel of her smooth, strong thighs. "Would that be so bad?"

His laugh was a little choked. "I'm a man, honey. What do you think?"

In answer, she slowly slid back down him again, the hard points of her nipples like points of fire every inch of the way.

Then her toes tickled the arches of his feet and he grunted, yanking them away.

"Ticklish, are you?"

He felt her lips on the small of his back. Then the nip of her teeth on his butt.

He shifted slightly, groaning a little. "Playing with fire, honey."

He felt her silent laughter work through him, and then she was slithering again, upward this time, and he was pretty sure his eyes were rolling back in his head at the sensations. She finally stopped sliding again when her breasts reached his shoulder blades and her arms came under his in a backward sort of hug. She kissed the nape of his neck and her breath was warm and sweet against his flesh. "Will you play something for me?"

He could hardly think straight for the feel of her body plastered against his. He exhaled slowly. Carefully. "Will you let me read one of your sort-of novels?"

"Touché." She moved her thigh a few inches along his, then back again. "If you promise not to laugh when you do."

"I promise not to laugh."

She slid her arms out again from beneath him and started to roll off him but he reached behind and caught her leg again. This time it was her knee.

"First you can finish having your fun back there," he said huskily.

"I don't know what you mean," she said in a prim little voice.

"Liar." He laughed softly. "You're as turned on as I am." He lifted his head and looked back at her. "How wet are you?"

Her cheeks were red. The bruised circles under her eyes were almost purple. But her aquamarine eyes met his with that combination of boldness and innocence that was proving to be his undoing.

"Very," she said.

He hardened even more and turned onto his back. "Show me."

Her pupils dilated a little. Then she slid her thigh over his and wrapped her hand around him.

He saw stars.

Then balancing on her knees, she slowly took him in. To all that heat. To all that sweet, wet heat that encompassed him so flawlessly.

The moan she gave then was the sweetest note he'd ever heard. It went on and on, singing inside his head, even long after he'd emptied everything that he was inside of her.

The story was about two penguins named Oscar and Aaron and the mischief they got into whenever Mama and Papa Penguin weren't looking.

"They're Toby and Tyler," he said after he closed the orange-colored binder. "You need to finish this." He handed it to her. "It's really sweet."

She took the binder and clutched it to her midriff. Her dress was still clanging around inside his dryer and after they'd showered together, she'd pulled on a shirt from his closet. She'd rolled up the too-long sleeves and the tails practically reached her knees.

As far as Jay was concerned, it would be his favorite way of seeing her dressed from here on out.

"You're just saying that because we've been playing doctor all afternoon."

"I'm saying it because you have a way with words," he corrected and went to reach for another binder from inside her bag.

But she pulled it away. "Not so fast, Mr. Cross." She waved her fingers at the piano behind the couch where they were sitting. "Your turn first."

He pulled a face. "I haven't played in a while." That much was true.

"I don't care." She dropped her binder in her bag and moved around to sit on the edge of the piano bench. She patted the space beside her. "Make your mama proud."

He chuckled, some of the odd tension that had been building inside him beginning to lessen again. He sat down beside her. "Don't remember ever playing piano wearing nothing but my boxers."

Her eyes sparkled. "Is it giving away too much if I admit I'm relieved to hear it?" She tapped two of the keys, discordantly. "Do you need sheet music or something?"

He shook his head and flexed his fingers comically before settling his index fingers on the keyboard.

He tapped out a fine rendition of "Chopsticks."

She laughed and bumped her shoulder against his. "Even *I* can play that."

The rest of his fingers joined in and "Chopsticks" morphed into the dramatic strains of Grieg's Piano Concerto in A minor.

He made it through the first couple dozen bars, which was a feat in itself since he hadn't played it since he was a kid.

But it was enough to leave Arabella staring at him slack-jawed. "That's not 'Chopsticks.'"

"Edvard Grieg." He gave her a quick kiss and got up from the bench. "Norwegian composer. Only piano concerto he ever wrote. I had to learn it for a recital back in school. I don't even remember the rest of it."

"If you can play like that, why did you ever go into *actuarial science*?" She followed him into the kitchen.

"Music might have been my first love, but I was way

better at math than I ever was in music theory and it paid for college." He kissed her nose. "We ate all the fried chicken. All I've got in the cupboard are boxes of cereal." He opened one to show her the truth of it. "And thanks to the workout you've put me through, I'm starving."

She smirked. "My dress is still in the dryer. So I guess you're stuck with—" She pulled out the nearest box. "Frosted Fruity Flakes. Seriously?"

"Don't make fun. Man's choice of breakfast cereals is sacred." He took the box from her and shoved it back on the shelf. "And your dress ought to be dry by now. We can go have dinner at Provisions." He went through the door that led to a powder room that was so small it always made him feel claustrophobic and into the slightly larger laundry room. When he went back out to her, he was holding her dress. "It's wrinkled but it's dry."

Even though they'd just spent hours discovering every cell on each other's bodies, she closed herself in the powder room to change.

"Not only wrinkled and dry," she said when she emerged a few minutes later, "but about a size and a half smaller." She twitched at the hem that was no longer midthigh but a good two inches higher. And while the zipper was done up, the denim hugged her figure in a snug way that it hadn't before.

It wasn't quite indecent, but he didn't want anyone else seeing her wear it now but him. "I'll buy you a new dress."

She laughed and waved off the offer. "I can buy my

own dresses, thank you very much. But," she said, as she twitched again at the barely-butt-covering hem, "if we're going to Provisions, I'd better stop off at Brady's and change first." She cast him a look. "Not that I'm protesting, but you might need a little more coverage in the clothing department, too."

He struck a pose. "Plaid boxers don't do it?"

"Anything about you does it for me. But the health code probably says otherwise." She leaned over to pick up her book bag and showed off a peek of her sunglass-strewn underwear. Then, as if she felt his gaze, she shot him a look over her shoulder and yanked on the hem again.

He spread his palms. "Only human, honey."

Her cheeks colored. Despite her bruised eyes, she was still the prettiest woman he'd ever known. From the outside to the inside, everything about Arabella Fortune was beautiful.

And now she'd narrowed her eyes to blue slits. "Why are you looking at me like that?"

Like he'd seen his future and didn't want to face what it would be if it didn't contain her?

"Just thinking about the next time Mariana sneaks us in to use the hotel's hot tub."

She made a stern face and pointed her finger at him. "We're not doing *that* again. Brady's already furious with me as it is." She dropped her hand to delve into her bag again. "But that reminds me. Your shoes are still in my housekeeping cart. And if I don't set a reminder for myself, I'm going to forget them yet again." When she pulled her hand back out, she had her cell phone in it. But instead of typing in her little reminder, she just stared at the screen. The color drained from her cheeks, leaving her bruises even more purplish.

"What's wrong?"

She turned the screen to show him. "Fifteen messages. The last time I had fifteen messages, it was after my mom found out Adam had a baby."

"Seems like Adam should have been the one getting the messages."

She sank onto the arm of the couch as her fingertip began swiping her phone screen. "You don't understand. Larkin was really sick for a while. Aplastic anemia. He might not have made it if Adam hadn't been a bone marrow match." She held the phone to her ear as she listened to a voice message.

Color reentered her cheeks as fast as it had fled, though, and she hopped off the couch arm. "There's been a flood at the hotel."

He frowned. "From the rain?"

"I don't know. I guess?" She was hunting in her bag again. "Where are my keys?"

"I'll drive." He bolted up the stairs and yanked on the first pair of jeans he came to. He pulled on socks and his boots, grabbed a shirt and hustled back down the stairs again. "We'll run by your brother's place on the way."

They left the barn at a jog, bypassing his grandmother's house altogether to go straight for the truck. He'd pulled on his shirt by then and she tossed her bag onto the floor, not even noticing this time the way she flashed her sunglass panties at him as she climbed up inside.

There was never any traffic on the road out to his grandmother's place, so he pushed the speed without regret. Not even thirty minutes had passed when he pulled up at the curb outside her brother's house.

Arabella's heart was hammering as she ran inside. Harper and the boys were sitting in the living room playing Candy Land and she hopped up, scattering the pieces when Arabella rushed inside.

"Bella! Brady's been looking—"

"I know." She tugged self-consciously at her dress. "I just found out." She headed up the stairs. "Just going to change," she called down as she went.

She replaced her shrunken dress with black leggings and a loose T-shirt, pushed her feet into her tennis shoes and pounded back down the stairs again. Naturally, Harper hadn't gone to the hotel because she was taking care of the twins.

"You were with Jay?"

"Yes." Arabella reached down and hurriedly provided the hugs that both boys were squawking for. "I just listened to the most recent message. How bad's the flood?"

"Really bad. Brady says he's not sure how much more the hotel can take."

Arabella scrubbed her fingers over Murphy's head when he jumped against her leg, then she hugged Harper as well. "It's going to be okay. It has to be."

She was still repeating those words inside her head when Jay pulled into the hotel parking lot a short while later.

Unlike the last emergency that had turned out to be a false alarm, there were no fire trucks this time. No police cruisers. No flashing lights, no people swarming around.

The parking lot was mostly empty, in fact, which for a Saturday evening wasn't exactly the best thing to see, either.

Jay parked near the entrance and they started to go inside. But even before they made it to the wide, shallow steps of the entrance, they could see the water flowing over them, pooling at the base and running off to the side in the general direction of the pool.

"Good grief," Arabella muttered, stepping more carefully because her tennis shoes were proving to be as useful as water skis. She looked upward. "Do you think it rained here harder than it did out at your place?"

"It's possible, I guess." Jay had closed his hand protectively around her elbow when he'd seen her slip the first time. "Careful."

They went up two more steps and when she slid yet again, she muttered an oath and pulled the shoes off altogether. Her bare feet had better traction but when they entered the lobby, the water was even deeper, covering her feet right over her toes. The water was bad enough. But there were brochures and reams of papers floating about in the mess. Flowers from the arrangement that always took center stage in the lobby drifted along with them.

It seemed like a dozen people were hustling around with big buckets while a dozen more swept at the water with everything from wide brooms to mops to other buckets.

Nobody was above pitching in. Mariana. Grace Williams. Callum and his brothers. Kane and Brady, who greeted her and Jay's arrival with a narrow-eyed glare. Even Beulah was there, her sour face tight with concentration as she mopped water into the bucket that Hallie was holding.

Arabella stopped next to Jason, whose trousers were wet up to his knees while he dragged a trash barrel around in an attempt to capture some of the non-liquid debris. "Here. Let me help." The poor kid looked about ready to bawl.

He gladly surrendered the plastic bin.

"I'm going to check in at security," Jay said grimly.

She nodded and watched him work his way through the mess before turning back to the task at hand. "Jason, what happened here?"

"Sprinkler system went haywire." He pointed to the ceiling. "Went off out of the clear blue sky and then nobody seemed able to shut it off again."

She shook her head, trying to adjust her thinking from a rain flood to a sprinkler system malfunction. "The fire department was just here two days ago because of the alarm going off! Shouldn't they have noticed then if something was wrong with the system?"

"There's no way this was an accident," Brady said, wielding a push broom nearby to send a wave of water hurtling toward the open front doors.

Grace Williams had tears in her eyes as she followed behind Brady with a broom of her own.

Just seeing the woman who was always the epitome of her name in tears was enough to make Arabella feel weepy herself. "What about the guest rooms?" She looked over her shoulder in the general direction of the restaurant. "Roja?"

"The restaurant's okay," Mariana said gruffly. She was out of breath and had wet splotches all over her pants and chef's coat. "Miracle of miracles."

"The guest rooms on the third and fourth floor were spared. But on the second?" Hallie shook her head. She was on her elbows and knees now, wielding a twisted towel like a squeegee to push water ahead of her, aiming, too, for the entrance. "They were evacuated as soon as the sprinklers went off." Her eyes rested on Arabella's face for a moment. "Maybe it's a good thing the vacancies have gotten as high as they have."

"What I'd like to know is why the police haven't been able to figure out who the hell has it in for the hotel." Beulah dumped a wad of soaking papers into Arabella's trash bin. "But then that's the police for you," she groused and sloshed her way across the lobby again.

Arabella nudged Mariana toward the leather chairs nearby. "I know they're wet, but go sit down," she urged. "Take a breather."

The fact that the older woman didn't argue spoke volumes. Arabella took over the broom that Mariana had been wielding and, leaving the trash bin to Jason once more, added her efforts alongside Grace.

She knew it was too much to hope that Brady wouldn't return to the topic of Jay, though she wished he could have waited until they weren't surrounded by a dozen other people.

"I've been leaving you messages for hours."

"My phone was in my bag." She pushed ahead of him, following her own personal wave of water right outside the doors. She watched the water flow down the terra-cotta steps. "I wasn't trying to avoid you."

"You were with Cross."

"All day." She gave him a tight smile. "So if you're thinking about trying to lay all this—" she swept out her arm "—at his doorstep, think again."

He frowned. "I don't think Jay did this."

"Don't you? Detective Teas seems to think he had something to do with the balcony collapse. Are you saying you didn't know about *that*?"

His expression told her well enough that he had. "I'm not saying I agree," he defended, following her back inside again. "But the guy's got too many blank spots in his background."

"So what if he does? Does anyone's background hold up perfectly under a microscope? Does *yours*?" Her annoyance with Brady was well placed in her broad sweeping against the water. No matter how much they pushed out of the building, it still seemed to maintain its depth above her toes. "Why doesn't the water go down?" Admittedly, she'd only been at it a short while in comparison to everyone else.

"The worst of it's been here in the lobby," Grace said as she wearily pushed her broom past them again. "It was almost ten inches deep before we were able to get the water cut off."

"Fire suppression system bypasses the regular water system," Jay said, reappearing. "Cutting one off doesn't cut off the other, but in this case, the suppression system's cutoff was bypassed, too." He had two long-handled window-washing squeegees in his hand and he gave one to Hallie. "You're going to ruin your back at that rate."

She sat up on her knees, stretching gratefully before pulling herself up to her feet using the squeegee as a crutch. "You'd think I'd still be used to crawling around cleaning under beds and such."

"Nothing prepares a person for this," Arabella said.

Brady propped his arm on top of his broom. "How did you know the sprinkler system's cutoff had been tampered with?"

"Guys in security told me," Jay said evenly before putting his back into helping sweep the water out of the lobby.

"I told you I've been with him all day," Arabella muttered through her teeth.

"Doesn't mean the damage wasn't planned another time," her brother said under his breath.

She huffed and walked away, moving to the rear of the lobby nearest the elevators. The doors were standing open and she stepped inside the furthest one. Every light on the panel was lit. Lord only knew how badly it would misbehave after this latest calamity.

She swept, swept, swept until she'd managed to push almost all of the water out of the car. Then, before it could flow back inside, she shoved a few of the sopping towels that Hallie had been using into the door track, creating a rough sort of dam. Then she did the same thing with the second elevator. Hallie had noticed and brought her several fresh towels.

"Here." She crouched down and helped wedge them into place.

"Thanks." Arabella watched her from the corner of her eye. "Hallie, I'm really sorry that I didn't mention—"

"Forget it," Hallie said, cutting her off brusquely. "I shouldn't have overreacted like I did."

Arabella turned to face her head-on. "We're okay then?"

Hallie made a face. "How can we not be? Look at you. Black eyes and on your hands and knees mopping up water."

"Oh, God." Arabella covered her face again. "All day long I've been forgetting how awful I look. First Jay and now—"

"Jay?" A smile played around Hallie's lips. "What's going on with Jay?"

Arabella's face went hot and Hallie's lips pursed in a silent whistle.

"Not bad," the other girl said under her breath. "Not bad at all, girlfriend." Then she pushed to her feet and started squeegeeing water out of the corridor and toward the lobby.

It was dark by the time they all successfully conquered the water well enough that there only remained a gloss of moisture on the terra-cotta floor.

All of the area rugs had been pulled out to the parking lot. So had all of the heavy wood furniture and everything else that was even capable of being moved at all.

Someone brought in folding chairs—Arabella thought it might have been Jay, but by that point she was too exhausted to really notice or care.

She was just glad to get off her feet and tuck into one of the sandwiches that Nicole and her sisters produced.

Callum, who'd spent much of that afternoon with his cell phone glued to his ear while he helped out with the cleanup, was sitting on the registration desk. His brothers were huddled nearby. One of them—Wiley—had his arm around Grace's shoulder. She looked as exhausted as Arabella felt.

"Obviously, we'll have to close while the restoration work gets completed," Callum announced to everyone assembled.

"What'd the insurance company say?" That came from Kane.

Nobody could miss the look that passed between Callum and his brothers. "They haven't said they'll deny this latest claim outright, but—" He shook his head and eyed everyone in the room. "I'm not going to lie here. The balcony was tampered with." His gaze fell on Grace and his brother Wiley. "We can just count our blessings that nobody was hurt worse than Grace with her broken leg. The food tampering at the Give Back barbecue was a passel more of bad publicity. We've beefed up security in and around the property. We've been trying to advertise the hell out of this place. The commercial we just filmed hasn't even hit the airwaves yet. We've had more cancellations in the last month than we've had reservations. And now this?" He spread his arms and dropped them wearily.

Wiley stepped forward then. "We're not giving up," he said flatly. "We're Fortunes and we don't give up."

Someone muttered a "hear, hear."

Callum clapped his brother on the shoulder. "Wiley's right. Fortunes don't give up." His lips tilted slightly as if he'd only needed that particular reminder. "But I wouldn't be doing my job right now if I didn't caution everyone here that the future right now as far as the hotel is concerned is anything but certain. So if you want to find a job elsewhere or—"

Brady stood. "I can't speak for anyone else, but I'm not going anywhere."

Arabella popped up. "Neither am I." She lifted her hands. "If I'm not cleaning rooms right now, then I'll help paint walls. Whatever it takes."

"So will I," someone echoed.

"Me, too."

Callum's smile widened slightly. "Well. We won't go down for lack of fight and support," he said huskily. "Now, it's late and you guys have lives to get home to."

"What do we do tomorrow?" That came from Beulah.

Grace stepped forward. "If I may?"

Callum waved his hand in invitation. "Everyone's opinion matters here, Grace. Particularly yours."

"If we could have all of the supervisors and department leads report as usual, we'll have enough staff on hand to deal with anything that crops up in the next week or so. Everybody else—"

"Will still receive your regular pay," Callum inserted. "It's none of your fault this is happening, and we're not going to pull the rug out from under anyone's feet."

"Not without due warning," Wiley inserted cautiously.

Arabella knew he was the family attorney. Naturally he had to add something to that effect.

"We'll have an all-staff meeting here a week from Monday," Callum added without missing a beat. "If you don't hear from Grace personally or one of the other managers here, then check in yourself for more details on the where and when. One way or another, we'll have more news by then." He clapped his hands together once. "Any questions?" He looked over the group, waiting patiently.

"Not a question," Hallie said, looking around rather nervously, "Just something to say." She smiled a little crookedly then punched her hand into the air. "Go Hotel Fortune!"

Arabella's eyes misted. She punched her fist, too, and smiled at Jay, who was leaning against a far wall, his arms crossed over his chest. "Go Hotel Fortune!"

In minutes, the cheer had filled the damp lobby as everyone chanted the phrase over and over and over again.

If a hotel could be saved through sheer enthusiasm, Hotel Fortune would end up being just fine.

Chapter Twelve

Despite the worrisome matter of the hotel's repairs, the days that followed were some of the sweetest days that Arabella had ever known.

Neither she nor Jay were heads of anything, which meant they had a vacation, forced or not.

They helped Louella harvest strawberries for half the day on Monday and spent the rest of the day in his barn loft bedroom making love.

On Tuesday, Jay talked Arabella into climbing inside the woefully tiny cockpit of a plane he rented.

They flew all the way to Houston—which wasn't all that far admittedly—and had lunch with his parents. On the return flight to Rambling Rose, Arabella didn't even remember to clutch her armrests in terror because she was so caught up with teasing Jay over the stories his mother had regaled her with over lunch. "You might have *told* me you were a child prodigy," she said. Loudly, because it was the only way he could hear her over the noise of the engine propeller.

"I wasn't a prodigy," he said dismissively, and just as loudly.

"You won a piano competition when you were nine! Against people who were three times your age! And you graduated from college when you were twenty!"

He rolled his eyes and pointed at the checkerboard landscape beyond the windows. "There's the barn."

She looked out and sure enough, she could see the rooftop of his barn and the water wheel beside it.

"Can we fly over the hotel?"

In answer, the wings of the plane banked slightly.

She whooped nervously and closed her eyes to the sound of his laughter. But only briefly, because it was much too interesting seeing the land below.

On Wednesday, he got her up on Loretta's back and with him on Waylon, they rode all over his grandmother's property. Then he heated the water for the tub in the peach orchard and pretended to wash Arabella's back even though he was a lot more interested in her front.

He admitted that he'd suspected, and now knew for certain, that that tub had always been big enough for two.

That evening, they had dinner at Provisions with Adam and Laurel. Stephanie, who was Callum's sister and had acted as Larkin's foster mom for a brief while, was watching the toddler with her husband for the evening.

By tacit agreement, they stayed away from the subject of the hotel. Instead, Adam and Jay talked beer brewing and Laurel and Arabella gossiped about the rest of her brothers—namely Josh and Brian who'd yet to find the loves of their lives as Kane, Brady and Adam had. The only thing she had a hard time doing was keeping Brady's secret about Harper's pregnancy.

But if he hadn't told the rest of the family, it was obvious that she shouldn't do so for him, no matter how badly she wanted to share that good news.

It was late when they all finally parted and much to Arabella's disappointment, Jay drove her back to Brady's house instead of his place.

She twirled her fingers down the front of his shirt when he walked her to the door. "Sure you don't want to…you know."

He laughed and caught her marauding fingers. "I definitely want to *you know*. But Brady already wants to strangle me for sleeping with his baby sister. You spent the night with me last night. And the night before. If he has any more stress about it, I'll feel guilty for causing his stroke."

"He's as bad as our father," she muttered, even though a part of her was charmed by Jay's version of gallantry.

"Besides." Jay kissed her chastely on the forehead. "We had the bathtub earlier today. And you still haven't finished Oscar and Aaron's story. You've left them locked in the back of a moving truck. I need to know that they end up okay."

She caught his hand before he could step off the porch and pressed it to her cheek. "I hope you know

I'm falling in love with you." The words just wouldn't be contained. Any more than the fullness in her heart could be.

The only light shining over them came from the porch light that Brady had left burning just exactly the way her father had always done when they'd been teenagers. It was just bright enough to be sure that any kissing that went on was visible to everyone up and down the block.

And it was also bright enough to see that Jay wasn't returning her sentiment anytime soon. His brows were pulled together and the corners of his lips were turned down. "Bella—"

She steeled herself and kept her smile in place through sheer willpower. "I don't expect you to say ditto, Jay. I just wanted you to know." She braced her hands on his shoulders and went up on her toes to kiss his lips. "Oscar and Aaron are waiting."

Then she quickly slipped inside the door and closed it behind her.

Her heart thudded heavily in her chest and she leaned her head back against the door.

A moment later, she heard the soft rumble of his truck engine as he drove away.

She exhaled and opened her arms for Murphy to jump up into them. The dog slathered her face in kisses. And if he tasted a few salty tears along the way, she knew she could trust him to keep her secret.

Jay stared blearily at the cop sitting across the table from him. He'd left Arabella at her brother's house eight hours earlier and he hadn't slept a wink in the minutes since.

Instead, he'd called Detective Teas and arranged to meet him at the police station at seven that morning.

"You wanted my confession," he told Detective Teas hours later when he'd finished his story. They were sitting in the same interrogation room that Teas had used with Jay weeks ago. "And now you have it."

Jay was pretty sure the cop didn't look stunned very often, but he looked stunned now.

He flopped his chair forward onto all four legs and reached one arm out to flip the lock on the door he'd already closed.

"You're Jett Carr," he repeated. "The one my daughter's been going around wearing a shirt that says she'd give it all up for Jett Carr. *That* Jett Carr."

Jay grimaced. "You don't have to rub it in, Detective."

The cop pushed his chair back again, balancing it once more. Only this time, he lifted his legs and crossed them at the ankle over the corner of the table. He propped his hands behind his neck and a broad grin crossed his face. "Why the hell didn't you just say so? And why now?"

Jay scrubbed his hands down his face. "Because I want to sleep at night without *you* hanging over my head." It wasn't the whole truth, but he didn't figure the officer needed to know it was the trust in Arabella's eyes that was driving him more. He pushed out of his chair. "I never even wanted to be Jett Carr." He paced from one corner to the next. "But everyone insisted I needed a name with more…salability than just Jay Cross."

"It's a name," Teas said on a laugh. "Who cares?"

"Everyone in Los Angeles." Jay rubbed the back of his neck and for some reason, found himself telling the detective all about the ways and means that had gone into turning him from a college student with a side hustle playing piano and writing songs into a full-time guitar-strumming singer. It was as if once he'd started confessing, he couldn't make himself stop. "I grew my hair. Grew a beard." He rubbed his jaw, feeling the prickles of day-old stubble. "Trademark shades. Cowboy hat. And one day I looked in the mirror and didn't even recognize myself. I was involved with a woman my family detested. Had a manager who cared more about booking the next gig than he did about the fact that I was losing my mind. Two record deals that barely made the needle jump. And then—" he spread his fingers "—poof. The label cut me loose. Tina followed the day after. My manager about a week after that."

"But that video of yours is all over creation!"

Jay laughed wearily and paced around the room in the other direction. "And it's ironic as hell, too. That was my sarcastic way of bidding it all adieu. Goodbye, LA. Goodbye, Jett Carr, whose skin I'd never fit, anyway. I recorded it on my damn phone for God's sake. Never intended to even upload it, but you know cell phones these days. Once it's got a setting, it's got it forever, and the next thing I knew 'Giving It All Up' was all over the airwaves. Everybody and their mother's brother suddenly wanted a piece of Jett Carr again and—" He shook his head. "I couldn't take it. I escaped home to Texas but the only place that people *really* didn't connect me to music at all was here in Rambling Rose."

"Living in a barn out back of your grandma's farmhouse."

"It might've been a barn," Jay muttered, "but I've put a little money into it over the years."

"Because you knew you'd need an escape hatch sooner or later?"

He exhaled. "Maybe. Jett Carr did earn me money over time. I worked my ass off for it, too. But I never really cracked the ice until that video."

"Well, hiding out after the fact seems like it was the best way you could have found to ensure even more interest in it. If you'd have just told me all this from the start, it would've saved the department a lot of time and money."

Jay threw himself down on the chair he'd vacated. "If I make a donation to the policeman's fund will that help?"

Teas smiled slightly. "How big a donation?"

Jay pulled out the checkbook he'd brought with him, because he'd figured one way or another he would be paying for the visit. He wrote out several digits and signed his name. His real name. He tore out the check and slid it across to the detective. "Will that do?"

Teas gave it a considering look and then nodded. "So if it's not you tinkering with things over at Hotel Fortune, who do you think it is?"

Jay grimaced. "Who the hell knows? Someone who's got a gripe against the Fortunes. The ones who built the place, I mean." He couldn't stand the thought that the vengeance might extend to Arabella.

"Yeah." Teas scratched his chin. "Only thing is, we can't seem to find anyone with a real gripe. That Callum fella and his brothers have done a lot of good things here in town. First they built that pediatric center. The veterinary clinic. Provisions has the best food in town. Took my wife to Roja and that's gonna be just as good. Retail shops. A fancy spa where my wife is constantly begging me to send her. They've brought in new money. Created jobs." He drummed his fingers against the table. "Even checked into that lady who went off the deep end a few years ago. Charlotte Robinson? Ex-wife of that Robinson Tech guy? Her permanent address is still the fancy sanitarium place she got checked into after she tried her hand and failed at kidnapping."

Jay vaguely remembered his mother recounting the sensationalistic story several years back. But he'd been in California then and couldn't have cared less about a bunch of people he'd never met, much less heard of.

"It's gotta be an inside job. But the only one who didn't have a good alibi has been you."

"I still don't have a good alibi," he pointed out. "You just know now what I was doing in the years between insurance and showing up here."

"You saying you tampered with the balcony?"

His lips thinned. "To what end?"

"Exactly." Teas slapped his hand down on the table. "I just need one thing from you." He flipped the pages on his yellow pad to one that was empty and sent it skidding across the surface toward Jay. He followed it with a pen from his lapel pocket. "Sign an autograph for my daughter. Her name is Keisha."

Feeling relieved, bemused and pretty much spent, Jay picked up the pen and scrawled out his autograph.

To Keisha.

All the best.

Jett Carr.

Then he set down the pen and pushed to his feet.

Teas stood as well. He carefully pulled off the sheet of paper and folded it in fourths to tuck into his pocket. "What're you going to do now?"

"About what?"

"Half the world's still looking for you, bud."

Jay unlocked the door and pulled it open. "Long as I can trust you not to out me now, they'll just have to keep looking. Far as I'm concerned, Jett Carr's dead and gone."

"And Jay Cross is happy being a hotel trainee in small-town Texas?"

Arabella's image danced in Jay's mind. Without Teas in his rearview mirror, looking into her beautiful eyes would be a lot easier. "Happier than he's got a right to be."

Teas clapped him on the shoulder. "Good luck with that, then. Just have t'say that I've learned one thing in all my years of police work. Secrets tend to come out."

Another thing on which the detective and Jay's grandmother would agree.

He pulled his hat down over his eyes as he walked out into the morning sunshine.

He was surprised at how much time had passed with

the detective. But then he hadn't intended to treat the meeting like the confessional it had become. He'd just planned to tell the cop the basics about his history in California, buy his silence if it became necessary and get on with his day.

Petunia's flower shop was down the street and on the spur of the moment, Jay pulled over and parked in front. Inside, he picked a pot of geraniums off the shelf only because the small clay pot wore a pair of pink sunglasses above a pair of equally pink painted lips. Then he added another fern to his choice because he couldn't seem to pass one without feeling he ought to buy it for his grandmother.

He'd inherited the habit from Herb. Because as many times as Jay had come to town with his grandfather to pay those parking tickets, when they drove back out to the farm, Jay had invariably been holding a potted fern on his lap.

He carried the pots over to Petunia where she was talking with her dad and set them on the counter. She gave him a smile, though she looked as if she'd had about as much sleep as he had. She rang up his selections on an old-fashioned cash register. "Heard about the trouble over at the hotel. How're things coming along?"

He pulled several bills from his wallet and handed them to her. "As well as they can, from what I know." Which, admittedly, wasn't all that much. "Figured I'd drop by on my way back to my grandmother's place just to check in."

"Give them all my best. They sure could stand a bit of good luck, couldn't they?"

Truer words. Jay looked at Norman. "Going to see you out at Mariana's this Saturday, Norm?"

"What business is it of yours?" The old man nearly barked the words.

"My grandmother's gonna have the last of her strawberry jam for the summer out there." He smiled cautiously. "Figure the way you go through it, you'll want to stock up while you can."

The old man blinked. Then as if a lightbulb had come on, he nodded. "You tell Louella I'll be there."

Jay wished he could say that his grandmother would be there, too, but since she was still prohibited from getting anywhere near Mabel, he was already planning on manning the booth for her. He was also counting on Arabella to keep him company.

He pocketed the change that Petunia gave him and with the box she'd settled the plants into in hand, went out to his truck.

He'd just placed the box on the passenger-side floor when Petunia knocked on his window. He rolled it down. "Did I forget something?"

She shook her head. "No, I just wanted to explain about Dad. He hasn't really been himself these days."

Jay nodded, not really sure how to respond. "My grandmother's already told me about the problem he has with his meds."

She looked relieved. "I'm trying to find a solution for him, but he's a determined old guy, you know? Independent as hell and the idea of having someone monitor anything he does is hard for him to swallow. The only person he tolerates these days is my nephew. I'm sorry if he sounded rude."

"No worries."

She reached in and squeezed his arm. "Louella's always said what a good boy you are and she's right."

He actually felt his neck get hot. "Um—"

She laughed slightly. "Now I've gone and embarrassed you, which wasn't my intention at all." She stepped back onto the curb. "One of these days, buy Louella something besides a fern!" Then she disappeared inside her shop.

He looked down at the plant. "What's wrong with a fern?"

It took only a few minutes to get to the hotel.

There was a sign posted on the front door that it was temporarily closed, but when he pulled it open, it wasn't locked.

He went inside.

The lobby smelled vaguely musty but there were big fans positioned in every corner blowing air noisily across the floor. Baseboards were gone, and the lower portions of drywall had been cut away from the walls, leaving the studs exposed. Whatever repairs were going to be needed, they couldn't even get started until everything was fully dried out.

The fans seemed to be the only occupants, though.

He looked into the office behind the registration desk but it was empty. So was the security office.

The elevators were locked on the first floor and he wandered past them, sticking his head around the door to Roja.

He earned a look from the group of Fortunes sitting at one of the tables.

Brady's eyes narrowed when he spotted Jay. "What do you want, Cross?"

To marry your sister.

The words popped into his head, making Jay forget for a moment why he'd even walked in there in the first place.

Callum rose and walked toward him. "Something on your mind?"

Jay swallowed and focused on the older man's face. It was a lot easier than the glaring one that Brady possessed. "I was just checking on how things were going. Insurance and all that."

Callum's brows rose. "You know about insurance?"

"I used to." He looked past Callum to Wiley. He was a lawyer. Nothing showed in his expression. But Steven and his brother Dillon were contractors. Easier to read. "They're denying the claim?"

Arabella's other brother Kane, who'd been involved with the hotel from the start, was the only one who nodded. "Wiley's been talking about filing a suit."

"They'll pay it if you'll agree to a higher premium," Jay said. "It'd be quicker and less expensive in the long run than a lawsuit."

"That's not news," Brady snapped. "You know how much of a higher premium?"

Jay calculated a moment, then named a figure that had all of the men sitting back with surprise. He figured he was at least within a few thousand dollars of being on target.

"That's oddly accurate," Callum admitted. "Problem is, coming up with that much is a bit of a problem. It's not as if it's a onetime investment. Collectively, we can pitch in from our own pockets but—"

Wiley's hands were fisted on top of the table. "But considering we don't know who's trying to sabotage the hotel in the first place, maybe it's safer for everyone if we just cut our losses now. Nobody wants to throw good money after bad."

No matter how many golden eggs *those* Fortunes had, Jay knew it couldn't be all that easy increasing their investments to such a degree.

"The town needs this hotel," Steven said quietly. Jay knew he was married to the mayor. "It's coming to stand for everything that Rambling Rose is. Embraces the past. Welcomes the future."

"Sounds straight from Ellie's lips," Dillon muttered.

"So what if it is?" Steven countered. "She's right."

Callum dropped his arm over Jay's shoulder and showed him right back to the door. "I'll trust you not to say anything about this before our staff meeting on Monday," he said quietly.

Jay nodded and felt Brady Fortune's eyes burning a hole into his spine as he left.

"Where's Brady?" Arabella slid into her seat at the breakfast table and reached for the stack of toast in the center.

"Went to the hotel again." Harper was nursing a cup of tea, looking vaguely green around the gills.

"You feeling okay?"

"Morning sickness," she admitted. "Why does it have to hit now when Brady's so worried about the hotel?"

"Maybe stress makes it worse." Arabella could see the twins through the doorway to the living area. They were bouncing recklessly on the couch and the fact that Harper didn't even seem to notice was enough to call for action. "Go back up to bed," she urged. "Sleep as long as you want. I'll keep the boys occupied today."

"I was going to take them out to ride again with Laurel."

"I'll take them," she promised.

"But you don't know how to ride at all."

"I know a little bit," she assured primly. "Jay showed me. And I'm sure he'd be willing to come with us, anyway, if you're so worried about my ability."

"I know you'll take care of the boys," Harper said quickly, looking horrified that she might have implied otherwise.

Arabella reached over and gave her a quick squeeze. "Go back to bed. Or take a bath. Whatever."

"Maybe I'll just hug the porcelain goddess," Harper muttered, but she got up looking grateful and left the room.

Arabella finished slathering Lou's jam on her toast and shoved half of it in her mouth as she went into the living room. She snapped her fingers at Murphy who obediently slunk off the couch where he wasn't allowed and then caught Toby around the waist mid-jump. She swallowed her mouthful and set him on the ground. "You know you're not supposed to bounce on the couch." She grabbed Tyler, too, and set him on the floor next to his brother.

"But—"

"No jumping on the couch!"

There were blocks scattered all over the floor. The Candy Land game they usually loved was upended in the corner, little pieces strewn about. Just looking at the mess made her actually long for the simplicity of cleaning a hotel room.

"Come on, guys. Let's clean up and later after you're dressed, I'll take you out to see Auntie Laurel and her horses."

"I want to watch TV," Tyler groused.

"Yeah, and I want a million dollars," she grumbled. Then she smiled and scrubbed her hand over his tousled hair. "Come on. Clean up and we'll negotiate the matter of TV." She knew that negotiating was something the boys were well-acquainted with, thanks to Harper.

Tyler halfheartedly tossed a block into the bucket where they belonged. "Harper's sneaky. She gives us five minutes before bed, but we gotta only read together."

Arabella laughed and went down onto her hands and knees alongside them. "The horror. Come on, we'll all do it together." Roving around, she gathered up a handful of blocks but before long, she was the only one cleaning up the mess on the floor, which proved her negotiating skills weren't up to Harper's level at all. Instead, Arabella was just a sucker for the boys.

At least the two eventually went upstairs and returned, suitably attired in mismatched shorts and T-shirts. Toby's hair was damp so she was fairly certain he'd washed his face and Tyler had a smear of toothpaste on his shirt, so she felt confident he'd brushed his teeth.

Considering all of that to be ticks in the win column, she handed them the television remote. "Your channels only," she warned. Brady had locked down their ability to unintentionally tune in to something too mature for them.

It usually meant that when Arabella actually felt like watching something on television, she was reduced to watching classic cartoons or kid-friendly videos on YouTube.

After a brief tussle for control of the remote, Tyler won and Arabella went back into the kitchen to have another piece of toast. It was cold by now, but the strawberry jam made up for it. She cleaned up the kitchen and realized she was humming along with the dreaded earworm song when it sounded from the other room.

She stuck her head into the living room, prepared to tell the kids to find another channel.

But they were standing there giggling and dancing the floss and she didn't have the heart. Instead, she pulled her own cell phone out of her back pocket and without their knowledge started filming them.

She'd send it to her parents later. They'd love it.

The song had a heavy beat. Oddly gut-wrenching really in comparison to the lively steps the boys were doing. She glanced at the TV screen above the boys' head.

The video was deliberately blurry in the way that some were. Sort of jerky, even. Focusing on the singer's long fingers as he strummed his gleaming guitar while his unbuttoned shirt fluttered from an unseen breeze. Then on his bearded profile as he crooned to some invisible lover. "Giving it all up. Gonna be someone new." His dark head dipped again, giving little more than a flash of dark sunglasses and a dip of his cowboy hat. "Never gonna trust again." His deep voice curled over the words and despite herself, Arabella felt a tingle down her spine.

Hallie wasn't exactly off-track, she decided. Jett Carr did have a sexy demeanor.

"Never gonna find someone like you."

He strummed harder, his fingers working the strings faster, and without volition, Arabella's feet carried her back into the living room. Closer to the television screen.

"You're not s'posed to stand so close." Tyler grabbed her hand and dragged her back two steps.

"Never gonna trust again, never gonna love again, never gonna find someone like you." After the buildup, the singer trailed off, though the music continued on. He stood up from the stool where he'd been sitting and set his guitar down. Then he walked away, the wind fluttering the tails of his shirt madly around his shoulders. She saw a flash of a tattoo and then Jett Carr looked over his shoulder straight at the camera.

He pulled his glasses down his nose, and Jay's distinctive green eyes stared straight at her. "Never find someone like you."

His husky words trailed off and the video went black before switching to a violently colorful commercial for Frosted Fruity Flakes.

I think you should know that...

"You're a liar, Jay Cross," she said thickly.

Because there was no question in her mind that he and the singer were one and the same.

She'd know those green eyes anywhere.

"Why's Jay a liar?" Tyler bounced onto the couch beside her, and then nearly fell over himself getting back off again when she looked at him.

"Here." She handed him the remote control again. Tyler hooted and quickly punched buttons but she barely noticed. She was too busy punching buttons on her own phone.

Only as soon as Jay's line started to ring, she chickened out and hung up again.

She was *such* a monumental fool.

How many times had she mentioned how much she detested that darned song? And he'd just...gone along!

Squelching a moan, she sank down onto the couch and didn't even protest when Murphy jumped onto her lap. She held her phone above the dog's head and opened a browser. She didn't even have to finish typing in the words *Jett Carr* before the video she'd just watched popped to the top of her list on her phone.

She turned down the volume and watched the video all the way through.

Even though she knew.

"Never gonna trust again," she whispered soundlessly. "Not even you."

Chapter Thirteen

Jay drove from the flower shop back to his grandmother's and carried the fern inside. She was in the kitchen, nursing the big metal pot she used to cook down her strawberries.

He set the plant on the table. "Are you tired of ferns, Gran?"

She glanced around the veritable jungle growing inside her house. "It's what your grandpa always gave me. How could I get tired of them?"

He leaned his hip against the table. "I told Detective Teas who I was."

She gave him a sidelong look. "Thought you were just Jay Cross."

"You know what I mean."

"Do *you* know what you mean?"

He muttered an oath and rubbed his forehead. "I'm too tired for your cryptic comments. Jett Carr's a stage persona. That's it."

She turned and gently drew her fingers along the fern's feathery edges. "Jet-pack. Your grandpa loved you more'n anything on this earth. And I loved him more'n anything on this earth. That's why I took on O'Brien when he asked young Louella *Carr* to marry him." She poked him once in the chest with a finger that was definitely not gentle. "Jett Carr isn't just some name you plucked outta thin air. Your problem with Jett Carr was that you were letting other people control who he was. Instead of being who *you* wanted to be."

"Some things aren't that easy."

She made a disgusted sound and returned to her pot.

He dropped it. "Was there ever something between him and Mabel?"

She threw back her head and laughed. "Lord no."

"And I know you didn't steal her jam recipe."

She snorted, still laughing. "No, sir, I did not."

"Then what the hell happened between the two of you?"

She gave him a look over her shoulder. "You really want to know?"

He spread his hands helplessly. "I'm asking, aren't I?" He'd been asking for days now.

She gave a huge sigh. "Shop-World wants to pay me a boatload of money to put my jam in all their stores. From California to Wyoming to Texas."

Jay was glad he was leaning against the counter, because he probably would have fallen on his butt otherwise. *"What?"*

She gave him an annoyed look. "You heard me." She tapped her long wooden spoon against the side of the pot. "My mistake was telling Mabel about it. She's always had a pea-green streak about her. She'll get over it in time."

"Why didn't you tell me about it? Does Mom know?"

"What good would that do?" She looked even more annoyed. "Wouldn't make your mama stop trying to get me to give up my home and move into a dinky bedroom at that house she shares with your dad. Nothing wrong with that house, mind you, but it isn't mine."

"Are you going to take the offer?"

"Would've done it already if it weren't for you."

"What have I got to do with it? Gran, you'll make a fortune."

"Never wanted a fortune," she muttered. "Just wanted my home and my family." She stuck her spoon back into her pot. "And soon as I take it, word is going to spread around this town like wildfire. Shop-World wants to do a whole advertising thing about me growing my strawberries and all that. How's that gonna play when my grandson's famous and afraid to get his face seen on some newscaster's camera?"

"I'm not famous."

"Jett Carr damn sure is now whether you like it or not." She gave him a fierce look. "I know you've been spending time with Arabella. *Quality* time."

"I'm not having a discussion about my love life with

you, Gran." He wanted to dunk his head in the stream outside his barn just thinking about it.

"There's nothing new under the sun," she told him tartly. "Why d'you think Herb and I had such a quick wedding? That's the problem with all you young people. Thinking you're the only ones who ever invented sex."

He covered his eyes and wanted to be anywhere other than there.

"You want to keep having your way with that young lady, you'd better do more than 'fess up to that detective person. Arabella's the one who matters, isn't she?"

He dropped his hand. "Yes."

She gave him a narrow-eyed glare. Then after a moment nodded decisively and pointed the end of her dripping red spoon at a drawer. "There's a metal box in there. Get it for me."

He pulled open the junk-filled drawer and managed to extract the flattish, rectangular box. He started to hand it to her but she just waved with her spoon. "Open it." He did so, expecting the deck of cards that he vaguely remembered it once contained.

Instead, sitting on a folded yellowed hankie were two delicate, glittering necklaces and one small diamond ring.

"I had t'stop wearing the ring when my arthritis got too bad." She waggled her slightly bent fingers. "But it's yours if you want it."

His gut tightened. "Granny—"

"Just take it." She sniffed slightly and focused on her bubbling jam concoction. "Give it to that girl. Pretty sure you love her just like Herb loved me. Or buy yourself something fancy and modern to give her. I don't much care so long as you get your head on straight and do what's right."

He slid the ring over the tip of his pinky finger. It was as far as it would go. She knew he'd never want modern and fancy. Then he kissed her lined cheek. "You're a helluva woman, you know."

She snorted. "Of course I know." But she patted his cheek the same way she'd done when he was five. "Now get on with you. I don't want to see your face until you've come clean with Arabella once and for all."

He hadn't slept. Hadn't showered.

He knew he probably ought to at least do one of those things before he went down on bended knee, but he did neither. Just got in his truck and drove back into town.

It was a sign of his own stupidity that he had to spend an extra hour getting gas when he ran out of it halfway there.

But finally he was standing on Brady's front porch step. The afternoon sun was high in the sky above him and he squinted against the glare because he'd also forgotten his hat back at his grandmother's place.

"You're falling apart, man," he muttered to himself before reaching out to knock on the door.

He heard the squeals of little boys laughing before the door opened up and he looked down to see Toby— or was it Tyler?—looking up at him. "Hey there. I'm here to see your auntie Bella."

"She's in the backyard," the boy said artlessly. "How come you made her cry?"

He frowned. "She's crying?"

The twin's twin popped his head into the doorway. "'Cause you're a liar," he said seriously. "We gotta get time out when we lie. Are you gonna get time out?"

The only thing Jay had lied about to Arabella was his past. "Can I come in?"

The two boys shook their heads. "We're not supposed to open the door."

"But you did."

They gave each other looks and promptly shut the door right in his face.

Jay started to knock again, but thought better of it.

Instead, he left the geranium on the porch and walked around to the back of the house. It was protected by a tall wooden fence all the way around the yard. Logically, he knew there had to be a gate somewhere, but he was way too impatient just then to try to find it.

Feeling like the biggest louse on the planet, he stretched up and caught the top of the fence, then grunting slightly, managed to heave himself up and over.

He landed in a pile of dog poop, which should have been his biggest warning to date that things were not going to go as he planned. He scraped his boot as well as he could against the grass and walked farther into the backyard, turning around the corner of the house.

And there she sat. Her flaming hair was spread around her shoulders. The temper in Arabella's blue eyes when she spotted him made them almost as black as the bruises that had faded over the last several days. She didn't even seem all that surprised to see him. "What're *you* doing here?"

He took a few cautious steps closer. She was holding

a baseball in her hands and the way she kept turning it between her palms was a little alarming. Particularly when she'd told his mother just two days earlier how she'd played softball in high school.

"I came to tell you something I should have told you a long time ago."

She tossed the ball lightly from one hand to the other. "I think you should know that—" She broke off, seeming to be waiting for some response.

"That I'm—" His voice came out croaky and hoarse. He cleared his throat. "I'm in love with you," he finished more clearly.

She made a harsh, buzzing sound. "Wrong."

"What?"

"Before the balcony collapse. You were going to tell me something. Remember?"

Time had been so full in the last several weeks that in comparison, the balcony collapse felt like it had happened years ago, rather than just six months. "I remember I wanted to tell you everything about me."

"Like the fact that you're a liar?"

Regret sank hard inside his gut. "Bella."

"Don't call me that."

"You know. Don't you?"

Her lips twisted. "That you're Jett Carr?" She bounced the ball twice in her palm. "And I'm the biggest fool on the planet?"

"You're not a fool."

She sent the ball whizzing two inches from his head. It bounced hard on the fence beyond him. "You should have told me," she said flatly and marched inside the house.

She slammed the door behind her.

Jay went over to it and tried the knob. No shock that she'd locked it.

He pressed his forehead against the warm wood. "I should have told you," he said loudly enough that if, by some miracle, she was still standing close to the door she'd be able to hear. "People used to only like me because I was Jett. And the longer things went on with you, the more I was afraid you'd like me only if I'd never been him at all. Bella, I'm sorry. I warned you that I wasn't good enough for you but I fell in love with you, anyway. You're everything that's right in this freaking world."

The door yanked open and he nearly stumbled inside. Tears glittered in her eyes, making them even more sharply blue. "I don't know why I didn't figure it out before I saw your damn video. You gave it all up. Became someone new. Never gonna trust again. Certainly not *me*. Not enough to tell me the truth. Was she the complication in California, Jay? The woman who broke your heart?"

His voice rose. "It wasn't a woman who broke my heart! It was the music that did that!"

She'd paled and taken a step back as he shouted the words, and he felt even worse.

"I would never hurt you," he said roughly.

"Bzzz," she said thickly. "Too late."

And she closed the door in his face yet again.

He sighed wearily. "Bella, please. There's no other woman. There's only you."

"Maybe you should go." He jerked his head back, looking up at the voice from above. Harper was leaning out an opened window. "Brady's going to be home soon and once he sees the state Bella's in—" She looked almost sympathetic. "Give her—give them—a little time, Jay."

He squinted up at her. The sunlight was creating a halo around her dark head. "You overheard, I guess."

"That you're the sexy missing Jett?"

He grimaced, feeling his neck get hot. He'd blushed more in the last twenty-four hours than he had in his entire adult life and he didn't much like it. "Just Jett," he muttered.

She propped her head on her hand. "I overheard."

He spread his hands and his grandmother's diamond ring on his pinky winked in the sunlight. "I should have told her. I know that. But I can't undo the past. So what am I supposed to do now?"

"Undo the future?"

"There *is* no future. Not without her in it."

She smiled slightly. "Find a way to make her listen," she suggested, and then disappeared back inside the window.

Jay blinked against the sun again. He looked around the yard. Spotted the gate finally, as well as the sturdy metal lock on its latch.

Resigned, he climbed back over the gate, this time at least managing to miss the dog crap.

He walked back to his truck, feeling the itch on his

spine of several pairs of eyes, but when he looked back at the house again, he saw nothing but the twitch of curtains in the windows.

He got behind the wheel and started the engine.

As if the fates were mocking him, the radio came on to his own voice singing back at him. He spun the dial and a droning voice reciting farm futures replaced his song.

Harper's words echoed in his head. *Find a way to make her listen.*

"How in the hell am I supposed to find a way to do that?"

He made it all the way back to his grandmother's place before the obvious hit him.

He drove around the house—something he never did—and parked next to the stone barn. Inside, he flipped up the piano bench and shuffled through the music books until he found a couple sheets of staff paper.

He flipped down the lid of the grand piano with shocking disregard for its value and dropped the paper on top of the gleaming black wood. He located a stub of a pencil and then he sat down at the keyboard and got to work.

"Ohmigod, have you heard it?" Hallie squeezed a folding chair in between the ones Arabella and Beulah were occupying.

It was Monday morning and even though Arabella would have preferred to be anywhere else, family loyalty had made her show up at the hotel for Callum's big staff meeting.

"Heard what?"

"Jett Carr's new song. It dropped just last night and every music station's been playing it practically non-stop. There's a rumor he was even spotted right here in Texas. Can you believe it?"

Arabella closed her eyes. "Hallie, I don't—"

It was too late. Hallie had already started the video playing on her phone. This time there was no shot of Jay. Or Jett. Or whatever he was calling himself.

Just hands on a piano keyboard. One raised scar on a long, tanned finger against ivory and black.

The melody was simple but haunting.

"Your love healed me," he sang softly. Much like the way he'd sung that shoe-tying song to her nephews that day that felt so long ago. "Your love revealed me—"

"Thanks to everyone for coming today." Callum's voice cut over the soft music from Hallie's phone that she quickly turned off and tucked away.

Healed me. Revealed me.

Try as she might, Arabella couldn't keep the words from circling inside her mind. To such an extent that she missed almost everything that Callum was announcing.

She'd been so afraid that Jay would also show his face at the staff meeting, but he was nowhere to be seen. More proof that he wasn't the man she'd believed him to be. Jett Carr might have been spotted and now it was Jay Cross who'd disappeared.

She ducked her head, surreptitiously swiping at the tears that kept leaking out.

She wasn't the only one who was crying, though that was more caused by the announcement Callum was making.

"This Friday night," he was saying. "That's just four days. So spread the word. The more people who turn out, the better off we'll all be."

Brady hadn't told her they'd be having a final party. But that was what it sounded like Callum was talking about.

Then the meeting broke up again and Arabella filed out miserably behind the others.

Hallie's car was parked next to Arabella's. "Think you'll go back to Austin?"

"You mean if this doesn't work?" Hallie shrugged. "How could it not?" Considering the situation, Hallie looked quite cheerful.

Arabella got into her car and drove back to Brady's. She went inside and her energy took her as far as the narrow twin bed in her bedroom. She threw herself down on it, staring blindly at the geranium plant sitting on the windowsill. She could hear the muffled sounds of Harper and the boys from the backyard accompanied by Murphy's excited yips.

She could sell her car. Maybe she'd get enough to pay for a one-way flight back to New York.

At least her dad would be happy.

She swiped her cheeks and pulled out her cell phone. She had two text messages, both from Tammy Jo Pendleton, containing photos of her and Ham wearing their wedding finery.

Arabella was so miserable she couldn't even summon a speck of annoyance. She texted back a polite congratulations and then dropped the phone like a hot potato when it vibrated and Jay's name popped up on the screen.

But he wasn't calling her. Just sending a text message. Even though she wished she had enough willpower to delete it unseen, she swiped her screen again and the new message appeared.

You don't have any reason to forgive me, but I still hope you'll come.

Below the message was a small image and she frowned at her own inability to just let it go.

She tapped the image and it blew up, the headlines filling the screen.

Jett Carr
One Night Only

She slowly sat on the side of the bed, expanding the image even more to read the smaller print.

And when she had, she bolted down the stairs, nearly plowing right into Brady as he came in through the front door.

Even though he had his own phone at his ear, she waved hers in his face. "Do you believe his *gall*?"

He pointed to his own phone as he brushed past her, dropping his tie on the couch as he passed it. "That's all it took?" he said to whomever was on the other end of his call. "Fifteen minutes?"

She followed him through the kitchen. "I should've listened to you all along. You said he was hiding some-thing and—"

Brady turned on his heel and held up a silencing hand. "That's good news, Kane. Thanks." He ended the call and waved his hand in front of her. "What's got you so wound up? As if I don't already know."

"He's having a concert! Right here in Rambling Rose. It wasn't bad enough that he lied, but now he has to rub our faces in it?"

"I wouldn't exactly put it that way." Looking entirely too calm about it, he picked up Murphy, who'd been dancing around his legs, and headed out the back door. Boyish squeals greeted him and he was kissing Harper when Arabella stomped out after him.

She propped her fists on her hips. "What way *would* you put it?" The wary looks she earned from both her brother and Harper annoyed her even more. "Why am I the only one who's upset here? Jay—" She shook her phone in the air. "*Jett* is having a concert. Right under our noses!"

Harper disentangled herself from Brady's arms. "Do you know why?"

"Because he's a deceitful—"

"Generous," Harper said firmly, as if Arabella were no older than Toby and Tyler.

"Generous!" Arabella snorted. "He's—"

"Donating his ticket sales to Hotel Fortune," Brady said. "Callum announced it at the staff meeting."

She felt poleaxed. "What?"

"You were there. What the hell did you think he was talking about?"

She blindly felt for a patio chair. "I wasn't listening," she mumbled.

Brady poked his finger at her nose. "For whatever reason, your crush is throwing us a lifesaving buoy and I don't want—"

"Brady." Harper closed her hands around his arm. "Arabella *is* the reason," she said gently. "And it's way more than a crush. Jay is in love with her."

"She's too young."

"I *am* not!" Arabella's ire instantly refocused on Brady as she shot to her feet.

"She's only a year younger than me," Harper added.

Brady frowned. "That's different."

Harper's amused eyes met Arabella's for a moment. "You think Jay—who has managed to keep his alter identity a secret all of these months—revealed himself to the public by volunteering his concert proceeds to Hotel Fortune because he's been so thrilled working there as a *management trainee*?"

Arabella sank right back down into the chair she'd just vacated. "He volunteered?"

"Criminy, Bella. Have you been listening at all?"

She shook her head, ignoring her brother in favor of Harper. There was a gnawing hole in the pit of her stomach, outsized only by the ache growing inside her heart. "Why would he do that?"

Harper smiled. "I think he found a way to be heard."

* * *

The days leading up to Friday were the longest days of Arabella's life.

She couldn't turn on the news without seeing some mention of Jett Carr. His mysterious disappearance from the public eye, now ended just as abruptly and just as inexplicably. There was speculation that he'd gone into hiding over a woman. That he'd been recording a new album for which his latest song was just a teaser. That he'd been abducted by aliens.

There seemed to be no end to it, and it wasn't helped by the fact that the singer, himself, was refusing all interviews until after the concert.

Posters of Jett Carr—bearded, sunglasses-wearing Jett Carr—cropped up all around town. They were in the grocery store. In the flower shop. At Provisions. Everywhere Arabella turned, there were people talking about the coming event. The motels miles outside of town were full.

Mariana's Market was supposedly even transforming itself into a campground of sorts for the weekend.

Meanwhile, aside from that one text message that Jay had sent her, Arabella didn't hear another word from him.

Not even when she went out to his grandmother's place—bearing the linen napkin that he'd wrapped Louella's chocolate chip cookies inside that very first time she'd been there with him—did she see him. Instead, Arabella had been stunned silly to see Louella and Mabel sitting together on her porch as if their brouhaha had never occurred at all.

When she'd finally just asked if Jay was there, Louella had shaken her head. "Gone to California."

Arabella's heart had fallen through the floor. "Is he coming back?"

His grandmother had merely peered cagily from beneath her shady hat. "Got a concert tomorrow night, doesn't he?"

Arabella hadn't had the guts to tell her she'd meant was he coming back to *her*.

By the next afternoon, the traffic lining up for the concert stretched all the way from the blocks surrounding the hotel that had been cordoned off by the police to the other side of town.

As she sat in the rear of the air-conditioned black SUV that had been sent for her and Brady, Harper and the kids, Arabella felt twisted tighter and tighter into a knot of nerves. If the ticket she had wasn't hanging around her neck inside a plastic lanyard, she would have twisted it, too, into a sweaty, pulpy mess.

"What're they doing?" Tyler poked his finger against the tinted window beside him. They were still several blocks away from the hotel but there were tables set up at irregular intervals along the curb and lines of people were already congregating around them.

"Selling concert merchandise," Brady said. He sounded almost as stressed out as Arabella felt.

She wondered what rabbit hole she'd fallen down and restlessly pulled the small mirror out from the purse she'd borrowed from Harper. Her black eyes had mercifully faded. But that was about all she could say about her reflection and she pocketed the mirror once again.

After another thirty minutes of crawling along in traffic, the driver—an amiable guy named Ted—pulled to a stop in front of a mass of yellow caution tape stretching across the main parking lot entrance of the hotel. "Okay, folks. This is where I drop you." He got out and opened the door for them. The sun was just starting to dip to the horizon and lights blazed across the parking lot, focused on the complicated metal framework that was nearly as tall as the four-story hotel behind it.

The stage was at the center of the framework with the hotel entrance immediately behind it. On either side, massive screens hung from the metal bars.

The first few dozen rows of chairs were also positioned beneath the soaring metal framework and Arabella was shocked to see several people moving about in the heights, anchored by safety belts.

"Holy cow." Harper murmured what Arabella couldn't manage to put into words. "Brady, are those cameras or lights up there?"

"Both. A crew came in yesterday and started building the staging. Callum's been working with some guy named Devane on security. The last thing anyone wants is some snafu tonight. That's why there are so many cops and security guards around." They joined the line of people waiting to pass through a metal detector.

In front of them, two teenage girls wearing headphones were dancing together. In back of them, two middle-aged couples were laughing and showing off the T-shirts they'd purchased outside the concert "gates."

Arabella felt dizzy. "I didn't know Jett Carr was so… big."

"Not sure Jett Carr knew it either," the woman behind Arabella stuck her head forward to say. She had a gleam of excitement on her face. "We used to see him once a month at a club he played at all the time in Los Angeles."

"You came from Los Angeles?"

The other woman with her leaned forward, too. "Plane tickets on such short notice were too expensive, so we drove. Took three days."

The line moved and feeling numb, Arabella opened the purse for a security guard to poke a flashlight into before waving her through the arch of the metal detector. She could only imagine how long it would have taken if she'd brought her usual bag.

A vaguely hysterical giggle rose in her throat as she left the metal detector and yet another guard shone a device over her plastic-encased ticket.

Then the lot of them were through and they started up the center aisle between two sections of chairs.

Each row was numbered and Arabella felt even dizzier when she realized there had to be at least a thousand chairs and their row—number 5—was actually the very first row. It was empty, except for Jay's parents and his grandmother, sitting in the very center. Louella saw Arabella and held out her hand.

With a knot in her throat, Arabella took it and sat beside her. She looked over her shoulder at the sea of chairs. Beyond the seats there was even more standing room.

"Exciting day," Louella said.

Turning back around, Arabella could only nod. She was too busy trying to keep her sudden tears at bay.

All too quickly, the seats around them began filling. When she saw Detective Teas and a pretty teenaged girl sit in the two seats at the end of their row next to Mariana, Arabella was even more disconcerted.

Music had been playing on the loudspeakers all along. But until it suddenly went up a notch in volume, Arabella hadn't even realized that none of the songs were Jay's.

The sky was nearly dark and the lights from the steel rafters overhead began swirling around. Shots of Jay playing guitar were spilling over the projector screens overlaid with horses running wild and waves crashing on a beach.

Jay's grandmother suddenly leaned toward her. "Breathe," she advised.

Arabella exhaled on a rush and laughed shakily.

Louella took her hand in hers and squeezed. She didn't let go.

Tyler and Toby were standing in front of Harper and Brady, dancing around with little Erin McCarthy. Kane's future stepdaughter was doing her level best to keep up with the boys even though she was half their age. A chant had risen in the crowd, getting louder and louder as people stamped their feet and clapped their hands. Their chant got even louder, almost drowning out the loudspeakers when a trio of men stepped out onto the dim stage. One went to the big drum set and the two others went to the standing mics and picked up guitars that Arabella hadn't even realized were there. The drummer suddenly rolled out a solo in perfect timing to the music on the loudspeaker and the chanting got even louder when the two guitar players started strumming. Then another trio—women this time—danced out onto the stage and took position to one side, where they started swaying and singing.

Arabella didn't even know the song and she suddenly wished she hadn't spent the past four days dithering over the fact that Jay hadn't called her when she ought to have been listening to every single piece of music he'd ever made.

Then the energy climbed to an even higher pitch and the lights that had been dancing over the skyline suddenly centered on the stage, beams crisscrossing.

Jay stood in the center.

His hat was pulled low over his face. A pair of sunglasses shielded his eyes and a guitar hung down his back. He wore black jeans and a plain white shirt with the sleeves rolled up his forearms and the buttons unfastened halfway down his chest.

Arabella had no way of knowing whether he knew she was there. Whether he was looking straight at her or at any of the people crowding into the parking lot and the street beyond as he pulled the guitar over his shoulder and launched into a hard-beating song that had everyone around her jumping to their feet.

Jay's grandmother pulled Arabella to her feet, too, and she pulled her close, an arm over her shoulder. "Jay's first song," she said into her ear, loud enough that she could hear. It was followed by three more equally fast and rowdy and wonderful tunes, and when the last notes trailed away and Jay lifted his guitar high above his head, Arabella was stomping her feet and clapping as loudly as everyone else.

Then Jay stepped close to the mic again and the crowd abruptly quieted. "It's good to see y'all here." His deep voice rumbled over them.

"It's good to see you," someone yelled from deep in the crowd. "Where've you been?"

"Been around." Jay's smile flashed and he chuckled, which set off another flurry of excitement. "Never had quite a turnout like this before," he drawled.

"We'll go anywhere you go, Jett," a woman screamed.

His smile flashed again. "That's real sweet of you, darlin'." He started strumming again, picking the recognizable notes that had been playing so incessantly on the radio for the last year. "Last year, I thought this was going to be the last song I ever wrote," he admitted and with the band and backup singers along with him, he sang it as he walked back and forth across the stage. When he finished and returned to center stage, a grand piano had been rolled into view. Its lid was lifted and the image of the strings and black-and-white keys filled the video screens.

"Wouldn't ever know they only had a few days to pull this all together," Louella commented in Arabella's ear. But she was barely listening because she was raptly watching every movement Jay made as he handed off his guitar and sat down at the piano.

He set his fingers on the keys and the crowd went quiet again as he slowly ran them up and down in a simple scale. "We spend so much of our lives pretending. I'm a piano player," he said quietly. His fingers danced again up and down the keyboard in a melancholy way. "There's only a handful of people here tonight who even know that."

"Play for me, Jett," someone cried out.

His dimple flashed. "And I can't help but think how much better off we would be if we could all just be who we really are. Folks want to know where I've been all this time." He swept out an encompassing arm. "And I've been right here all along. Just me. Figuring out who I really am." He banged out a couple chords that earned another burst of applause, and just as deftly returned to the haunting notes up and down the keyboard. "I play piano. I love my family. I ride horses. I write songs and I make more mistakes than I can count." He pulled off his sunglasses and tossed them into the blackness outside the lights focused over him. "And I've realized how badly everyone wants to be loved exactly the way we are. Even me." He cleared his throat softly. "So I wrote a little song about that. This song."

Then he looked straight at Arabella.

His long, strong fingers picked out the notes with impossible delicacy as he sang right to her.

Even though they were surrounded by hundreds and hundreds of strangers, even though he was helping to save the hotel from financial ruin, she knew in that moment that this song, this moment, was the real reason for it all.

For her.

"I think you should know that your love healed me,"

he sang, his voice turning gruffer. Huskier. "Your love revealed me. You're my Bella. And I never want to let you go. My Bella, please don't go."

By the time the final notes of the hauntingly beautiful piano notes faded into the night, Arabella didn't even care anymore that tears were sliding down her face. Nor did she need the little nudge that Jay's grandmother gave her as she stood and walked to the corner of the stage where a slim man dressed all in black helped her up the steps.

At the top, she turned and was shocked at the way the lights blurred out everything beyond their glare. But at the center of it all was Jay.

Her Jay, standing next to the piano and watching her oh-so-closely with those green eyes. The same green eyes that she'd fallen headlong into on a January night.

A pin drop could have been heard as she slowly crossed the stage, not stopping until she stood toe to toe with him.

"I think you should know that I could never stop loving you." She didn't care that the mic picked up her words. She reached up and slowly pulled off his cowboy hat. "Not even if I tried."

When his arms swept her tight against him, she heard only his whispered words. "I love you—"

But suddenly a spotlight swerved and Arabella felt a sudden *whoosh* of heat.

She didn't even understand that it wasn't normal until Jay swore and shoved her down. Her knees hit the stage and she cried out, blinded by light and Jay's body covering hers, flattening her right down.

She heard shouts. The sound of cymbals crashing. A discordant guitar twang. The stage beneath them vibrated with running footsteps.

"What's happening? What's wrong?"

He raised his head and she could finally see the wall of orange flames licking at the edge of the stage.

She gasped.

Beyond the flames, beyond the spotlights, she could hear but not see the people who were yelling. Then Jay, on his knees, pulled Arabella farther away from the flames. They knocked into one of the standing mics and it toppled, adding yet another screech to the cacophony.

Hands grabbed at them and in a panic, she hit back with all the ferocity her brothers had ever taught her. "Leave him alone!"

But Jay caught her flailing fists. "They're security, Bella. It's okay."

"Nothing about this is okay." She wrapped her arms around him, glaring at the guards who seemed perfectly useless considering the state of things. "We need to get you somewhere safe." They were farther away from the flames now, but the heat was still searing.

"Ah, Bella." She felt his lips against her ear. "You're my somewhere safe. Come on. We're almost at the steps." His lips moved away. "Devane," he yelled. "Where's the crew?"

"Safe." The slim man in black appeared, the sweat on his face shining. "Everyone's off the stage except you. Nobody's been hurt. The audience is being pushed back." He was shining a flashlight on the stage floor. Arabella barely spotted the steep steps before the security guards surrounding them hustled them down them and well away from the stage.

From the other side—the audience side—Arabella could only stare in horror at the tableau.

The images of horses and rolling waves on the big screens were still playing, accompanied now by the sounds of the retreating crowd and the hungry flames hissing and popping.

Jay's arm kept her close to his side. "I told you no pyrotechnics."

Devane lifted his hands. "And there weren't any. This isn't our doing. I already told the cop there, that."

Arabella realized he meant Detective Teas, who was pacing back and forth some distance away, a cell phone at his ear.

Several guards were wielding fire extinguishers which didn't seem to be having any effect. The wall of flames just kept flowing up and over the metal framework of the stage, long fingers flicking back and forth into the sky, neither growing nor shrinking.

If it weren't so shocking and horrible, it would have been almost mesmerizing.

She obviously wasn't the only one who thought so, Arabella realized when she spotted Jason on the other side of the chairs. He was staring at the fire in much the same way she'd been.

She squeezed Jay's hand. "I'll be right back."

He frowned slightly, but when he followed her gaze toward the young man, he nodded and let go of her.

Giving the first dozen rows of chairs a wide berth, she crossed over to him and realized his shoulders were shaking from sobs even before she reached him. "Jason." She slid her arm around him. "It's okay. Nobody's hurt. Listen. You can hear the sirens already. The fire department will put out the fire."

His shoulders heaved even harder. "My grandpa's under the stage."

She stiffened. "Norman? Your grandpa Norman?" She looked back toward Jay and as if he sensed it, he separated from the cluster of people around him. Dragging Jason with her, she dashed toward him and met him halfway. "Jason says that Norman is under the stage."

He swore and gestured to the guards. In seconds, they'd fanned out and were approaching the stage once again from the sides not engulfed in flame.

"It's my fault," Jason was moaning where he'd collapsed in a chair.

She sat beside him and covered his fisted hands with hers. "Of course it isn't," she soothed the same way she would have soothed Tyler or Toby. She knew the young man was close to his grandfather.

"He said he just wanted to see how it was all set up. He's always interested in how things are built. How they work. So I got him backstage."

"Backstage doesn't mean under it," Jay reasoned.

Arabella nodded. "Jay's right." Despite the height of the stage, it was still difficult imagining the gray-haired man clambering beneath the metal framework. But even if he had, the flames hadn't gotten beneath the stage. Hadn't surrounded it or engulfed it. She was nevertheless grateful to see the fire engine creeping through the congested parking lot. "I'm sure your grandpa's fine. There're a lot of people here for the concert. He'll turn up."

"You don't understand. When he was in the army, he used to blow things up."

Her mouth dried and her eyes met Jay's. Because she suddenly realized that Jason wasn't concerned because his grandfather was a curious man in danger. "You think he has something to do *with* the fire? Why would he want to hurt Jay?"

"I don't think it's him he wants to hurt." Jason swiped his face with his arm and held out his hand, opening his fist to reveal his hotel name badge. "I found this in my grandpa's car tonight."

Jay plucked the badge from the young man's palm. "Did you forget it there?"

The firelight danced over Jason's pale face. "I lost that one the first week I started working at the hotel. Before they even opened up in January." He turned slightly and she saw an identical badge already pinned to his chest. "He's had it and he never told me. He could get anywhere in the hotel."

Because the badge was an access key.

Jay grabbed Jason's arm and hauled him to his feet. "You need to tell this to the police."

"Aunt Petunia's gonna lock him away if she finds out."

"He'll be lucky if that's all that happens," Jay muttered. He was aiming toward Teas but Devane caught up to them first.

"Nobody's under the stage," he reported.

Feeling shaky, Arabella didn't know whether to be relieved or not.

"Find Callum and fill him in," Jay told him and the man set off again.

The fire engine had made it through the parking lot, and in practiced choreography, firefighters in full gear began dragging hoses from the truck.

Jason had barely finished stammering out his story for Detective Teas when the crews conquered the fire. The cessation of heat was immediate.

"Jason." Arabella suddenly turned back to him. "You said before that you didn't think it was Jay your grandpa wants to hurt. Why?"

Jason looked more miserable than ever. "When I first started working at the hotel, I was on the cleaning crew at night. I found him sleeping inside the kitchen at Roja. It was locked up tight." His gaze flicked over the name badge that Jay had handed over to the detective.

"Just sleeping," Teas repeated.

"Yeah. When I woke him up to get him outta there, he was all confused. Talking about my grandma and how he—"

"How he *what*?" Teas asked flatly when Jason broke off.

Arabella sat beside him again and squeezed his hand.

He swiped his cheeks again. "He was talking about how he was gonna get her back from the Fortunes and—" his voice dropped to a hoarse whisper "—and make them pay."

Detective Teas swiped his hand down his face. "Is

there anything *else*? Any other details you should have shared before now?"

"He's been in Roja after it's closed more than once," Jason admitted, slumping in his chair.

Jay leaned his head closer to the detective and Arabella knew he was telling the man about Norman's problem with his meds.

Teas lifted his cell phone again to his ear. "Get someone over to Roja now. And I want an all-points on Norm—" she heard him saying as he paced away from them.

Jason's eyes sought Arabella's. "I told you he's just confused. My grandma hasn't lived in Rambling Rose since before I was born. I doubt she's ever even met anyone named Fortune."

A confused man—for whatever reason—with a grudge and unfettered access to a hotel that had been besieged with one inexplicable challenge after another.

Arabella looked over her shoulder at the rows of chairs. What had been neat and orderly when they'd arrived had been knocked askew by the vacating audience.

Only they hadn't really vacated at all, she realized. The outer edges of the parking lot were crammed with faces. The streets beyond, equally packed.

They'd all come for a show, and they'd gotten one none of them could have expected.

"Norman or not, we need to finish the concert," Jay said, as if he were reading her mind. "People paid good money that the hotel still needs."

She looked at the stage. The fire was out, but the foamy substance used to douse the flames flowed over the stage, dripping off the sides while the firehoses still snaked all over the ground. "How?"

"He's how." Jay nodded toward Devane who was jogging their way again, this time with Callum Fortune keeping pace with him. "If there's one thing Michael Devane is good at, it's turning a situation right-side up."

And he did.

In thirty minutes, they had a plan. And while Devane went off to address the crowd, everyone else set to work. The fire chief said that even though the fire appeared to have been set more as a distraction than to cause damage, nothing from the original staging could be used until it was inspected for damage. But there was backup equipment that was pulled off trucks and repositioned squarely in the center of the parking lot. Chairs were repositioned. And before another thirty minutes had passed, the crowd was chanting Jett's name again and when a spotlight suddenly came on, picking out Callum Fortune standing in the center of the impromptu "stage," the chanting got even louder.

"Let's give it up for Jett Carr," Callum shouted and his voice rang out from the speakers. "Thanks to his generosity, Hotel Fortune's gonna be here for Rambling Rose for a long time to come." He stretched his arms, clapping his hands rhythmically over his head and the backup band started playing again and the women were singing something that had the crowd singing along, too.

Arabella looked up into Jay's eyes. "That's your call, Jet-pack. Your fans are waiting. Tonight. Tomorrow."

"Give me my Jett!"

She smiled as the piercing yell was swallowed in the night and the music. "From the sounds of it, every day from here on out."

She felt the fine tremor in his fingers as he stroked her cheek. "None of that out there counts for anything if you're not a part of it."

"Jay."

"I'm serious, Bella. I walked away once but it wasn't for the right reason. Once these shows are done, I could walk away happy. Because *you* would be the right reason. Music's my first love." He kissed her fingertips and pressed them against his chest. "But you're the very heart of me. And if you want to raise strawberries and babies with me, then I'll spend the rest of my life doing just that."

Sudden tears sprang to her eyes. "Babies? You want babies with me?"

He reached in his pocket and pulled out a small ring. A diamond ring. "I want everything with you," he said huskily. "Laughter. Tears. Triumphs. Fears. And babies who'll have all of their mother's beauty and hopefully none of their father's failings. And I'll read them bedtime stories about Oscar and Aaron. If you'll have me."

She laughed through her tears. If she hadn't already fallen so far in love with him, she would have tumbled for good right then and there. "And you'll teach them piano," she added huskily, holding out her hand.

He slid the small ring into place. "Of course it would fit perfectly." He sounded a little choked. "Trust my grandmother. It's her ring."

Arabella's tears spilled over as she pressed her lips to his.

Then she pulled back and gave him a little shove. "Now go make your music, Jay. And I'll be right here waiting."

His eyes glittered. "You're absolutely sure?"

She took the guitar that Devane was holding nearby and held it out to Jay. "I told you. I couldn't stop loving you even if I tried."

His fingers caressed hers as he took the guitar. Then he turned and jogged into the spotlight, holding it high above his head.

The cheer that went up could have probably been heard all the way to Houston.

And even though his smile was directed at the crowd beyond the spotlight, Arabella knew it belonged, most of all, to her.

Epilogue

He sang straight for the next three hours. Then, while the fireworks that shot off into the night sky during the finale were still flickering into nothing, everyone involved in the show gathered inside Roja where, they all learned, Norman had been found and taken unresistingly into custody.

There was coffee. Champagne. There was toast and jars of strawberry jam and fried chicken Arabella knew could only have been prepared by Louella herself.

Mostly, there were kisses and lots and lots of hugs as Jay officially introduced her to Michael Devane. "He's the one who managed to pull together this whole show in a matter of days," Jay explained. "Found the guys in the band. The singers. All of it."

Even as tired as she was, Arabella couldn't help staring. "You'd never performed together before?"

Devane clapped Jay on the shoulders. "Started rehearsals two days ago in a sound studio in California. And we did pretty damn well, considering everything." He looked at his watch. "But now I'd better check on things for tomorrow's show."

"That'd be *today's* show," Brady said, throwing himself down into a chair nearby. "At least we can count on it being less exciting than this one was." He rubbed his fingers through his hair. "God knows how much worse it could have been if Norman had been really trying to burn things down."

Arabella pressed her head against Jay's shoulder as she glanced across the restaurant to where Mariana— her blond bun atypically askew—sat at a table with Jason and his aunt Petunia. "There won't be any charges against Jason, will there? He was genuinely shocked that his grandfather had his badge."

"I doubt there will be charges." That came from Kane, who looked as tired as Brady when he joined their table. "I can't speak for everyone, but I know I'm not interested in hanging the kid on a peg because his grandpa's got it in for the Fortunes."

"From everything Brady said, it sounds like he blames them—us—for losing his wife," Arabella said.

Nicole set down the coffeepot she'd been carrying around to refill cups and perched on the edge of the booth next to her sister Megan. Both Nicole and Mariana had been in the restaurant when the police apprehended Norman. "He kept calling Mariana his wife when Detective Teas took him away. He's always liked hanging around her, but obviously he'd become fixated."

"His meds." Jay shook his head. "Now we all can see why Petunia was so worried about him and his meds."

"He'll get the help he needs with that now," Callum said, sliding onto the table, because that was the only place left. He stuck out his hand toward Jay. "And thanks to you, we've got the help we need now, too."

Jay smiled faintly and shook the man's hand. "It was nothing."

Callum snorted and so did a lot of others. "The revenue from tonight alone should put us back in the black. In fact, it was so successful they're going to play two more shows over the weekend, so what happens tomorrow and Sunday needs to stay in your pock—"

But Jay was already shaking his head. "Now you know that Norman's been behind all of the mishaps around the hotel, you'll have bargaining power again with the insurance company, too. But after making sure the crew's paid, the Rambling Rose concert revenue is all yours." He smiled down at Arabella. "I'm already getting everything I need out of the deal."

"I've got just one question for you," Brady said, sounding pugnacious. "When's the wedding?"

Arabella raised her eyebrows at him and waggled her finger with the ring on it. "When's yours, Brady," she shot right back at him.

"That's actually a good question." Megan bumped her sister's shoulder. "You and Collin are the only ones who've made it legal. But you've still got a honeymoon to take. When's he getting his next leave of service?"

Nicole smiled brilliantly. "He's getting transferred stateside. Should be here in the next several weeks."

Kane sat forward and held up his fingers and started ticking them off. "So who've we got? Grace and Wiley. Me and Layla. Megan and Mark." He nodded at Brady. "You and Harper. Even Dillon and Hailey need to get the deed done. S'pose there's a discount wedding service to get us all hitched at once?"

None of them even noticed when Arabella and Jay started creeping out of the restaurant.

"There you go," Megan said on a laugh. "Always looking for efficiency. But that would finish us all up in the marital department, wouldn't it?"

"Not if you count Josh and Brian—"

The restaurant door closed on Kane's voice and Arabella looked up at Jay. "Now what do we do?"

"We're in a hotel with a couple floors of empty rooms that were never even touched by water damage and that group in there will never find us. What do you think?"

She was tired right down to her bones but she laughed delightedly and wound her arms around his shoulders. "I think I'm very glad we know where the master keys are kept."

I think you should know that...

...the future is ours.

And it was.

* * * * *

Catch up with the rest of
The Fortunes of Texas: The Hotel Fortune

Look for these titles:

Her Texas New Year's Wish *by Michelle Major*
Their Second-Time Valentine *by Helen Lacey*
An Unexpected Father *by USA TODAY*
bestselling author Marie Ferrarella
Runaway Groom *by Lynne Marshall*
An Officer and a Fortune *by Nina Crespo*

Available now wherever Harlequin books
and ebooks are sold!

WE HOPE YOU ENJOYED
THIS BOOK FROM

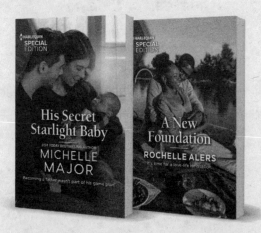

Believe in love. Overcome obstacles. Find happiness.

Relate to finding comfort and strength in the
support of loved ones and enjoy the journey
no matter what life throws your way.

6 NEW BOOKS AVAILABLE EVERY MONTH!

#2845 A BRAMBLEBERRY SUMMER
The Women of Brambleberry House • by RaeAnne Thayne
Rosa Galvez's attraction to Officer Wyatt Townsend is as powerful as the moon's pull on the tides. But with her past, Rosa knows better than to act on her feelings. Yet her solo life is slowly becoming a sun-filled family adventure—until dark secrets threaten to break like a summer storm.

#2846 THE RANCHER'S SUMMER SECRET
Montana Mavericks: The Real Cowboys of Bronco Heights
by Christine Rimmer
Vanessa Cruise is spending her summer working in Bronco. Rekindling her short-term fling with the hottest rancher in town? Not on her to-do list. But the handsome rancher promises to keep their relationship hidden from the town gossips, then finds himself longing for more. Convincing Vanessa he's worth the risk might be the hardest thing he's ever had to do...

#2847 THE MAJOR GETS IT RIGHT
The Camdens of Montana • by Victoria Pade
Working with Clairy McKinnon on her father's memorial tests Major Quinn Camden's every resolve! Clairy is still hurt that General McKinnon mentored Quinn over his own adoring daughter. When their years-long rivalry is replaced by undeniable attraction, Quinn wonders if the general's dying wish is the magic they both need... or if the man's secrets will tear them apart for good.

#2848 NOT THEIR FIRST RODEO
Twin Kings Ranch • by Christy Jeffries
The last thing Sheriff Marcus King needs is his past sneaking back into his present. Years ago, Violet Cortez-Hill disappeared from his life, leaving him with unanswered questions—and a lot of hurt. Now the widowed father of twins finds himself forced to interact with the pretty public defender daily. Is there still a chance to saddle up and ride off into their future?

#2849 THE NIGHT THAT CHANGED EVERYTHING
The Culhanes of Cedar River • by Helen Lacey
Winona Sheehan and Grant Culhane have been BFFs since childhood. So when Winona's sort-of-boyfriend ditches their ill-advised Vegas wedding, Grant is there. Suddenly, Winona trades one groom for another—and Grant's baby is on the way. With a years-long secret crush fulfilled, Winona wonders if her husband is ready for a family...or firmly in the friend zone.

#2850 THE SERGEANT'S MATCHMAKING DOG
Small-Town Sweethearts • by Carrie Nichols
Former Marine Gabe Bishop is focused on readjusting to civilian life. So the last thing he needs is the adorable kid next door bonding with his dog, Radar. The boy's guardian, Addie Miller, is afraid of dogs, so why does she keep coming around? Soon, Gabe finds himself becoming her shoulder to lean on. Could his new neighbors be everything Gabe never knew he needed?

HSECNM0621

*Rosa Galvez's attraction to Officer Wyatt Townsend
is as powerful as the moon's pull on the tides.
But with her past, Rosa knows better than to act on her
feelings. But her solo life slowly becomes a sun-filled,
family adventure—until dark secrets threaten to
break like a summer storm.*

*Read on for a sneak peek at
the next book in
The Women of Brambleberry House miniseries,
A Brambleberry Summer,
by New York Times bestselling author RaeAnne Thayne.*

"Everyone has secrets, do they not? Some they share with those they trust, some they prefer to keep to themselves."

He was quiet for a long moment. "I hope you know that if you ever want to share yours, you can trust me."

She trusted very few people. And she certainly wasn't going to trust Wyatt, who was only a temporary tenant and would be out of her life in a few short weeks.

"If I had any secrets, I might do that. But I don't. I'm a completely open book."

She tried for a breezy smile but could tell he wasn't at all convinced. In fact, he looked slightly disappointed.

She tried to ignore her guilt and opted to change the subject instead. "The lightning seems to have stopped for now. I am sure the power will be back on soon."

"No doubt."

"Thank you again for coming to my rescue. Good night. Be careful going back down the stairs."

"I will do that. Good night."

He studied her, his features unreadable in the dim light of her flashlight. He looked as if he wanted to say something else. Instead, he shook his head slightly.

"Good night."

As he turned to go back down the stairs, the masculine scent of him swirled to her. She felt that sudden wild urge to kiss him again but ignored it. Instead, she went into her darkened apartment, her dog at her heels, and firmly closed the door behind her. If only she could close the door to her thoughts as easily.

Don't miss
A Brambleberry Summer *by RaeAnne Thayne,*
available July 2021 wherever
Harlequin Special Edition books and ebooks are sold.

Harlequin.com

Get 4 FREE REWARDS!

We'll send you 2 FREE Books plus 2 FREE Mystery Gifts.

Harlequin Special Edition books relate to finding comfort and strength in the support of loved ones and enjoying the journey no matter what life throws your way.

FREE Value Over $20

YES! Please send me 2 FREE Harlequin Special Edition novels and my 2 FREE gifts (gifts are worth about $10 retail). After receiving them, if I don't wish to receive any more books, I can return the shipping statement marked "cancel." If I don't cancel, I will receive 6 brand-new novels every month and be billed just $4.99 per book in the U.S. or $5.74 per book in Canada. That's a savings of at least 12% off the cover price! It's quite a bargain! Shipping and handling is just 50¢ per book in the U.S. and $1.25 per book in Canada.* I understand that accepting the 2 free books and gifts places me under no obligation to buy anything. I can always return a shipment and cancel at any time. The free books and gifts are mine to keep no matter what I decide.

235/335 HDN GNMP

Name (please print)

Address   Apt. #

City   State/Province   Zip/Postal Code

Email: Please check this box ☐ if you would like to receive newsletters and promotional emails from Harlequin Enterprises ULC and its affiliates. You can unsubscribe anytime.

Mail to the **Harlequin Reader Service:**
IN U.S.A.: P.O. Box 1341, Buffalo, NY 14240-8531
IN CANADA: P.O. Box 603, Fort Erie, Ontario L2A 5X3

Want to try 2 free books from another series? Call 1-800-873-8635 or visit www.ReaderService.com.

*Terms and prices subject to change without notice. Prices do not include sales taxes, which will be charged (if applicable) based on your state or country of residence. Canadian residents will be charged applicable taxes. Offer not valid in Quebec. This offer is limited to one order per household. Books received may not be as shown. Not valid for current subscribers to Harlequin Special Edition books. All orders subject to approval. Credit or debit balances in a customer's account(s) may be offset by any other outstanding balance owed by or to the customer. Please allow 4 to 6 weeks for delivery. Offer available while quantities last.

Your Privacy—Your information is being collected by Harlequin Enterprises ULC, operating as Harlequin Reader Service. For a complete summary of the information we collect, how we use this information and to whom it is disclosed, please visit our privacy notice located at corporate.harlequin.com/privacy-notice. From time to time we may also exchange your personal information with reputable third parties. If you wish to opt out of this sharing of your personal information, please visit readerservice.com/consumerschoice or call 1-800-873-8635. **Notice to California Residents**—Under California law, you have specific rights to control and access your data. For more information on these rights and how to exercise them, visit corporate.harlequin.com/california-privacy.

HSE21R